❦ BRIDES OF CULDEE CREEK • BOOK 2 ❧

WOMAN OF GRACE

Kathleen Morgan

Fleming H. Revell
A Division of Baker Book House Co
Grand Rapids, Michigan 49516

© 2000 by Kathleen Morgan

Published by Fleming H. Revell
a division of Baker Book House Company
P.O. Box 6287, Grand Rapids, MI 49516-6287

Printed in the United States of America

Library of Congress Cataloging-in-Publication Data

Morgan, Kathleen, 1950–
    Woman of grace / Kathleen Morgan.
            p.   cm. – (Brides of Culdee Creek)
    ISBN 0-8007-5727-0 (paper)
        1. Women pioneers–Fiction. 2. Married women–Fiction.
    3. Colorado–Fiction. I. Title.
    PS3563.O8647 W66   2000
    813'.54–dc21   00-027187

Scripture is from the King James Version of the Bible.

For current information about all releases from Baker Book House, visit our web site:
                    http://www.bakerbooks.com

For Chris Lewis and Nancy Praiswater,
two of my dearest friends

A Word from the Author

The stories authors write often mirror issues beset-
ting them in their own lives. That certainly was the case
when I wrote *Daughter of Joy,* the first book in this
series. At the time, my characters' search for joy in the
midst of tragedy was a primary issue for me.

Though it was perhaps not readily apparent to me in
the course of writing this book, I now realize the same
principle held true this time. From the beginning, I knew
Hannah Cutler's journey would be one of discovery and
acceptance of God's grace. It had to be. After the horrors of her past, she desperately needed to learn not only
that the Lord loved her, but that nothing she had ever
done could keep her from that precious gift.

The more I delved into Hannah's story, the more I
came to realize how important a role grace has played
in my life. Grace, after all, is about a second chance.
Such was the second chance God offered me after my
youngest son died.

Pain and sorrow opened me to Him like no amount of
happiness ever could, quieting my soul and sharpening
my hearing until I finally began to discern that small,
still Voice. The Lord presented me with yet another
opportunity to make my life really count–another chance

to come to know and love Him person-to-person, heart-to-heart.

Grace . . . God's second chance. His hands outstretched in love, the Lord offers the most wondrous miracle any of us could ever hope to experience. We have only to take that one small step to find ourselves in His arms. Yet how hard that one step can be!

Woman of Grace is the story of a journey back to that grace-filled haven of God's loving arms. Like many of our journeys—mine included—it's not one easily begun or completed. But oh, the wonder, exquisite self-discovery, and depths of joy found in such a quest! A quest filled with riches untold—not just for us, but for all those who come to know the Lord thanks to one, small, courageous step.

Kathleen Morgan

HANNAH
"Given to Much Grace"

By grace are ye saved through faith.
Ephesians 2:8

1

The plains east of Colorado Springs, Colorado, April 1897

Wherefore dost thou forget us for ever, and forsake us so long time?

Lamentations 5:20

There were days, increasingly now, when the deep, dark, shameful secrets no longer seemed so hard to bear. Days that filled Hannah Cutler with such wild hopes for the future, she thought she might finally put the horrors of the past behind her. Days when she was so overwhelmed by the kindness and generosity of others she nearly wept with gratitude.

But then there were other days. Days like today, as Devlin MacKay greeted her with yet another sour look, when Hannah knew those shameful secrets were best kept hidden away. Best kept clasped tightly where no one could threaten the tenuous hold she had on this new, far better life.

Only fools gave others the weapons to destroy them, and Hannah had learned long ago, in many painful, degrading ways, how to survive.

"Well, come in, will you?" the dark-haired, powerfully built man growled, making an impatient motion for her to enter. "The house is cold enough without you standing there with the door open."

Hannah hurried inside, a bundle of clean towels and sheets tucked beneath her arm. When Devlin offered no assistance, she turned and shut the door against the blowing snow and howling winds. A dusting of powdery flakes followed in her wake, coating the threshold and floor. With a surreptitious glance at the man who scowled even more fiercely, Hannah tried to brush the snow back toward the doorway with the side of her black, high-buttoned shoe.

"I'm sorry," she said, choking back her irritation at his lack of manners.

Though Hannah wanted to say more, to refute his harsh words and implied insults, she didn't dare. Admittedly, she was tired of Devlin's hostility. It had never been his right to pass judgment on Conor and Abby's decision to invite her to stay at Culdee Creek Ranch. Or to belittle her relationship with Evan either. Indeed, it should hardly be any of his business. But he hadn't seen it that way. The proud ranch foreman wasn't the kind of man to easily—or ever—let go of a grudge.

To challenge Devlin would be, as it had been with others before him, to risk dire punishment. Though he might not stoop so low as to actually beat her for any implied impertinence, he could do far worse. He could jeopardize her continued stay at Culdee Creek. He could ruin everything.

So with gritted teeth and clamped lips, Hannah did what had always served her well. She hid her true emotions. Keeping her glance cast downward, she strode across the small kitchen. It didn't matter, at any rate, what Devlin thought of her. She would never have come if it had been just for him. He could have lain here in this house and rotted for all she cared.

No, it wasn't for Devlin that Hannah had dared enter. It was for his wife, Ella, who lay writhing in her childbed, and for Abby. It was for the two women who had first welcomed her to Culdee Creek almost a year ago when, nine months pregnant, she had escaped the bordello where she had been forced to work as a prostitute. It was for these two women, women who had tirelessly championed her when almost no one else would.

As Hannah moved past Devlin, who sat at the kitchen table with a mug of coffee clenched in his hands, a soft, low moan rose from the bedroom at the end of the small house's short hall. Her footsteps quickened.

"One thing more." Devlin's voice, hard as steel, sliced through the tension-laden air.

She slid to a halt, shoulders rigid, and waited for the blow she knew was about to come. "Yes, what is it?"

"You can stay because Abby needs your help right now. But just as soon as Doc gets here, I want you out of my house. Women like you aren't fit to be near decent folk or innocent children."

Rage boiled inside Hannah. How dare he? *How dare he?*

She turned, her gaze meeting his. A look of mutual fear and distrust arced between them. "I'm done with that life, and you know it, Devlin MacKay," she spat out finally.

"Are you?" He gave a harsh bark of derision. "Don't fool yourself. When the going gets rough, women like you always go back to your old ways. After all, it's the only thing you ever learned to do well. Mark my words. You'll go back."

13

No, I won't, she thought with fierce, fervent determination, even as old doubts plucked at her anew. I'd rather die than go back to that life. I'd rather die than prove people like you right. People like you, who have sinned in ways far greater than I ever could.

She almost uttered those very words, almost turned and pointed an accusing finger. But she didn't. Devlin MacKay was too blinded by his own guilt and complicity to ever see the truth. It sat far better with him to lay all the blame on her. In some twisted way, she supposed he also imagined it absolved him. Absolved him and washed his soul as white as snow.

Or as white as dead men's bones, scattered and forgotten in some desolate, whited sepulchre.

The afternoon burned on. Through the ever-worsening storm, Hannah periodically came and went. Ella's screams grew weaker, her moans lower and farther apart.

The light began to dim, and still Devlin sat hunched over his now cold mug of coffee, staring blindly into its black, murky depths. Bit by agonizing bit, he felt the life, the hope drain from him. Drain away as surely as it seemed to drain away for his beloved wife. His dear, sweet Ella who now struggled to birth their third child—a child she should've never dared to conceive, much less carry.

The truth of that statement cut through him as cruelly as the bitter winds howling outside his window. Ella should never have risked this pregnancy. Yet what choice had he given her after Mary's birth, when Doc Childress had warned them of Ella's fragile condition?

Devlin hadn't been able to accept the consequences of that pronouncement. Rather than honor his wife, he had turned to drinking and visiting Grand View's bordello to ease his pain. Though his guilt had made him stop long before Ella finally confronted him, he secretly wondered if she could really believe he'd remain faithful, if continually denied the marriage bed. And now, because of his failure to properly love her, Doc's grave predictions were coming true.

It seemed like hours since he had sent two of the ranch hands riding out to Grand View to fetch Doc Childress. Devlin knew the men wouldn't fail him. But he was also well aware of the vagaries of spring weather on the high plains. He knew how viciously the winds could blow, how quickly the snow could fall, blanketing the land and swirling so thickly you could barely find your way. Even strong men got lost in blizzards like today's. Even strong men died.

Doc would arrive as soon as his men could safely get him here. Meanwhile there was nothing to be done but wait. Wait, and endure Ella's gut-wrenching cries, knowing there was nothing, absolutely nothing, he could do for her now.

Once more the kitchen's back door opened. Devlin looked up. Lamplight spilled into the room, illuminating Hannah's pale, drawn face with red-gold radiance.

No one, he thought bitterly, should be allowed to look like she did. No one deserved, after the life she had lived, to appear so much like an angel with that pale blond hair, those big, blue-green eyes, and that soft, guileless face.

Those looks had seduced him to choose her nearly two years ago when he had called on Sadie Fleming's bordello. They had also helped cement her cozy little sanctuary here at Culdee Creek. Against his cousin's better judgment, Abby had somehow convinced Conor to let Hannah deliver her child at the ranch. Yet what had been intended as just a brief reprieve for the young prostitute had now stretched to almost a year.

15

Yes, that guise of injured innocence had fooled the lot of them, Devlin recalled, seething with resentment. But then none of them knew Hannah Cutler like he did. Few realized the power she held over him.

She could ruin everything.

He eyed her for an instant longer, then turned away. His aversion for Hannah Cutler notwithstanding, nothing was served berating the girl each time she entered his house. She was, after all, trying to help Abby with Ella.

At the admission, guilt plucked at him. Here she was, coming and going all day through the raging storm to fetch whatever Abby required, and all he could do was sit glaring and snapping like some wounded, cornered animal.

The comparison struck too close to home. Devlin's mouth twitched sadly. A wounded, cornered animal . . . yes, that was exactly what he had become.

All he seemed to do anymore was lick his wounds in suffering silence, hoping against hope for some miracle to heal him. Sit here in helpless impotence and pray to a God he had long ago turned his back on. A God who had long ago ceased to listen.

Behind him, Hannah closed the door, then headed across the kitchen. The wind momentarily died. In the sudden silence her hard-soled shoes clicked with a staccato rhythm on the wooden floor. Her long skirt, swirling about her legs, made soft, whooshing sounds. As she drew near, the scent of apples and cinnamon filled the air.

"I brought you and Abby some fresh-baked, dried apple pie." She placed a large, covered basket on the table.

Devlin glanced up. An infinite number of replies—none of them kind—rose to his lips. He bit them back. Such repeated, intentional cruelty wasn't like him. But then he hadn't been much like himself since Hannah came to Culdee Creek.

16

"I also brought cold roast beef, potato fritters, and boiled peas. You're probably not very hungry right now," she hastened to add when he sent her a hard, slanting glance, "but it's important both you and Abby keep up your strength. I've already seen to it that your children ate."

Devlin's six-year-old son and two-and-a-half-year-old daughter had spent the day at the main house, safely out of the way of the goings-on here. Devlin had visited them for several short periods today, but he felt compelled to stay primarily near Ella. He couldn't do much more than that for their mother, but at least the children would be spared the agony of knowing her pain. At least they would never have to experience the long, torturous hours wondering, worrying, fearing she would die.

"Just leave the food, will you?" he growled. Yet again, the memory of Ella's labor swamped him, laden with its humiliating reminders of his inability to ease her torment—and of his selfish desires that had brought her to this life-threatening moment. "I'll fetch Abby and see if she's hungry."

He scraped back his chair and stood. "She needs a long overdue break, and I need to be with my wife."

Hannah's turquoise gaze locked with his. "Yes," she whispered. "Yes, you do."

Something flickered in her eyes, something that smacked, to his way of thinking, of kindness, compassion, and even understanding. Fury swelled in him. It was all Devlin could do to choke back a savage curse.

He didn't want anything from the likes of her. He had been fool enough to buy her favors all those months ago when Ella, for fear of another pregnancy, had turned him from her bed. It just wasn't fair that his good, God-fearing wife suffered now, while a woman like Hannah had so easily delivered her own, illegitimate child. But then, when had God ever been fair, or good?

17

Such fruitless considerations, though, only served to stir painful, chaotic emotions Devlin couldn't deal with tonight of all nights. Before he said something that would heap further insult onto those he had already flung at Hannah Cutler this day, he turned on his heel and strode away.

"Mama, Mama! Mama, Mama!"

The insistent drone of Jackson's voice, punctuated by squeaks and squeals from his swaying crib, woke Hannah late the next morning. She turned over, forced one eye open, and smiled. "Hungry, are you, sweetie?" she asked softly.

Jackson grinned, revealing six little white teeth, and jumped all the harder. "Mama, Mama, Mama!"

With a weary groan, Hannah slid out of bed and fell to her knees for her morning prayers. Just as Abby had taught her, she folded her hands, bowed her head, and uttered the words with fervent deliberation. Sometimes, as she prayed, she almost imagined she felt a connection with God. Then there were other times, too many to count, when Hannah felt nothing.

It seemed, she reluctantly admitted, just as difficult to love God as it was to love most of His children. He had let her down so often. Indeed, as the all-powerful being He was purported to be, wasn't He responsible for allowing all the evil wrought in the world?

Still, Abby encouraged her not to give up on God. She urged her to be patient, to trust in the Lord and His promise that all things good would come in time. So Hannah doggedly kept on trying. She trusted few people, but she trusted Abby and everything she said with her whole heart. She would try her best to please Abby in every way—even if that required trying to make peace with God.

Jackson's cries grew more strident. The crib threatened to collapse beneath the relentless impact of his chubby little legs. With a sigh, Hannah finished her prayers and climbed blearily to her feet. She walked to Jackson's crib and lifted him from it, then pulled the rocking chair close. He was soon nursing greedily at her breast, his moist, pink lips pursed, one small hand clutching a lock of her hair.

Gazing down at her son, Hannah's heart filled with peace. These were indeed the moments she lived for, the moments when she thought her heart would break with happiness. She wondered if, even now, Ella was feeling the same thing as she cradled her newborn daughter in her arms.

The doctor had finally made it through the blizzard at six last evening. By midnight the exhausted Ella had delivered. The next hour, however, was spent in a frantic battle to staunch her heavy bleeding. There were moments when Hannah feared they'd lose her. But, at last, as if by some miracle, the bleeding had all but ceased.

Hannah had then headed back to the little bunkhouse that sat between Devlin and Ella's house, and the main house shared by Abby, Conor, and their family. She wasn't sure when or even if Abby had ever gone home. If she had, Hannah was certain that she, too, must be exhausted.

Once Jackson was nursed, bathed, and dressed, and her own morning ablutions were completed, Hannah decided to head to the main house and see what help was needed there. It was the very least she could do. Until Hannah had first met Abigail MacKay that December day in Gates' Mercantile, she had despaired of being treated with tolerance, much less love and compassion, ever again. Now, in whatever way she could, she wanted to return the kindness Abby had always shown her.

A half hour later, her long hair neatly braided down her back and a dark blue woolen dress covering her slender frame, Hannah paused just long enough to slide her stockinged feet into tall, leather boots, throw on her short wool coat, and tuck a shawl over her head. Then, after bundling Jackson and his bag of wooden blocks in a warm blanket, she forced open the bunkhouse door.

To her surprise and immense gratitude, she found that someone had already shoveled a path through the snow-drifts to the main house. It would have been impossible, otherwise, she soon discovered, to traverse the hip-high snow with Jackson in her arms. As it was, the shoveled snow piled on either side of the path rose to her shoulders, forming almost a tunnel within which to walk.

It was a tunnel, Hannah realized as she closed the bunkhouse door and began her trek, that had its definite advantages, serving as a very effective windbreak for the blustering winds. Of course, its powdery top layer did still swirl and scatter, coating Hannah's face and making it hard to breathe. After such a storm, though, she was thankful for every and anything that made life easier.

As she neared the main house and climbed the back porch just off the kitchen, the acrid stench of burning grease reached her. It was quickly followed by the sound of an angry male voice and footsteps hurrying across the hardwood floor. Hannah grinned. If she didn't miss her guess, Evan had just fallen victim to Old Bess, Abby's much maligned if sometimes recalcitrant cookstove.

After pausing to shake off as much snow as she could from her boots and skirt, Hannah entered the kitchen. Sure enough, Evan had scorched one of the cast-iron skillets. At her entrance, he glanced up from his task of pumping water into the pan from the sink's kitchen pitcher pump.

"Well, you're a sight for sore eyes," the young man exclaimed, his face lighting with a mix of relief and delight. "Not to mention"–he made a wry grimace as he indicated the still steaming skillet–"a lifesaver."

Hannah chuckled. One couldn't stay glum for long when Evan was around. Conor MacKay's son, nineteen-year-old Evan had his father's height, impressive build, and the same smoky blue eyes and blue-black hair. He certainly possessed the MacKay good looks.

Evan's grin was just as engaging as his father's and Devlin's, too. Though he lacked the benefit of Devlin's long, dark mustache to add drama and maturity to his youthful features, Evan was at least spared his cousin's roguish look of a desperado. His features were more refined, and his nose–unlike Devlin's, which had apparently once been broken–was straight and strong. Surely Evan was, Hannah decided, one of the most handsome men she had ever met.

"What exactly were you attempting to do?" Hannah squatted and deposited Jackson, blanket, toys, and all, in a corner near the two tall cupboards. "In case you hadn't noticed, cooking has never been one of your particular talents," she added as she ambled over to stand beside Evan at the sink.

The young man shrugged. "I was hungry. Abby's still asleep, and Pa headed out early with the hands to feed the cattle stranded in the far pastures. A man's got to keep up his strength, you know."

Hannah reached out and lightly squeezed his muscled biceps. "You don't strike me as a man who's wasting away, Evan MacKay."

"No," he agreed solemnly, "and I don't intend to start anytime soon either. Who do you think spent the last two hours shoveling that path from here to your bunkhouse?"

She grinned. "I'll bet that was just so I could cook you some breakfast."

Evan gave a snort of disdain. "If I'd been hoping for some breakfast, I'd have starved a long time ago. It's nearly noon. I'd say you need to cook me some lunch."

"Do I now?"

Hannah sashayed over to the apron hanging by the cookstove and quickly tied it on. She so enjoyed the harmless teasing they shared, even as she knew Evan wanted far more than just a brotherly relationship from her. He had been in love with her for months now.

Always the gentleman, Evan courted her as gallantly, and patiently, as would any man a fine lady. He bought her presents. He wrote her poetry. He went for long walks with her.

She should be grateful for a man like Evan. She did have feelings for him, even if they were more sisterly than passionate. When it finally came down to it, though, Hannah just wasn't sure she wanted to marry him—or any man for that matter—right now.

But she was also no fool. Evan MacKay offered her far more than just affection. As Culdee Creek's heir, he offered her security and maybe even a return to respectability someday as the wife of a prosperous rancher. Both were potent inducements for a woman with nowhere else to go, especially now that she had a child who depended on her.

From his corner Jackson played in contented silence, seemingly fascinated with the bag of wooden blocks Hannah had brought along for him. She smiled in satisfaction. The kitchen was snug and warm. Evan's company was pleasant. She had her precious son and a safe place to raise him.

Life was good . . . just the way it was.

"So it's to be lunch, is it?" She walked back to the sink and pulled out the now cooled skillet.

"Lunch would suit me just fine."

22

"And how would the last of the roast beef, some fried potatoes, and canned green beans do?"

"It'd send me straight to hog heaven."

Hannah laughed. "Why don't you go, instead, and see when Conor and the hands are due back? Might as well cook up a whole mess of vittles while I'm at it. They're all bound to be pretty hungry."

Evan's face fell. "But I was planning on having a cozy little meal with just the two of us. We hardly have any time alone together these days."

"We've plenty of time, Evan MacKay, and you know it." She made a shooing motion with the big butcher knife she had just picked up. "Now, skedaddle. I've got work to do, unless you want to be eating this meal at supper time."

The look of horror on Evan's face almost made Hannah laugh again. He was quick, though, to grab his jacket and Stetson and head through the kitchen and parlor to the front door. Few things motivated a man better than the needs of an empty stomach.

Hannah's smile faded. Few things, anyway, that asked so little for such simple effort, and still left a woman with her pride and sense of decency. But the memory of those other needs, she was quick to remind herself, was best left hidden away . . . with all the rest of the pain and shame.

"I don't like it." Abby sighed and shook her head later that evening. "The baby's not nursing well, and she cries all the time. I don't like it at all."

Hannah glanced up from the sinkload of soapy dishes she was washing. "Well, little Miss Bonnie MacKay isn't even a day old," she offered. "Considering what Ella went through in birthing the little one, perhaps her milk just hasn't had time to come in."

"Perhaps." Abby finished drying the dinner plate and laid it aside. She took up another from the rinse basin. "Still, I'm thinking we should send for Doc Childress first thing in the morning. Ella needs her rest. The baby's constant crying isn't helping her state of mind much either."

"I could take—" Hannah bit off further words.

"Take what?" The brown-haired woman cocked her head, and paused momentarily.

"Never mind." Hannah flushed crimson. She found sudden fascination in the soapsuds. "It would never work. Devlin wouldn't stand for it."

"What? You taking little Bonnie for the night and wet-nursing her so Ella could get some sleep?"

Hannah's head jerked up. She should have known Abby had been thinking the same thing. Abby was always thinking of others and how best to help them.

"Yes," was her simple reply. "You know how Devlin feels about me. He'd most likely believe my even touching his daughter, much less sharing my milk with her, would somehow corrupt her."

"But you'd do it anyway, if Ella was willing? Just until she had her strength back, of course, and her milk came in?"

"Of course, I'd do it for Ella. She's never been anything but kind to me."

With a few quick swipes, Abby had the plate dried and stacked with the others. "Good." She tossed the dish-cloth aside and headed for the door.

Hannah stared after her. "What are you doing?"

"I'm going to have a talk with Ella." Abby shrugged into her warm coat and pulled on a pair of boots. "Just don't be surprised if I come back with another baby for you."

2

For sin shall not have dominion over you: for ye are not under the law, but under grace.

Romans 6:14

"There, there, little one," Hannah cooed as she lifted Bonnie to her shoulder the next morning. Ever so gently, she began to pat the baby's back. "It's going to be just fine."

The infant snuggled close, made a few soft, mewling sounds, then settled. Hannah smiled. There was just something special about a newborn. She hadn't realized how much she enjoyed them at this age. With a wry grin, she watched Jackson scoot across the bedroom floor, reach her chair, and pull himself up using her nightgown. Her son's increasing activity level had all but erased those easier, more relaxing times from Hannah's memory.

Still, she was so very happy she had been blessed with Jackson. Only one thing marred that happiness—the fact that her son would never know his father. And all the mother's love in the world, Hannah feared, might not make up for that.

"Mama, Mama, Mama." Jackson's dark blue eyes lit with interest at the white bundle in Hannah's arms. He reached toward Bonnie.

She quickly banished her bittersweet thoughts and turned her full attention back to her son. "It's a baby, sweetie. A *ba*-by."

The toddler peered up at her, puzzled. "Ba Ba?"

"Yes," Hannah nodded her encouragement. "A *ba*-by." Bonnie burped her agreement.

"Hannah?" Abby's voice came from the front door. "Is it all right if I come in?"

Hannah leaned as far over in the rocker as she dared, and peeked through her open bedroom door into the bunkhouse's little parlor room. "Yes, come on in," she called. "I'm just finishing up with Bonnie."

She took Jackson by the hand and lowered him carefully to the floor. Then she rose and carried Bonnie to the bed. Laying her down on a section of rubber sheeting, Hannah began to remove the baby's rubber diaper drawers. Abby walked in and came to stand beside her.

"So, how's our little one doing?" her friend asked. "She looks well enough."

"Oh, she's doing just fine," Hannah replied with a laugh. "She woke me every three hours last night, nursed her fill, then immediately fell back asleep until her next feeding. And every time I feed her, it seems I have to change her." She unpinned both sides of Bonnie's diaper, removed it, and laid it aside. After sliding a dry cotton diaper under the baby, she dusted her lightly with cornstarch, then pinned the diaper snugly shut.

"So lack of milk *was* the problem," Abby observed thoughtfully. She sat beside the baby and brushed a finger tenderly down her cheek.

26

"Maybe so." Hannah rebuttoned the diaper drawers, pulled down Bonnie's nightgown, and hefted the baby back to her shoulder. "How's Ella feeling? Has her milk finally come in?"

Abby frowned. "No, or at least not that either of us can tell. She's feverish this morning. I sent a hand out first thing to fetch Doc. He should be on his way by now."

"So you want me to keep Bonnie for a while longer."

"If it wouldn't be too much of an imposition, it would take a load of worry off Ella's mind."

Hannah was tempted to ask what Devlin thought of her wet-nursing his daughter, then thought better of it. No sense stirring the pot if it wasn't yet boiling.

She forced a cheerful smile. "No imposition at all. You make sure Ella knows that. And tell her her daughter's doing fine, too."

Abby smiled, patted Hannah's hand, then rose. "I will. And you can be sure that both Bonnie's mother *and* father will know."

"And now, atop it all," Devlin complained to Conor the next day as the two men loaded hay into the buckboard, "I've got to allow that young tart free run of my house. Blast, but I'd thought I was finished with her after Bonnie was born!"

Devlin was beside himself. The news from Doc Childress hadn't been good. Doc pronounced Ella ill with childbed fever and recommended that at least temporarily she not nurse her baby. With a wet nurse so readily available, there was no reason to further risk her health. She needed to direct all her strength toward overcoming the infection–an infection that could kill her just as easily as childbirth could have done.

27

"Hannah hasn't done anything but help you, Devlin." Conor grabbed the bale of hay his cousin had just lifted up to him, and shoved it across the wagon bed to pack it in tightly against the others. "Don't you reckon it's past time you eased up on the girl?"

"Eased up!" Devlin bit off an oath. "Conor, none of you knows Hannah like I—" He caught himself. Even Conor, his best friend and closest living relative, didn't need to know everything.

"Oh, come on now." The ranch owner paused in his work, walked to the side of the buckboard where Devlin stood, and squatted in the bed. "Let's just spit it out once and for all, then be done with it," he continued, his voice gone low. "None of us knows Hannah like you do because she's one of the women you called on at Sadie Fleming's, isn't she?"

The blood rushed from Devlin's face. He should have known he couldn't keep the full truth from his cousin for long. After a furtive glance around him, he shook his head. "I didn't say that," he whispered hoarsely. "All I meant—"

Conor cut him off. "Ella's going to find out about Hannah sooner or later. Best you tell her sooner, than she find out from someone else later."

Devlin bit his lip and looked away. "She already knows I paid several calls at Sadie's. She's forgiven me, and we've put it all behind us." As he met Conor's piercing gaze, a heavy ache throbbed in the middle of his chest. "And that's where I want it to stay. How can it, though, if Ella finds out about Hannah and has her nose rubbed in it each time that girl walks by? Blast it, Conor! Haven't I hurt Ella enough without telling her about Hannah?

"When will this nightmare be over?" Devlin groaned.

"I don't know." With a sigh, Conor leaned back. "Maybe when it's all out in the open and there are no more secrets or surprises. Have you talked with Hannah about this?"

Devlin gave an incredulous laugh. "Talk to Hannah? Why that would be like falling back in with the devil himself! I'd never give a woman like her a chance to use that to her advantage. And she would. That's all those kind of women know how to do."

"I think you're wrong about her, Devlin. From what Abby tells me, the girl doesn't sound likely to jeopardize what she's got here. You aren't giving either her or Ella a fair shake in this."

"Well, I sure in tarnation can't tell Ella right now." Devlin spun around, turning back to the next bale of hay. There was work to be done. No purpose was served wallowing in his misery. "News like that, on top of everything else she's had to endure, might be the death of her."

"Then let Hannah be. It wouldn't hurt to share a little of the forgiveness *you've* received with her. No sense hoarding it all for yourself."

"Can't say as how I'm in the mood right now to think very kindly of Hannah, much less feel forgiving." The big foreman sighed and shook his head. "Maybe it isn't very honorable, but I can't help it."

His cousin nodded. "Well, a man's got to come to forgiveness in his own time. I sure had to. But just remember. Right now Ella needs Hannah to care for the baby, not to mention do the cooking, cleaning, and help little Mary and Devlin Jr. Abby can't spend every waking moment with Ella and the children anymore. The two hands you sent to fetch Doc Childress that day of the storm have come down with a fever and chills, and Evan told me just this morning he's not feeling all that well either. I'm thinking it's the influenza. Talk has it a mess of folks in Grand View are sick with it."

Devlin slipped his gloved hands beneath the twine encircling another bale, then heaved it to his shoulder. "Yeah, I heard about the influenza that's been going around Grand View." He swung about and tossed the hay into the buckboard. "Talk has it Mary Sue Edgerton nearly died from it, and two of Sadie Fleming's girls finally did."

"It's bad this year. Since Abby's already been exposed in caring for Wendell and Frank, it's probably best she stays away from Ella. And that leaves only Hannah to help you. As much as you might hate to admit it, right now she's the only solution to your problems."

"Easy for you to say," Devlin muttered, not feeling at all mollified. "But then your mistakes aren't thrown in your face every time she walks into your house."

"Sounds like you shot yourself in the foot one time too many, cousin." Conor managed a wry grin. "Just hope you're man enough to take it."

Devlin's lips quirked. Leave it to Conor to always point out the obvious, if sometimes painful, truth. "Yeah, I hope so, too. Guess, for Ella and my kids's sakes, we'll find out."

Hannah finished buttoning the lace collar of the fresh nightgown she had just put on Ella. After pulling up the sheet and blankets to cover the other woman, she retrieved the basin of now dirty wash water, washcloth, and towels.

"Is there anything else I can do for you, Ella?" She glanced down at the woman's pale face. "If not, a nice nap before dinner is in order."

Ella smiled wanly. "Yes, I am rather tired. Do you think, though, that I might hold Bonnie for a few minutes? My fever's been gone for two days. I thought I might try to nurse her."

It had been over a week now since the baby's birth, and almost as many days since Ella had last tried to nurse. It seemed likely, by now, her milk had all but dried up. Still, Hannah couldn't blame her for wanting to try. She had given life to the child; she wanted to be the one to nourish and mother her.

"I'll fetch Bonnie. I nursed her two hours ago." Hannah shot her a quick smile as she began to walk away. "She's a greedy little feeder, that one is, though. She just might be hungry again."

"You've been such a blessing to us, Hannah. What would we have done without you?"

Hannah halted, embarrassed and not knowing quite how to respond. "Abby said it's our Christian duty," she offered finally, "to help each other in any way we can. I'm trying hard to learn to do that."

"And you're learning it well. I'm just thankful I'm here to reap all the benefits."

Hannah laughed and headed again for the door. "Well, I'm just as thankful to be here, too."

"Another blessing, I'd say."

"I suppose so," she amicably agreed, before walking from the room.

As she reached the kitchen, she found Devlin seated at the kitchen table, working on some ledgers. In spite of their unspoken if temporary truce, Hannah couldn't help but stiffen defensively. Though he said nothing, she could feel his barely restrained hostility. Only a thin veneer of civility coated the still evident loathing he felt for her.

She marched to the sink nonetheless, emptied the basin, rinsed it, and set it aside to dry. Then, after washing her hands, she strode to the wooden cradle set near the cookstove and picked up a sleepy Bonnie.

"Where are you going with my daughter?"

Hannah stiffened. Whatever was wrong now? she wondered. "Ella wants to hold her for a few minutes, before she takes a nap."

He glared at her briefly, then tugged at his mustache and resumed his scribbling in the ledger. "Good. It's about time Bonnie got to know her mother."

Rather than waste more of it with me? Hannah silently finished Devlin's sentence for him. She bit the inside of her lip, then chewed on it in frustration. Would nothing she did matter to him? Was there any restitution she could *ever* make that would wipe the slate clean? But then, why should she even care?

"I agree," Hannah forced herself to reply. She cuddled Bonnie closer and inhaled deeply of the baby's sweet scent, then straightened. "Well, if you don't mind, I've got an eager mother waiting to see her child."

Never once looking back up, Devlin made a dismissing motion with his hand. "I just wanted to make it clear who her real mother is."

"Oh, you did, Mr. MacKay," Hannah said through gritted teeth as she walked from the kitchen. "You most certainly did."

The next week passed in a crazy, frantic haze of activity. Three more hands came down with the influenza, as did Conor's ten-year-old daughter, Beth. Save for the most minimal of maintenance duties, such as feeding and watering the livestock, work at Culdee Creek virtually ground to a halt. Those not stricken were called into caring for those who were.

Though Ella improved a bit each day, her condition was still too precarious to risk her catching the dreaded influenza. Devlin—one of the few still healthy workers—

tried to do his part by limiting contact with his wife, even going so far as to bed down at night in the kitchen. As much as she could Hannah also tried, for Ella's sake, to avoid Culdee Creek's other residents—Evan included. Though she wrote him a short, daily note to cheer him up as he recovered from his own bout of influenza, his return missives made it clear he missed her sorely.

For Hannah, time not required preparing meals, washing clothes, and caring for the children was spent talking with and reading to Ella in her and Devlin's bedroom. She helped the other woman when she needed it and played games with Jackson and Ella's two older children when she didn't. From time to time, the confined quarters became too close, and Hannah would bundle up Devlin Jr. and Mary to play outside in the snow.

She also continued to nurse Bonnie, for Ella's milk had indeed dried up. Each time the infant was finally sated, however, Hannah quickly changed her, then laid her in her mother's arms. It was a time Hannah came to cherish. The two women talked of many things. As the days passed, the cordial relationship that had been slowly developing over the past year grew into a deeper trust and friendship.

"You know," Ella said one particularly overcast, windy day as she rested in her bed with Bonnie sleeping contentedly at her side, "I used to think she'd have my red hair, but now I'm not so sure. It's already"—she fingered the fuzzy thatch on her daughter's head—"much darker than mine."

Hannah glanced up from the embroidery work she was applying to a hand-stitched, lace-edged table runner. She leaned forward in the rocker she had pulled up close to Ella's bed and studied Bonnie's hair. "Yes, it is darker, but I still see glints of red. Perhaps she'll have auburn hair."

Ella smiled. "That'd be nice. A pleasing combination, at long last, of Devlin's and my hair colors after my carrot-topped son and brown-haired little Mary."

"They'll make a pretty trio, won't they," Hannah observed, "all lined up and ready for school?"

"Yes, they will."

The conversation eased then into a comfortable silence. Hannah resumed her careful stitching. The rose and ivy motif was filling in nicely. She was quite pleased with the various shades of vermilion she had chosen for the flowers. Combined with the vibrant blooms, the rich emerald and forest green threads of the ivy leaves made a striking contrast against the ivory linen cloth.

"You've really a talent with the needle," Ella commented from beside her. "I've never seen such even, delicate stitches, or such a flair for design and color."

Hannah could feel the heat rise in her cheeks. She still found it hard to accept, much less believe, a compliment. "I learned from a true artist," she replied finally. "My dear friend, Hu Yung, taught me how to sew. It passed the long hours after we were both finally free from our night's work, filling the day with a semblance of refinement and beauty.

"Or at least so it seemed to us." Hannah smiled in sad remembrance. "We were deluding ourselves, of course, but at least it helped us endure the nightmares to come each night. We always had each other and our beautiful sewing to look forward to on the morrow."

"What happened to Hu Yung? Did she, too, finally escape?"

Hannah looked down. At the memories that had been so carefully stored in the deep recesses of her heart, tears swelled. "In a sense, yes, she did. Hu Yung fell in love with a young miner who promised to come back and marry her once he struck it rich. Some months later, though, she got word he'd died in an avalanche. After that all the hope seemed to drain from her. She soon took an overdose of morphine, killing herself."

"Oh, I'm so sorry to hear that." Ella touched Hannah's arm. "She deserved better."

"Yes. Yes, she did." Hannah brushed away the tears that had flooded her eyes. Hu Yung *had* deserved better. Better from life, and better from a friend. A true friend would've known the right thing to say and do to comfort her, to prevent her from taking her life. But she hadn't, Hannah thought, the old, guilty sense of failure rising to engulf her anew.

"She was sold into the brothels, too, you know. Not as early as I was," Hannah hastened to add, forcing her morose thoughts back to the present, "but forced into it nonetheless. A Chinese man from San Francisco returned to his village in China, wooed and wed her, then brought her back to San Francisco, promising her a better life. One day, though, he informed her he would be going on a long trip, and asked if she'd sign an agreement to stay with a friend of his. Only as she was being dragged into a brothel did Hu Yung realize she'd signed her own bill of sale."

"How terrible."

"Yes," was Hannah's stark reply.

She scanned the room. Her gaze snagged on Jackson, who sat near the window engrossed in play with Mary and Devlin Jr. Each time the three children built a tower of blocks, one immediately knocked it over to the accompaniment of much squealing and shouting from the others.

Outside huge, fat flakes drifted past the frost-edged, glass panes. With each blustering gust, the wind sent the snow twirling in a wild, white, blinding dance. From time to time the house timbers rattled, and the wind shrieked high along the roof.

It was a good day to stay inside, Hannah thought, safely snug and cozy warm from the heat radiating from the big kitchen cookstove. At times like this the old life, rife with bitter recollections, seemed far away. This room, alive with love, hope, and children's laughter, was all that mattered.

"Unlike poor Hu Yung," Ella observed, meeting Hannah's gaze with a wise one of her own, "you have so much to live for." She shifted in bed, raising herself up. "I know Jackson makes you happy. I can see it in your eyes every time you look at him. But I'm not always so sure how happy you are being *here,* at Culdee Creek."

Bemused, Hannah turned to face her. "I don't understand why you'd say that. If it weren't for Abby and the life she's given me here . . . well, I don't want to think about what would've happened to me and Jackson."

"I know you're grateful to Abby, Hannah." Ella's gaze locked with hers. "It's just that there always seems a tension in you, a tension . . ." She sighed. "A tension I particularly note whenever you and Devlin are together."

The blood drained from Hannah's face. For a fleeting instant the room whirled before her. She felt sick, dizzy.

She had dreaded this would happen someday. Dreaded the inevitable confrontation over her past involvement with Ella's husband, even as she did her best to deny its existence. This was why she had yet to confront Devlin to iron things out between them. She supposed she had secretly, if foolishly, hoped the whole, horrible mess would just go away.

"I reckon he doesn't care for women like me," she forced herself to reply, knowing Ella expected some sort of answer. "Some folk don't think a fallen woman can ever reform."

"Perhaps," her friend admitted. "But I think there's more to it than that." Ella paused. "There is, isn't there, Hannah?"

36

Suddenly, she couldn't bear to meet Ella's piercing gaze. A wild impulse to rise and run from the room filled her. But Hannah knew it was already too late. She looked away. "I don't know what you mean."

"I think you do. You were one of the women Devlin called on, weren't you, when he went to Sadie Fleming's?"

Ever so slowly, Hannah turned back. So, she thought with a curious mixture of anguish and relief, the secret was out at last. Ella *did* know about Devlin's unfaithfulness.

"Don't you think that's a question better asked of your husband?" Her words came out a husky whisper.

"It *is* a question I must ask of him," the red-haired woman agreed, her gaze calm, her smile serene. "But it's also one to ask you. How else can there ever be an end to all the secrets and pain?"

How else, indeed? Hannah asked herself sadly.

Ella sighed. "Devlin's been so guilt-ridden ever since . . . since he began calling at Sadie's that summer, that he can barely stand to be near you, much less look me in the eye." She shook her head. "I can't begin to tell you how angry it made me."

"You had every right to be angry."

The red-haired woman gave a wry laugh. "Oh, and I was. I assure you. I'm no saint. From the first day you came here, I suspected something between you and Devlin, and it near to ate me up with suspicion and jealousy. In the beginning, though, I tried to convince myself Devlin hated you because you reminded him of his unfaithfulness—an unfaithfulness I suspected long before he finally confessed it to me. But, in time, I realized his guilt and anger at you went far deeper than that."

"I'm sorry . . . so sorry, Ella," Hannah whispered. "I never meant to hurt you. I swear it."

"I know." Tears brightened Ella's eyes. "Still, for the longest time, I had to force myself to be kind to you. Oh, how I fought to hide the bitterness and pain!"

A single tear trickled down her cheek. "The Lord finally pierced the darkness that held me, though," she continued at last, earnest intent now gleaming in her eyes. "I love you both. I don't want either of you to go on suffering because of what you did. The Lord long ago showed me the only way to truly love Him was to love others as He does, and forgive them as He did."

Tears filled Hannah's eyes. "After what I did to you, however unintentionally, I don't deserve your forgiveness, Ella, much less your love."

"Just as none of us can ever deserve God's forgiveness or love." Ella took Hannah's hand. "But that's the mystery of grace. No matter how good we are, we're still never worthy of it."

"Perhaps he offers it to people like you and Abby." Tears clogged Hannah's throat and, for a moment, she couldn't speak. "But never to people like me."

"And who told you that?"

"People. Many people. Even if their lips didn't utter the words, their eyes sure did."

"But never God. Never Jesus Christ, who ate, drank, and associated with harlots, unclean Gentiles, and even hated tax collectors. He saw the soul of each and every person, knew their heart." Ella squeezed her hand. "As He knows your heart."

Hannah managed a watery smile. "I don't deserve a friend like you."

"That's grace then, too, I suppose."

As Ella released her hand and fell back against her pillow, the kitchen door opened and closed. The sound of heavy footsteps echoed on the hardwood floor. Hannah glanced at the small, brass and wood clock sitting on Ella's bureau. Noon. It must be Devlin, home for dinner.

She rose from the rocking chair and smoothed the wrinkles from her dress. "I'd better get the table set. Devlin's sure to be hungry."

"Take the children out with you and send Devlin in to me." Ella's mouth tightened with grim resolve. "It's past time we set God's grace into motion, and begin healing your wounded souls."

3

There is no fear in love; but perfect love casteth out fear.
1 John 4:18

"Come along, children." With Jackson in her arms, Hannah herded Devlin Jr. and Mary into the kitchen ahead of her. "Time to wash up for lunch."

From the bench near the back door, Devlin watched Hannah pull a stool to the sink, then help his son step up to wash his hands. She was fitting in right nicely, he thought, the now familiar surge of irritation swelling anew. If a body didn't know better, one would think she almost fancied herself part of the family.

Well, Devlin resolved, one way or another it wouldn't be for much longer. He had begun to make inquiries for a wet nurse in Grand View. Just as soon as Ella regained her strength and the influenza epidemic was over, he intended to ride to town and bring back the Widow Ashley. Then Miss Hannah Cutler could high-tail it back to her snug little bunkhouse, and the equally snug little life she had managed to make for herself here.

Taking up a rag, Devlin leaned down and used it to wipe as much snow as he could from his boots and blue denims. Then he tossed the cloth aside, stood, and strode to the sink. "What's for dinner?"

Hannah half-turned from her task of drying Devlin Jr.'s hands. "Potato soup, baked chicken, rice, and mashed turnips. Dessert's a bread pudding. Everything's already in the warmer but the soup, and that's simmering nicely."

"You can eat your meal with Ella, if you like. I'll stay with the children in the kitchen."

"That's fine with me." Hannah hesitated. "First, though, Ella wants to talk with you."

His eyes narrowed, suspicion flaring. "What about?"

"I-I think you should ask her."

Devlin didn't like the way Hannah suddenly avoided his gaze. Unease filled him. He grabbed her arm as she turned to put his son down.

"I'm asking you. What does Ella want to talk about?"

"What do you think?" The girl jerked free. "She knows about us, has known for a while. And now she wants things settled."

Bending, Hannah put the little boy down. Mary immediately toddled over, was quickly picked up, and soon had her hands washed and dried. Watching her, the bottom slowly dropped out of Devlin's stomach. Ella knew . . . knew about him and Hannah. He choked on a vicious curse. Now the fat really *was* in the fire!

Fury surged through him. Blast the woman! What had she gone and told his wife? And how, at this late a date, was he to explain himself?

Well, there was no avoiding the issue any longer. He had waited too long as it was. Whatever Hannah had revealed to Ella, his only recourse now lay in trying to make his wife see his side.

Devlin dragged in a deep, steadying breath. Then, his hands clenched at his sides, he headed down the hall to their bedroom.

"Close the door, please," Ella said, as he walked into the room.

He did as requested, coming to stand at the foot of the bed. "Hannah said you wanted to talk with me." He paused for an instant, then forged on. No sense pretending ignorance of the reason for their meeting, Devlin decided. Might as well seize what little advantage remained him in a bold, frontal assault. "Seems she went and told you about her and me."

"She didn't need to say much." Ella met his unflinching gaze. "I figured it out months ago. Who wouldn't, what with the grudge you've held against her since the first day she came here?"

"I didn't want a woman like her keeping company with my wife and children!" Devlin cried out in his defense, feeling as if his world had suddenly turned upside down. "No decent man would."

"Your rancor sprung from a much deeper source than the act of a decent man, Devlin." Ella clenched the edge of her quilt until her hands fisted knuckle-white. "It's long past time you accepted full responsibility for your actions, and stopped trying to lay it at Hannah's door."

Tears of anguish glimmered in her eyes. Frustration filled him. Would there never be an end to it then? Devlin wondered. Would he never, ever, be free of the guilt and shame and pain?

"You need to make your peace with Hannah," his wife said softly. "Not just for your sake, but for the sake of me and the children. We can't be a whole family, a truly happy family, until you do."

Distractedly, Devlin ran his thumb and forefinger down both sides of his mouth, smoothing his long mustache. Whatever did Ella mean by that? he wondered, struggling for time in which to sort through his confusion.

"The only peace I need to make is with you," he finally said. "I'm sorry. I did wrong in keeping the rest of the truth from you, but I only did it to spare you further pain."

"The pain that mattered most to me was the pain you caused when you committed adultery. It was never principally in the fact you committed it with Hannah, though that hurt, too, once I finally figured it out."

He closed his eyes against the tears now trickling down his wife's cheeks. "I did what I saw fit," he groaned. "I did the best I could—"

"You did the best you could to protect *yourself,*" Ella gently corrected him. "And the only way to do that was to place all the blame on Hannah. Yet *you* were the one who sought *her* out."

"I said I was sorry, Ella, and you know I am," he ground out the hated, humiliating words. "What more do you want from me?"

His wife sighed. "Oh, Devlin, you see everything through the eyes of a man rather than through God's eyes! Your sin encompasses not just me, but Hannah, too. Don't you realize, for your contrition to be complete, you must also forgive *and* ask forgiveness of her? Don't you know you must open your heart to God, and accept the healing power of His grace?"

As if he had been struck square in the face, Devlin staggered backward. Surely he had heard wrong. Forgive Hannah and ask her forgiveness? Open his heart to God? Did Ella know what she was asking of him?

It was one thing to beg his wife's forgiveness. He loved her with all his heart and had hurt her deeply. But he had done nothing that justified asking Hannah's forgiveness.

Or had he?

43

She had offered him a service, which he had paid for fair and square. It had been purely a business transaction, sordid and illicit though it was. He had to believe that. To regard what he had done any other way compounded his guilt. To consider it in any other light was to admit he had not only betrayed Ella, but also used Hannah in the basest, most degrading of ways.

Ella's deep religious faith prompted her to bring healing to all who needed it. It was vitally important to her that he and Hannah make peace. It had also always been her dream that he return to the Lord. Yet he couldn't. He just couldn't. And that was the greatest shame, the deepest betrayal, and the most heart-wrenching failure of all.

"I love you, Ella," Devlin finally replied, lowering his head in despair, "but this time you ask too much. I'm sorry. You know how I feel about God, and I can't ask Hannah's forgiveness. I just . . . can't."

She gave a low, anguished cry. Startled, Devlin jerked his gaze to hers. Ella stared up at him for a long, poignant moment, then turned away in dismissal. "It's in the Lord's hands, then," she whispered, "if only you ever open your ears to hear, and your heart to His love."

Two days later, Ella came down with the influenza. It started with a fever, sore throat, and chills. It soon progressed, however, to a severe cough and lung congestion. Doc Childress was called in on the eve of the fourth day of her illness, when Ella began to have breathing difficulties and sporadic bouts of delirium.

"I'll tell you like it is," he informed the small group seated around the kitchen table when his examination was complete. "Ella's bad. She's got pneumonia in both sets of lungs."

Devlin groaned and buried his face in his hands. "What else can go wrong? Isn't she *ever* to have a fighting chance?"

Abby, sitting beside him, reached over and took his hand. "What can we do, Doc?" she asked, meeting the older man's concerned gaze.

"Keep Ella warm, but if her fever gets high, begin sponging her down with tepid water." Doc opened his black bag and removed two dark amber, glass bottles. "Here's a bottle of cough medicine and another of willow bark decoction to help lower her fever. Give Ella a teaspoonful of each every four or five hours as needed."

Devlin looked up. As hard as he fought to contain it, terror filled him. "You're not going to stay? You said she was bad."

Doc Childress sighed and shook his head. "I'll get back here just as soon as I can, but there are other folk who need me, too. This influenza outbreak hasn't run its course yet. Besides, much as I hate to admit it, there's nothing more I can do for Ella than what I just said."

Abby nodded. "We understand. We'll do what you tell us."

"I know you will, Abby." The old man closed his bag. "How many at Culdee Creek are still sick?"

"Three hands and now Beth. But I think the worst is over for them."

Doc Childress rose. "Well, since I'm already here, no harm in paying them all a quick visit."

"I'll come along." Abby released Devlin's hand and stood. "Hannah can stay with Ella in the meanwhile." She shot the girl, who stood looking out the kitchen window, a quick glance. "Can't you, Hannah?"

Hannah swung around. "Yes. Yes, I'd be glad to." She walked to the stove, grabbed a towel, and picked up a steaming kettle of water. "Would you like a cup of tea before you go, Doc?"

He shook his head. "No. I'd best be on my way if I'm to see to my other Culdee Creek patients, and still get back to Grand View before dark. Perhaps another time."

Hannah smiled bleakly. "Yes. Perhaps."

With a sinking heart, Devlin watched as Abby and Doc left the house. A heavy silence fell in the kitchen. Gradually, from down the hall, he could hear the voices of children. *His* children . . .

His heartsick, burdened mind lurched back into action. He needed to keep them away from Ella, or risk them, too, becoming ill.

"You need to move Bonnie out of our bedroom." Once more his glance fell, this time to the table's worn, pitted wood surface. "And I don't want Mary or Devlin Jr. visiting with Ella or playing in our room either."

"I understand."

He looked up at her then. Once again that expression of compassion and empathy seemed to burn in Hannah's striking eyes. It was a compassion and empathy he desperately needed right now, but he didn't dare turn to her for comfort.

"I think I'll give Ella a dose of Doc's medicines," he muttered, rising. Suddenly Devlin felt uncomfortable, restless in Hannah's presence. Ella's words that day in their bedroom had weighed heavily on him ever since, and he couldn't help but wonder how deeply his inability to forgive really went.

"Could you prepare a basin of tepid water?" He met her wary gaze with a steady one of his own. "When last I touched her, Ella felt very hot. I think I'll sponge her down."

"Devlin." Hannah's softly spoken word halted him as he turned to go.

"Yeah, what is it?" He paused, glancing over his shoulder.

"Whatever you need for Ella, please let me know. I mean, if you want me to stay here to be close in case you—"

"Abby'll bunk in until Ella's out of the woods." Devlin knew his words must sound curt, even harsh, but he didn't know how to behave anymore with Hannah. Indeed, he hadn't known for a long while how to deal with the woman who slowly but surely seemed to be emerging. "You're doing more than enough in caring for my children."

"Still, I mean it. Ella's my friend."

"Yes. I know." And the funny thing was, Devlin finally did.

In the middle of the night, Ella took a turn for the worse. She woke up burning with fever, struggling desperately for breath. Devlin and Abby sat her up in bed, propping her with pillows, and still she didn't improve. As the minutes passed and Devlin watched his wife panting and gasping, his sense of helpless panic grew.

"I'm going for Doc," he finally said. "I can't stand here and watch Ella like this, and not try to do something."

"Fetch Hannah on the way out, will you, and send her over here?" Abby glanced up from her task of bathing Ella's brow. "I may need her help."

He nodded. Bending, Devlin tenderly brushed aside the damp, red ringlets clinging to his wife's ashen face. "I'll return soon, dearest. I'll bring back Doc. He'll know what to do."

Ella leaned toward him, reaching to touch his chest. "I-I love y-you. A-always . . . f-forever. I know . . . you think . . . you've failed me . . . but you h-haven't. You're a good m-man, Devlin. . . . You'll s-see that . . . someday."

Her words sounded so much like a farewell that tears sprang to Devlin's eyes. Quickly, furiously, he blinked them away. "I'll hold you to that," he rasped, his throat gone tight with emotion, "just as soon as you're better."

She managed a tremulous smile before falling back against the pillows in exhaustion. Devlin hesitated at her side a moment longer, then turned and strode from the room.

With a heavy-lidded Jackson in tow, Hannah arrived ten minutes later. She took one look at Ella, and promptly carried her son down the hall to where the MacKay children slept. A pallet on the floor was prepared, and Jackson was soon once more sound asleep.

Hannah hurried back to Ella's room. "What do you need me to do?" she asked Abby.

"Make some tea, would you please?" The chestnut-haired woman briskly carried some towels to a small bench that served as a table of sorts. "Perhaps if Ella takes in some fl-fluids." Her voice cracked, then broke. Her knees buckled, and only Hannah's quick response kept Abby from sinking to the floor.

"Come here." Hannah grasped Abby firmly about the waist and guided her to the rocking chair. "I'll make us all some tea. You sit here by Ella. What she needs most now is someone close by."

Abby nodded. With the back of her hand, she swiped away her tears. "Yes, you're right, of course."

Hannah forced a bright little smile. "Of course I'm right," she said before walking from the room.

Ella looked bad, very bad, Hannah thought as she filled the teakettle and placed it on the cookstove. Next she stoked the firebox full of narrow, split dry pine, then opened all the appropriate dampers and regulators. She soon had a hot, fast fire going.

48

As the water in the teakettle warmed, Hannah busied herself setting mugs, spoons, a bowl of sugar, porcelain teapot, and silver tealeaf strainer on a small wooden tray. Her quick work, however, soon left her with extra time—time she would rather not have had. Time to consider the full implications of Ella's condition—and her own, awful helplessness in the matter.

Hannah had seen her share of prostitutes die of one thing or another. She had been present when several actually succumbed to pneumonia. They all, in their final hours, had fought for breath and looked like Ella did.

Fleetingly, an angry frustration warred with her fear for her friend. Devlin should have been made to stay, rather than allowed to ride off on some futile quest for a doctor who could do nothing more. He should have remained with his wife when she needed him the most. He should've been here, for he would surely never see her alive again.

Then shame filled Hannah, and she buried her face in her hands. She wasn't being fair to Devlin. He was as scared as the rest of them. He was only trying to do what he could. Besides, what really mattered now wasn't Devlin, but Ella.

Ah, Lord, Hannah prayed. Abby claims You are a merciful, loving God. If that's really so, and You must take Ella this night, don't let her suffer long. Take her gently up to You, and gather her into Your loving arms.

She blinked back hot tears. Her hands fisted, and she ground them into her eyes. If anyone deserved to die peacefully and painlessly, it was Ella MacKay. Yet the cruelest irony was that Ella didn't deserve to die at all. Not now at least, in the prime of her life, with young children to care for and a husband who loved her.

It was so unfair. How could a truly good and merciful God do this to one of His most faithful servants? And, even more horrible to contemplate, if He would permit this to happen to a woman as kind and virtuous as Ella, what would He someday do to one such as she?

From somewhere outside, a chill wind found a chink in the window frame and swirled into the room. Hannah shivered. The night, dark and cold and lonely, closed in on her. Fear and confusion swallowed her. She floundered in a storm-tossed sea of despairing memories, feeling so alone and afraid she almost cried out from the pain.

The worst pain, the most bitter memory of all, though, was of that sweltering summer night three years ago when she had found Hu Yung, dying from her morphine overdose.

"Alone," the young woman had whispered. "So alone . . . and afraid . . . " Then, with one final, shuddering sigh, she had died in Hannah's arms.

Alone and afraid . . . Even now, the memory of those piteous words struck a chord of terror and remorse in Hannah's heart. Poor Hu Yung had finally lost hope in life and in herself, and she had given up. No one had been able to help her, not even Hannah, who had thought they were friends.

But then, what kind of friend had she really been? Obviously not enough of a friend to recognize the depths of Hu Yung's despair. And not a wise enough friend to know how to help her.

She didn't know how to help Ella either. All she could do was be with her, but that seemed so paltry and insufficient. Ella deserved much more from her than that, as had Hu Yung.

A high, thin whistle shrilled in the distance. Hannah jumped, momentarily disoriented. Then reality returned.

The teakettle . . . The water was ready.

She pushed to her feet, walked to the stove, and mechanically took up the now steaming kettle. She set the tealeaf strainer over the painted porcelain teapot, then poured the boiling water through it. It felt good to do something that grounded her in the here and now, Hannah thought, suddenly thankful for anything that drew her back to the real world.

That real world, she noted as she finally, tray in hand, reentered Ella's bedroom, didn't seem all that frightening anymore. A sense of peace, even joy, now pervaded the room. Curious, Hannah set the tray on the bureau then turned to study Ella more closely. Eyes closed, the red-haired woman clutched her Bible to her breast, her expression startlingly beautiful.

Perplexed, Hannah joined Abby. "What . . . what's happened? She looks . . . different."

"I read her the twenty-third psalm, and then her favorite verses from the first book of John, chapter four. It filled Ella with such joy and comfort." Abby sighed, then smiled. "Oh, Hannah, I wish you'd been here to see the effect those words had on her!"

"I can see enough. That joy and comfort is with her still," Hannah observed, strangely unsettled. "I only wish I might someday find even half that for myself."

Abby took her hand and squeezed it. "You will. Trust in the Lord, and you will."

"H-Hannah?" Ella's lids lifted. She looked straight at her, then extended a shaky hand.

"Go on," Abby whispered. "I think she needs to say good-bye."

Instantly, an urge to turn and run flooded Hannah. She was no good at such heart-wrenching times. She knew no words of consolation that might ease Ella's way.

But Ella was her friend. No matter how desperately she wished to do it, she couldn't run away. Hannah dragged in a steadying breath, then walked over to sit beside her. "Yes?" She laid a hand over Ella's. "I'm here."

"Th-the children . . . " The woman forced out the words with great difficulty. "H-help take care of them . . . for me. L-love them."

"I will. I promise."

"And D-Devlin," the dying woman whispered. "F-forgive him." Tears filled her eyes and coursed down her cheeks. "He needs . . . forgiveness . . . so b-badly."

Frantically, Hannah looked to Abby. Concern and understanding gleamed in her tear-bright eyes. She gave a slight nod. Hannah knew she was urging her to acquiesce.

But to render such a promise, when Hannah harbored no illusions about how Devlin still felt about her . . .

Forgive him.

What had Ella said, just before she had gotten her to fetch Devlin from the kitchen that day? Something about how truly loving God was to love and forgive as He did? Even those who didn't seem to deserve it, like Devlin MacKay.

Such was also the gift of God's grace, she recalled Ella saying, that unearned, undeserved favor He had bestowed on all. God only asked the same as He gave.

"Gr-grace, Hannah." As if she had seen into her innermost thoughts, Ella reached up and clung to her, gasping out the words. "Grace . . . "

"Yes, Ella," Hannah repeated softly, leaning close. "Grace. It's what I need, what I'll pray for, in order to find some way to forgive Devlin. I promise to try."

Ella smiled and nodded, then fell back onto her pillows. Her grip on Hannah loosened; her eyes slid shut. A few minutes later, she was gone.

4

The LORD gave, and the LORD hath taken away, blessed be the name of the LORD.

Job 1:21

Two days later, on a bright, balmy, late April morn, Ella's funeral took place. She was buried near Sally MacKay, Conor's first wife and Evan's mother, in Grand View's pine-studded cemetery. As he had for Sally, the Reverend Noah Starr presided at the internment ceremony.

Afterwards, as Hannah helped Abby load the children into the buckboard, the young priest walked over. Watching him approach, she had to admit she found his dark blond, wavy hair, brown eyes flecked with gold, well-molded mouth, and finely hewn features quite attractive. Though only of moderate height, Noah Starr moved with an athletic grace that bespoke great power and strength.

That physical presence, however, was only enhanced by his personality, which was gentle, patient, and seemingly very compassionate. Though only twenty-four and out of seminary just six months, he already promised to be a far more impressive pastor than his aging, infirm uncle under whom he currently served. But he also seemed, to Hannah's way of thinking, too good to be true. She always felt uneasy in his presence.

She couldn't pretend to ignore him, though, when the Episcopal priest finally drew up beside her. Abby was busy helping Beth settle Devlin Jr., Mary, and Jackson in a snug little nest of quilts and blankets behind the buckboard's front seat, while Hannah, with only baby Bonnie to hold, stood there relatively unencumbered. There seemed no polite way to escape Noah Starr, so she plastered on her most welcoming, social smile and faced him down.

"Is there something more we can do for you, Father?"

He returned her smile with one Hannah wagered was far more natural and sincere than hers had been.

"Is there anything else needed for Mr. MacKay and his family?" the blond man asked. "The ladies of the church have offered their services—cooking meals, taking in the children for a time, mending clothes . . . you know . . . things like that."

Did this priest seriously think they weren't capable of taking care of Devlin and his family? Or was it something more, Hannah wondered, perhaps involving some prejudice against her because of her past? She could well imagine the furor in Grand View that news of her helping with Devlin's children would cause.

Nonetheless, Hannah clamped down on her immediate swell of anger. She shot Abby, who had joined them after finishing with the children, a quick, sideways glance.

"Can't say as I know of anything we need right now," she finally replied. "I've been doing the cooking and cleaning for Devlin's family since Ella delivered, as well as caring for his children. Perhaps you'd do better to ask him if he still finds anything lacking."

Noah's gaze moved to where Devlin stood at the gravesite, head bowed, hands fisted at his sides, his stance rigid and angry. For a fleeting instant, the young priest's features softened. "I would," he said, a pensive note in his voice, "but right now he hardly seems open to any assistance, especially from the religious domain."

"Please thank the ladies, will you, Father?" Abby interjected briskly. "We're managing as best as we can right now. In time Devlin might be open to speaking with you, but for now"—she sighed and nodded in affirmation of his words—"for now I don't think any offer from the church would be well accepted."

"He's blessed to have a strong, supportive family." Once more the Reverend Starr's gaze swung back to the two women, and settled finally on Hannah. "And good friends, too."

"Ella was my friend. Unfortunately, the same can't be said for Devlin and me."

At Hannah's blunt reply Noah Starr's eyes momentarily widened. He studied her for a long moment, then nodded. "Still, Devlin will need friends to help him get through the pain and loss. Frequently, losing a loved one changes a person and opens his heart to the truly important things in life."

Though Hannah couldn't ever conceive of being Devlin's friend, she *could* feel some compassion for his grief. He didn't deserve a wife like Ella. Still, for all his faults, Devlin *had* deeply loved her and had lost much with her death.

"Perhaps," she conceded grudgingly. "I never said I wouldn't continue to offer him my assistance, no matter how I feel about him. For Ella's sake I *will* be there for her children."

The priest smiled. "I'm glad to hear that, Hannah." He cocked his head. "Can I hope that we might see you in church someday? I'm sure Abby–"

"With two babies to care for"–blushing furiously, Hannah quickly cut him off–"both of us can't be gone from the ranch at the same time. And it's just too hard to bring all the children along to town very often."

"Well, in time as the babies grow older," Noah persisted, "things might change. Then–"

"Things will never change!" she blurted, at the end of her patience. Perhaps it wasn't wise to speak her mind so forcefully, but she was tired of pretending she didn't care how people thought of her. "I know you're new to Grand View and to the ministry, but it's time you faced facts. The townspeople know about my past all too well. They'd never hold with having me in their precious church."

"God's house is meant for all, Hannah." The priest's words were gentle, softly spoken now. "In time, the congregation would accept that."

"No." She firmly shook her head. "No, they wouldn't. You'd probably lose most of your congregation if I dared step foot in church."

Fervent zeal burning in his eyes, Noah opened his mouth to reply as Abby laid a hand on Hannah's shoulder. "Though I'm sure Hannah appreciates your intentions as much as I, Father," she interjected with quiet emphasis, "this isn't the time or place for such a discussion. We need to get the children home."

He flushed, nodded, then stepped back. "Yes, of course you're right, Mrs. MacKay. Sometimes my good intentions do overstep themselves." Noah turned back to Hannah. "We'll talk again soon. The Lord always prevails, and I know He wishes for you to join us."

Gazing up at him, Hannah suddenly knew why the Reverend Starr made her feel so uneasy. Not only did he seem too good to be true, but he was also extremely naïve in the ways of people and the deep-seated prejudices they held. Because of that, he possessed the potential to do her great harm.

He could bring fresh attention to her. He could inadvertently stir up public resentment, causing problems for Conor and Abby. Even if only indirectly, he could, Hannah realized with a ripple of fear, threaten her secure life at Culdee Creek.

But the young and idealistic priest could and would not see it that way. Only time would remove the blinders from his eyes. Meanwhile, Hannah didn't intend to be anyone's sacrificial lamb.

She turned and climbed into the buckboard. "Good day, Father Starr."

The priest recognized the dismissal and rendered them both a quick nod. "Good day, ladies." He turned and walked away.

The ride back to the ranch was somber and sad. Conor and Evan rode on ahead with Devlin, one man on either side of him. Abby and Hannah—Bonnie in her arms—followed a short distance behind with the children. A small group of ranch hands brought up the rear.

Beside her, Abby drove the team of horses pulling the buckboard with calm expertise. Hannah studied her covertly. She knew her friend deeply grieved Ella's passing. Ella had been the one to welcome Abby when she had first arrived at Culdee Creek to work as Conor's cook, housekeeper, and tutor for his then nine-year-old daughter, Beth. Ella had been the one who had supported her through the difficult months with an embittered, irascible employer and his love-starved, troubled daughter. The bond between the two women had grown deep and strong.

The strain of the past month showed on Abby. She looked pale and exhausted, and had lost weight. Though she had never contracted a full case of the influenza in the weeks of caring for those stricken, Hannah knew Abby had been fighting nausea and feeling poorly almost the whole time. She imagined her friend was near sick to death with grief, too.

Hannah vowed to make more time to help Abby. It was the least she could do for a good and true friend.

The day had turned cool but remained sunny, and a brisk spring breeze rattled the winter-browned grass. At the ground, Hannah could see tiny flashes of green. It made her smile.

Spring was definitely upon them. Another few weeks and everything would brighten with color. Another few weeks and the risk of winter would finally be over.

It was strange, though, to anticipate nature's rebirth on this day. Ella had died. Her life was over, yet the world went on around them as if seemingly unaffected.

Somehow, that seemed callous and cruel. But then why should she be surprised? Hannah asked herself, her mood taking a dark, painful turn. In the end they were all destined for suffering and death. Only Abby's unwavering faith in God seemed to hold out hope for something better. Yet some days, Hannah wasn't so sure she would ever possess a faith as strong as that.

Movement behind her pulled Hannah from her thoughts. For the first time in the past few days the children began to giggle. Hannah glanced over her shoulder.

A feather had worked free from one of the old quilts and had somehow stuck to the tip of her son's nose. He looked at it cross-eyed and swatted awkwardly at it, but kept missing.

Mary and Devlin Jr. pointed, but did nothing to aid him. Beth smiled in amused tolerance. Finally, when Jackson's frustration level reached its limits and tears filled his eyes, Hannah leaned back and sent the feather flying with a quick flick of her thumb and middle finger.

"Funny thing, isn't it, how just when you think life is the most dismal, hopeless fate a person could endure," Abby observed with a backward glance and smile, "something funny or endearing happens to make you think twice. Then you remember all the blessings you still have, and thank the dear Lord for reminding you."

"I just hope Devlin can remember that when he sees his children," Hannah muttered, turning her attention once more to the three men riding ahead. "I fear they'll be all he has to cling to for a long while to come."

Her friend shot her a slanting look. "You care more for Devlin than you let on back there with Father Starr. I'm glad you don't hate him anymore. That's the greatest tribute you could pay Ella."

"No, I don't hate him anymore." She sighed and clutched Bonnie closer, her emotions suddenly all ajumble. "I can't say as I particularly like or trust him, though. It's just so difficult at times . . ."

"No one ever said following the Lord would be easy, Hannah." Abby's lips quirked. "Sad to say, most of our biggest crosses in life turn out to be other people."

Once more, Hannah's gaze settled on Devlin, shoulders slumped, head down. "Well, he's certainly one of *my* biggest crosses. I only wish I knew how to get him to like me. It would make things so much easier with me in his house, taking care of Bonnie and—"

"You aren't going to be taking care of the children anymore." As if to add extra emphasis to her words, Abby slapped the reins over the horses' backs, urging them to a quicker pace.

59

Hannah's stomach gave a great lurch. Frowning in confusion, she turned in her seat to face Abby. "What do you mean? You heard Ella ask me to help take care of them, to love them."

Abby shot her a quick, apologetic glance. "Devlin's made arrangements with a Widow Ashley to come out to the ranch this afternoon. She lost her husband in the influenza epidemic, and needs some sort of employment to support her and her infant son. She'll be Bonnie's new wet nurse, besides care for the children and the house."

Hannah felt sick. She also felt hurt, betrayed, and totally disoriented. She had hoped she'd be permitted to continue to nurse Bonnie and take care of Mary and Devlin Jr. But then she had also hoped that, in time, Devlin would come to accept and forgive her.

Now it seemed it was never to be. She swallowed hard. "Where will this . . . this Mrs. Ashley be staying?"

"Devlin thought it best if she bunked in with you. There is the spare bedroom . . ."

Through the haze of pain and disbelief, anger gradually filled Hannah. So it had all been planned, and she had never once been privy to it.

"When exactly was he intending on telling me?" she demanded hoarsely. "When the woman pulled up at the bunkhouse with her son and all her belongings?"

"Please, Hannah," Abby pleaded, "try to understand. I suppose I should've told you, but I kept hoping Devlin might change his mind." The chestnut-haired woman sighed and shook her head. "Seems, though, he's had this planned for a while. Even before Ella took sick with the influenza."

She reached over and grasped Hannah's hand. "I'm so sorry. He's not being fair to you."

Tears stung Hannah's eyes. "He's never, ever, been fair. And now . . . now for him to do this." Her hand fisted and she pounded her thigh. "He has never valued what

I did for him and his family. I've never been anything more to him than something to be used and tossed aside at the first opportunity!"

"Oh, Hannah," Abby cried softly. "Don't say that. Devlin's not himself right now. Maybe in time, once things settle down and he has a chance to think things through more clearly . . ."

"No." The girl shook her head. "He won't change his mind. Not Devlin."

The tears fell unchecked now, and she found she didn't care. She had been a fool to hope Devlin would ever change. She had been even more of a fool to care. But, blast it all, she *did* care.

Hannah had always wanted to belong, to be accepted. She supposed, over time, Devlin MacKay had come to represent that goal. In some crazy, mixed-up way, Hannah imagined if she could gain his respect, the respect of a man who had used and then discarded her, she would have finally achieved her dream. She would finally have redeemed her lost purity—and her soul.

But that was exactly all it was and ever would be—a crazy, mixed-up dream.

"No," Hannah repeated softly, "he won't change his mind. But it doesn't matter anymore. I won't *let* it matter."

Martha Ashley was an impressive woman. Tall, big-boned, and possessing a very ample bosom, the fiery-cheeked, ebony-haired woman swept into Devlin's house with all the authority and might of a conquering army. She soon marshaled Mary and Devlin Jr. into their bedrooms in submissive, overawed silence, ensconced her own six-month-old son, Harold, in a crib in the kitchen, then immediately set about rearranging the kitchenware into what she described as a "more efficient system." She didn't, however, stop there.

Clucking her tongue as she went, Mrs. Ashley swept and scrubbed the floor, washed down the cabinets and table, and cleaned and oiled the cookstove. "I know your poor wife, God rest her soul, was in no condition to maintain this kitchen," she explained as she worked, "but that last girl you had—what was her name? Anna?—was really a most disappointing housekeeper."

"Her name's Hannah," Devlin patiently corrected her. "And considering the state of things at the time, she managed well enough. None of us went hungry or had to wear torn or dirty clothes."

Even as he uttered the words, Devlin couldn't quite believe he was defending Hannah. But then, he also had no idea the Widow Ashley was such a dynamo. In the space of but an hour he was already beginning to recall Hannah's presence as a soothing balm. Soothing at least, he thought wryly, in comparison to this other woman's frenetic manner.

Mrs. Ashley shot him a dubious look from beneath a pair of finely arched black brows. "I'm sure you're being far too kind in your assessment of the situation. Most men are. But never you mind. I'm here now. Things will be run in a proper, orderly manner."

Glancing about the already pristinely clean, efficiently organized kitchen, Devlin had no doubt that they would. In the end, it didn't matter to him one way or another, just as long as his children were well cared for and there were decent meals on the table. That was about all he could deal with at any rate, he admitted as a freshened wave of grief washed over him. Ella was gone, and the only things left in life that mattered to him were his children.

"I'd appreciate some calm and order, Mrs. Ashley," he mumbled, wanting nothing more at the moment than to retire to a darkened room and the solitude of his thoughts. "I'll be in my bedroom for a while. I'm tired and think I'll lay down."

"Please, call me Martha. And yes, you do that, Mr. MacKay," the woman cooed, fluttering her hands at him in a strangely incongruous shooing motion. "Take all the time you need. I'm sure I can find everything just fine."

"I'm sure you can . . . Martha." He began to walk away.

"Oh, one thing more, Mr. MacKay."

Wearily, Devlin halted and turned. "Yes? What is it?"

"Before you lie down, could you bring the baby and her cradle out here to stand beside Harold's? That way whenever it's time to nurse her, I won't have to disturb you. It will work out far more efficiently."

Somehow, the thought of leaving Bonnie out here, in the midst of all the noise and activity he was certain Martha Ashley would create, didn't set well with Devlin. The woman, however, seemed to put a premium on getting everything done in an expedient manner.

Still, what other choice was there? Perhaps, in time, the Widow Ashley would relax and slow down. Maybe she was just trying overly hard right now to impress him. Yes, surely everything would soon settle back into some semblance of the way it used to be.

Except that Ella was gone forever, Devlin recalled, the memory stabbing through him with a fierce, freshened agony. Because of that, surely nothing could or would ever be the same again.

5

Thou shalt not harden thine heart, nor shut thine hand from thy poor brother.

Deuteronomy 15:7

"Well, she certainly didn't waste any time moving in and taking charge, did she?" Abby observed a week later, after returning to the main house from a short visit to Devlin's.

Hannah glanced up from the freshly plucked roasting chicken she was stuffing with corn bread and herbs. "Widow Ashley, you mean?" The memory of Abby's report of the woman's brisk efficiency in rearranging Ella's kitchen filled her with misgiving. She sighed, then returned her attention to the chicken. "I suppose she means well. I just hope she has a care for the children. What they need most now is a lot of hugging and loving, not a spotless kitchen and strict routine."

"How true," her friend murmured. She removed her coat and hung it on a peg by the back door, then walked to the big cast-iron cookstove and took down a white cotton apron from the peg beside it. "Problem is," she said as she donned the apron, "I'm worried Devlin's new housekeeper won't see it that way. And Devlin certainly isn't in any frame of mind to offer much comfort to his children right now."

Sadly, Abby shook her head. "Conor says he can barely drag himself out to do his work, and most of what he does needs redoing."

Hannah skewered shut the chicken's now stuffed cavity, placed it in a roasting pan, then quickly sprinkled it with salt and pepper. "He needs to stop thinking just of himself and his own pain," she muttered, her irritation beginning to rise. "Most of Devlin MacKay's problems arise from his own, self-centered outlook."

An angry frustration filled her as she carried the chicken to the stove and thrust it into the oven. It was bad enough he treated *her* so badly. It was unconscionable if he began to neglect his own children because he allowed himself to become mired in his sorrow.

"I know he loved Ella," Hannah hastened to add when she turned and noted the pain in Abby's eyes, "but he also needs to remember he's the father of her children. Ella doesn't need his grief. She needs him to take care of and love her children!"

"It's not that easy, Hannah." Abby walked to the nearest of the two kitchen cupboards and took down two thick pottery mugs. She placed them on the table, filled a silver tea strainer full of tea leaves, then walked to the stove and took up the teakettle. "Come on," she urged as she placed the tea strainer over one mug and poured hot water through it, then did the same with the other, "let's take a short break and talk."

Her words about Devlin were uncharitable. Hannah knew it, yet she still couldn't keep silent. As much as it might disappoint Abby, she thought as she took her seat

65

at the table, she was tired of always having to be the one to turn the other cheek.

"Devlin's still in the very early stages of his grief." Abby slid a mug of tea over to her. "Right now, all he feels is pain. It consumes him so completely he can't see outside himself. He'll pass through this in time, but until he does, it's up to us to help him. It's up to us to accept his limitations and carry the responsibilities he's not able to bear right now."

Shame filled Hannah. In so many ways, she was no different from Devlin. So many times, in her own pain and need, she, too, forgot about everything but herself. "Like the responsibilities of his children? Is that what you're saying?"

"Yes." Abby nodded, a gentle smile on her lips. "Like his children. We need to help Devlin see the blessing he has in them. But we must accept Devlin, as well, allowing him the time he needs to come to terms with his loss. And that time must be his, never ours."

Hannah gripped her mug of tea, savoring the reassuring warmth that radiated through the thick pottery. "I know I should be more patient and understanding of Devlin, especially just now." She expelled a long, frustrated breath. "But it's hard when I don't trust or even like him. If the truth be told, sometimes I actually even fear him."

"Fear him? Why? Has he ever threatened you or raised a hand to you?"

"No." Hannah shook her head. "He's never physically threatened me. For all his animosity toward me, I don't think Devlin's that kind of man. It's just"—she dragged in a deep breath, hesitating over whether she should reveal this even to Abby—"it's just that he's family, and I'm not. In the end, if it came down to choosing between Devlin or me, I know you'd have to choose Devlin."

Abby reached across and grasped her hand. "And you're still afraid he might force it to that, is that it? That, although Conor and I have never, since that first night you came to Culdee Creek, discussed you leaving, you might yet be asked to do so?"

"Yes." Hannah hung her head. "And what would I do then? I haven't many skills save what housekeeping ones you've taught me, and what I've learned in a brothel." She lifted her tear-filled gaze to Abby's. "Still, it's more than that. I can't help it, but even after all this time I feel so unclean, so unworthy. I still doubt my strength sometimes. I still don't trust myself not to return to the old life.

"Don't get me wrong, Abby," she hastened to add, when her friend opened her mouth to protest. "If it were only me, I'd die before ever going back to that life. I'd scrabble out any kind of a living I could, even beg and wear rags if need be, just to stay out of another brothel. But it isn't just me anymore. Now I also have to think of Jackson."

"Ah, Hannah, Hannah." Her friend expelled an exasperated breath. "You talk as if you've no other options, but that's not true. You could always get a job somewhere cooking or cleaning. Maybe not in Grand View, but the Springs is a big town and far enough away that no one there would know about your past.

"And what about Evan?" she continued. "We haven't had much time to talk in the past few weeks, and I know you've had your doubts about rushing into marriage, but have you come to any decision about him?"

Hannah paused to take a tentative sip of her tea. It was still quite hot, but it tasted good, soothing chamomile overlaid with a faint bite of mint. "I'm not ready to marry anyone," she replied finally. "Besides, it wouldn't be fair to Evan. My feelings for him are still so confused. I don't know if I could ever love him like a woman should love a man she wants to wed, and he deserves better than that."

"You deserve better than that, too." Abby smiled and patted her hand. "After what you've been through, it's quite understandable you might need a good amount of time to set your heart and head straight. I didn't mean to imply Evan was the answer to all your problems, unless *you* saw him in that light. And I'm grateful you've never chosen to take advantage of his affection for you."

Hannah smiled ruefully. "You give me too much credit. Marriage to him as the answer to all my problems *has* crossed my mind many a time. Especially when things get bad with Devlin. But that's not it."

"Then what is it?" Abby leaned forward, concern now darkening her eyes. "Tell me, and let me help."

Hannah gave a wry laugh. "That *is* the problem. You're a comfort and help to everyone, and I . . . well, I fail everyone who ever needs me."

Her friend frowned in puzzlement. "I don't understand. You're a kind, generous woman."

Pain lanced through Hannah. It was so hard to reveal such a shameful secret—especially to Abby, who trusted and cared for her. "It's all a lie, a face I put on to please others and protect myself," she blurted at last. "But there's nothing of any value beneath that pleasant shell. I have nothing to offer to others. Nothing!"

"You were there for Ella in her last moments. And she told me the story about that poor Chinese girl you befriended. You didn't fail them . . ." Abby's voice faded as Hannah gave a soft cry and buried her face in her hands.

"Yes. Yes, I did!" Muffled through the barrier of her hands, her words sounded strangled and harsh, but Hannah didn't care. "I'm no good at being anyone's friend. You might as well know it now, rather than later when you might really need me."

"Oh, Hannah, Hannah." Abby rose from the table and came around to hug her. "Why do you see only your failings and limitations, and ignore all the other, far more numerous times you've done good?"

"Because I c-can't see how I've h-helped," she sobbed. "All I know is I failed Hu Yung and Ella when they needed me. Hu Yung might still be alive if I'd been more sensitive to her pain, and Ella . . . well, I didn't know what to say or do to comfort her."

"You can't save everyone, Hannah," Abby crooned, stroking her hair. "All anyone can do is try. Be there for another, do your best, and love with all your heart. That takes a lot of trust, courage, and patience, though. After all, we don't always know for quite some time what impact we've had, or how it all fits into God's plan."

Hannah lifted her tear-streaked face. A tiny ray of hope touched her heart. "I do try to believe that—about God, I mean. It's just so very hard to accept, or to trust in Him sometimes." She gave a shaky little laugh. "It's also so very hard to wait patiently for His results."

Abby chuckled. "Ah, yes. Patience is hard. I struggled a lot with that when I first came to Culdee Creek. Conor and Beth set about testing me at every turn . . . Believe me, I questioned the Lord and His will a lot in those days."

By now, Hannah knew Abby's story well—the loss of her first husband in a tragic railroad accident and then, less than a year later, the death of her five-year-old son from diphtheria. It had taken great courage to accept the job of housekeeper and tutor at Culdee Creek. Especially considering Conor MacKay's less-than-commendable reputation in those days.

"But you persevered," Hannah said, finishing her story for her, "and now you have your reward."

"Rather, I've received a glorious gift," Abby corrected gently, "in Conor and his children. And in receiving it,

I've learned that everything God gives us is good–the pain as well as the happiness."

"I doubt Devlin thinks so just now." Or me, either, for that matter, Hannah silently added. Sometimes, especially when talk turned to things spiritual, Abby could speak in such riddles. How could the pain of someone's death ever be something good? What good had come of Hu Yung's and Ella's deaths?

"No, I don't imagine Devlin would be inclined to see any hope in his loss," Abby agreed with a soft sigh. "He's a man beset with personal demons, many of which he carried into his marriage with Ella. He's come a long way since then, but the wounds of his childhood pain him still."

"Well, mine pain me, too," Hannah ground out, struggling to contain a sudden surge of bitterness, "but I haven't let it eat me up, or used it as a club against others."

"I know you haven't, Hannah." Compassion warmed Abby's eyes. "I remember you telling me how hard you tried to care for your poor mother when she turned sick after your papa died. And then how you were sent to that orphanage . . ." As if in remembrance, she shivered. "I don't know how you managed to stay at that terrible place as long as you did."

"One way or another, I should've," the girl muttered, the memories flooding back. "If I had stayed just a few more years, until I came of age, I might have left with a passel more opportunities than I ever gained by being forced to work in a brothel."

"Conor would say you make your own opportunities out of what life deals you. And *I'd* say that's what you've done in the past year since you came to Culdee Creek."

The savory, herb-laden scent of roasting chicken reached Hannah. She rose, walked to the cookstove, and opened the oven door to check on the bird. It was beginning to cook nicely. She took a moment to baste it before closing the oven and returning to the table. "The chicken should be ready in an hour. Guess I'd better get the water on to boil some potatoes."

Abby drained the last of her tea. "Yes, and I'd better get to icing the spice cake." She paused. "Devlin's really a good man at heart, Hannah. I hope you'll see that in time."

"Maybe I will," Hannah grudgingly agreed as she filled the pot from the pitcher pump. "All I know is he still blames me for cheating on Ella, and it colors everything he says and does." She carried the pot to the stove and placed it on a back burner. "You had guessed by now, hadn't you, that I was one of the girls he visited there?"

"Yes, I had."

"A lot of married men came to me like that, full of excuses why they couldn't help themselves, why it was someone else's fault they were there." Angry now, Hannah turned to Abby. "But that's all their stories ever were to me. Excuses. They took vows to love and honor their wives until death. Yet they were also the same men who sat in church each Sunday with their families, piously praying and singing hymns. A bunch of bald-faced hypocrites is what I call them." She gave a sharp, bitter laugh. "I'm sorry if this makes me sound mean, but I'm tired of always having to carry all the blame."

Abby's mouth quirked in sympathy. "You've a right to feel hurt and angry, Hannah. But you also have to someday move past them to forgiveness or you'll never be healed. Just remember. We all have our weaknesses, our personal demons. Thank heavens God loves us in spite of them."

"Well, maybe God can see past Devlin's weaknesses," Hannah muttered, "but it's not that easy for me."

"All I can say in Devlin's defense is that he made a mistake, and he regrets it to this day."

71

At the thought, Hannah shivered in revulsion. "Men and their lusts! I'm so sick of how totally it controls them, and of the terrible destruction it wreaks on innocent women."

"It's not all disgusting or destructive, Hannah," Abby said. "When a man and woman come together in a loving, holy union, it can be so very, very beautiful. As are its fruits—the children they conceive."

Hannah closed her eyes, unwilling to accept such a consideration. How *could* she? Until Hannah had come to Culdee Creek, all she had ever known was shame, selfish manipulation and, sometimes, even pain at the hands of men. She had been forced to hide her true feelings and needs and subject herself to depraved desires, pawing hands, and sweating, heaving bodies. Few men had seen her as anything other than an object of pleasure meant to serve them. She had hated them all—even Devlin MacKay.

It was that hatred—and shame—that had pushed her to run away from Sadie Fleming's that night, climbing onto the roof outside her window and scrambling down the rose trellis beside the front porch. The vicious thorns had pricked her skin, leaving deep scratches that oozed and bled, but it didn't matter. Heedless, she had run off into the darkness, bringing nothing with her but the clothes on her back. She had run all night until a passing freight wagon bound for the Springs had stopped, and the grizzled old driver had taken pity on her.

Six weeks later, the two bodyguards Sadie sent out after her found her and dragged her back. Six weeks . . . long enough for Hannah to discover she was pregnant.

She could never be certain whose child she carried, but it didn't matter. She clutched the secret to her like a priceless jewel, managing to hide her advancing girth far past the time any unscrupulous doctor would've dared take the baby from her. She had needed to—she had seen what Sadie had done to other girls who had revealed their pregnancies too early.

Her lips curved in scathing disdain. Yes, a man had indeed gifted her with a beautiful child, but it hadn't been through some loving, holy union. And no man had stepped forward to claim that child either, or offered to care for it.

It was all her fault, after all, that she had conceived. It was her shame, and her shame alone, that she flaunted each time she dared bring Jackson with her to town.

Her shame . . . her fault . . . and never, ever, that of the men who had paid for and used her. There was nothing beautiful about that.

6

As thou hast done, it shall be done unto thee.
Obadiah 15

Late that night, Hannah awoke to a pounding on the bunkhouse door. Groggy with sleep, she stumbled out of bed, threw on a wrapper, and staggered through the parlor to the front door. Evan stood there, a stricken look on his face.

"Come quick!" He grabbed her hand and tugged her forward. "Abby's real sick. She needs you."

"Abby?" Hannah's heart gave a sickening lurch. "What happened? What's wrong?"

"We don't know. Pa said she just woke up with pains and then began to bleed. I've already sent a hand to fetch Doc Childress."

"Give me a moment to dress," she urged with a quick squeeze of his hand, "and I'll be right over."

He managed a nod and lopsided grin, then turned on his heel and strode away. Hannah wasted no time slipping into a plain, blue cotton dress and her shoes. After changing Jackson's wet diaper and dressing him warmly, she clutched her son close and hurried to the main house.

Evan awaited her in the kitchen. Hannah's glance immediately went to the stairs leading to the house's second story. "Is Abby in her bedroom?"

"Yes. Pa's with her."

"Here." She deposited Jackson in Evan's arms. "Hold him."

Hannah quickly stoked the cookstove and filled the teakettle and a large pot with water. "Keep an eye on the water," she then instructed Evan. "We might need some once Doc gets here. And keep an eye on Jackson for me, too."

"Uh, Hannah, I don't know much about babies." As if to add further credence to his words, Evan shifted Jackson from one arm to the other, then back again. "What do I do if he cries, or makes a mess in his drawers?"

She shot him a long-suffering look. "I just changed him, so odds are you won't have to endure a dirty diaper. And if he gets fussy, rock him and he might go back to sleep. If not, find him a biscuit or something else hard to chew on."

Before he could utter further protests or excuses, Hannah brushed by Evan and headed for the stairs. When she reached the top, she paused for a moment as, once again, the old panic threatened to overwhelm her. What if something was seriously wrong with Abby? she asked herself. She didn't know what she'd do if she failed Abby, too.

Then the memory of her friend's words earlier in the day wafted gently through her mind. *All anyone can do is try. Be there for another, do your best, and love.*

Love . . . Hannah knew her love for Abby was deep and strong. She also knew she'd do her very best for her friend. That was all she—or anyone else—*could* do.

Squaring her shoulders and lifting her chin, she stepped out once more, heading toward the door she knew to be Abby and Conor's bedroom. As she passed Beth's room, the girl's door opened a crack.

"Hannah?" A tawny-skinned little face with bright brown eyes peeked around the door.

She halted. "Yes, Beth?"

The door opened all the way. "Abby . . . I'm so scared," Conor's daughter whispered. "Is . . . is she going to die?"

What could she say, Hannah wondered, when she feared the very same thing. She squatted, and took the ten-year-old by the arms. "I don't know. First, I need to see and talk with Abby. Then I need to hear what Doc Childress has to say."

The girl's lower lip began to wobble. "Don't let Abby die. Please, Hannah!"

"You know we'll all do our very best for Abby, sweetheart." She hugged Beth, then released her. "I'll come and tell you everything that's happened, just as soon as we know more. Okay?"

Beth nodded in solemn agreement. "Okay."

Hannah rose. "Evan's in the kitchen with Jackson. Why don't you go down and help your brother? While you watch Jackson, he can fetch some milk from the springhouse. Then you all can have some cookies and milk."

Once more, Beth nodded, but this time the action was a bit more animated. "Okay, Hannah."

Hannah watched the girl, her long black hair tousled, her feet bare, head down the hall in her pink, flowered nightgown. Then she turned and resumed her journey to Abby and Conor's bedroom. Their door was closed, so she rapped softly.

In response to her knock, booted footsteps moved across the hardwood floor. The door opened. Conor stood there, fully dressed in a red cotton work shirt, and his usual blue denims and scuffed boots.

For all his kindness to her, especially since he had at long last returned to the Lord, Hannah still found Conor intimidating. Maybe it was his piercing, unwavering gaze. Maybe it was his air of authority and presence. Whatever it was, looking up at him, she felt a tremor vibrate through her.

Hannah swallowed hard and took a step back. "Abby," she croaked. "Evan said she was ill."

The big rancher moved aside, swinging open the door. "Yes, she is. Come in." He gestured for her to enter. "She woke up a few hours ago with bad cramps, then began to bleed."

Hannah hesitated, then decided there was no point pretending modesty. "So she doesn't think, then, that it's just the beginning of her monthly fluxes?"

"No." Conor firmly shook his head. "Abby just informed me she missed her last one. Plus there are other changes . . ." He met her gaze. "She thinks she's in a family way."

The blood drained from Hannah's face. If Abby had indeed conceived and was now cramping and bleeding, it was possible she might lose the baby. "There's not much I know to do," she said, "except keep Abby quiet and in bed until Doc gets here."

As she made a move to go around him, Conor took Hannah by the arm. "Take care of her the best you know how," he rasped. "I don't want to lose the baby but, even more, I don't want anything to happen to Abby."

A deep concern burned in his eyes. She heard it, as well, in his voice, felt it in the strength of his grip. Conor loved his wife more than life itself. The realization filled her with equal parts of joy for Abby and envy for herself.

In a sudden, totally unexpected surge of emotion, a fierce yearning swamped Hannah. What she wouldn't give to be loved–and love–with the ardent devotion Conor and Abby had for each other. Such grandiose hopes, though, were but false illusions for a woman such as she.

Perhaps that was why she hesitated to encourage Evan any further. As wonderful as he was, he somehow didn't seem the man for her—the man capable of helping her mend her tattered heart and soul. More and more strongly each time she was with him, Hannah was overcome with the feeling Evan wasn't meant for her, but for someone else.

She carried too much pain in her heart ever to be strong and whole again. Just as brutally as her body had been violated, so had her soul.

Despite his protests to the contrary, she could bring Evan little of any worth, save perhaps the comfort of her body. But physical needs eventually waned. When they did, he would see her for what she was—an empty shell.

"I understand, and I'll do all I can for Abby," she whispered, once again locking gazes with Conor's tormented one. "I love her, too. Above everything else, I want her to be okay."

Conor seemed to relax then. With a shuddering sigh, he released her arm and stepped back. "I'm sorry. I didn't mean to frighten you." He ran a hand raggedly through his hair. "I'm . . . I'm just so worried."

"I know." Hannah forced a tight smile. "So am I. But we're not any good to Abby if we let our fears get the best of us. Right now, she's all that matters—she and the baby."

He nodded. "What can I do? Just tell me, and I'll do it."

She stared up at him, her brow furrowing in thought. Just like his cousin, Conor was a man of action. He didn't like feeling helpless.

"A nice, soothing cup of herbal tea would probably do Abby a world of good right now. I put on some water to heat before I came upstairs. Could you make a pot of tea and bring it up to us?"

Conor's eyes brightened with resolve. "Yes. Yes, that's a good idea." He walked to the bed and took his wife's hand. "Hannah's here now, and we've sent for Doc. I'm going downstairs to make you some tea, but I'll be back soon."

Though her face was taut with worry, Abby still managed a smile. "That's thoughtful of you, Conor. I'd love a cup of tea."

He bent down and kissed her tenderly, then straightened and strode from the room.

Hannah watched him leave, then turned to Abby.

"Thank you for finding something for Conor to do," her friend said. "His agitation was beginning to wear on me."

"I suspected as much." Hannah walked to the bed and sat in the rocker next to it. "Besides, a nice cup of tea *would* be good for you." She glanced at Abby's belly. "This is quite a surprise, you being in a family way, I mean."

The chestnut-haired woman managed a sheepish grin. "I should've known. It's not as if this was my first child. But what with Ella's birthing problems, and then the influenza outbreak, and then . . . then Ella dying . . ." Her voice quavered, then faded in sobs that rose from deep within her. "Oh, Hannah, if I should lose this baby–Conor's baby–because of my own carelessness and n-neglect . . ."

"Hush." She took up Abby's hand and squeezed it. "You did the best you could, considering the circumstances. When did you once, in the past month, have a moment's time to think of yourself?"

Abby's head jerked up, and she stared at Hannah. "I-I suppose I really didn't, did I?"

"No, you didn't." Once more, Hannah squeezed her hand. "And now that the Widow Ashley has come to help Devlin, I'm totally free to help *you* take care of yourself. You're always telling me how all things work together for good to them that love the Lord. Well, if the Lord's hand isn't in this bit of perfect timing, I don't know what is."

Abby smiled in wry amusement. "Rather, I'd say, if the Lord's hand wasn't in *your* coming to Culdee Creek, I don't know what was."

Gladness filled Hannah. Gladness and a sweet, warm sense of satisfaction. It felt good to be needed and appreciated. At least in a small way, she at last felt of use, of substance and value to someone she admired and loved.

Once again, the wild hopes stirred anew. Once again Hannah felt as if she might weep with gratitude. Then the old doubts and fears assailed her.

Abby was a rare, wonderful being, precious in the eyes of God and man. She didn't, however, represent the rest of the human race. Though Conor and Abby's offer to stay at Culdee Creek had become open-ended, someday she might still have to venture back into the midst of other, less loving and forgiving people. People like Devlin MacKay.

She must never forget that.

The sound of approaching footsteps reached her. Conor. Hannah shook aside her morose thoughts. His hands might be full. He'd need help.

She released Abby's hand and rose. "I think your tea has arrived." Turning, Hannah walked to the door, her fierce determination to help Abby undimmed, but refocused by the harsh light of reality—and the bitter knowledge of her true place in the world.

Doc Childress's prognosis was guarded but optimistic. The cramps and bleeding had stopped by the time he arrived. There was still a chance, he informed them, that the baby might make it.

His advice, however, was stern and unyielding. Abby must remain on complete bedrest for the next two weeks. After that, he would determine a schedule for gradually increasing her activity level.

Conor and Hannah exchanged relieved looks, then immediately set about planning how to care for Abby. By midmorning, a call-bell system was devised, a bedside commode procured, and Hannah began concocting simple, nourishing, and easily digestible meals. Abby watched the flurry of activity with a tolerant smile, then continued her reading.

The days passed, and Abby remained healthy. Hannah began to breathe easier, her hopes for the continued safety of her friend's unborn child growing. She lingered longer outside in the warm sunshine while she hung up the laundry, or worked for a short while in the flowerbeds. There was even time for evening strolls with Evan. As the month of May began to wane, the daylight hours lengthened; the rolling pastures of Culdee Creek–thanks to an unusually wet spring–transformed to a verdant green. The hummingbirds and butterflies returned.

Hannah's concerns about the Widow Ashley, however, only worsened. As soon as Devlin left to do his chores each morning, Mary and Devlin Jr. were hustled outside to play. Save for a short break for the noon meal when she officiously hustled them back into the house before their father returned, the children seemed to spend the entire day outside. Hannah could only wonder–and worry–about the amount of attention baby Bonnie received.

She kept her concerns to herself, though, loathe to distress Abby during such a delicate time. And so the frustration grew, until Hannah could bear it no longer. Finally, more than three weeks after the woman's arrival, Hannah summoned the courage to broach the subject with the widow.

"How is everything going at Devlin's place?" she asked one evening as they both sat in the little bunkhouse parlor, catching up on some mending.

The Widow Ashley glanced up from the sock she was industriously darning. Her glance narrowed, and her mouth pursed. "Very well, thank you. Did you think there'd be problems?"

Her hand poised in midair over a torn petticoat hem she was stitching, Hannah shook her head. "From all I've seen and heard, you seem to be running the household aspects with great success. I must say I admire how much you get done each day."

"Well," the woman said smugly, "I have a system, you know, as to how I approach each task, and I never permit anything to interfere with it."

"But surely that must be difficult, considering people—especially children—tend frequently to set all the best laid plans awry. What do you do then?"

"As I said before, I never permit anything—or anyone—to interfere." Martha Ashley lowered her gaze to her darning, deftly weaving threads to and fro across the worn heel. "Children must adapt to my needs, not the other way around. One cannot maintain any sort of an efficient schedule otherwise."

Just as she had feared, Hannah thought. The children were being shuffled about to suit the Widow Ashley, most likely to their detriment. She wondered if Devlin had even the slightest inkling of what this woman was about.

Hannah opened her mouth to reproach the widow. Then, thinking better of it, she clamped her lips shut. Martha Ashley was too self-important and certain that what she did was right to ever listen to her. Already, the woman had made it clear how little she thought of Hannah. The girl was certain the widow viewed her and

Jackson's presence in the bunkhouse as just a temporary imposition.

No, without Devlin's support—which wasn't likely to be forthcoming anytime soon—Hannah knew she hadn't any authority over the woman. For his children's sake, though, Hannah had to find some way to ingratiate herself with Widow Ashley. Ella was depending on her.

"I was wondering," Hannah began, choosing her words with care, "if you might like some help with the children."

The other woman cast her a withering look. "Are you implying that I am somehow amiss in my responsibilities toward them?"

"No, not at all." A twinge of guilt assailed her for the deception, but Hannah forced an innocent smile. It was for the children's sake, she reminded herself. She meant the woman no harm. "It's just now that Abby's feeling better," she explained, "I've some extra time on my hands. I thought you might like a bit of assistance.

"I mean," she hastened to add when the widow arched a dark brow, "it doesn't seem fair that you're working from dawn to dusk with hardly a moment for yourself, while I've plenty of time to loll around."

"True enough." The raven-haired woman nodded in brisk agreement. "I'm just surprised to find you so eager to help, after all this time of hanging back and allowing me to bear such a heavy burden."

Baby Harold, sleeping in his cradle near her feet, chose that moment to waken and begin to squall. Without even a glance in her son's direction, Martha Ashley placed a stockinged foot on one of the rocker arms and began to pump it up and down. Eventually, lulled by the rhythmic swaying, Harold fell back to sleep.

For several minutes, Hannah watched the woman. Then she sighed. "Of course you're right. Abby keeps urging me to do my Christian duty and help others. I guess I've finally had an attack of conscience." She pretended a happy eagerness she didn't particularly feel, and smiled brightly. "So, if you'd like some help with the children . . ."

"Yes. Yes, I would." Once again, Martha Ashley nodded briskly. "Whenever you're free tomorrow, come over to the house. Just wait, if you please, until Mr. MacKay has left for the day." She smiled and Hannah thought she saw a hint of malicious satisfaction in the widow's eyes. "We both know how intolerable he finds your presence, so there's no point in causing any unnecessary scenes, is there?"

"No, there isn't," Hannah agreed, clamping down on her rising irritation. All that mattered, in the end, were the children, she reminded herself yet again. Not her pride, not the fact she sensed the widow wanted to take all the credit for herself, and certainly not any favor she herself might curry with Devlin by looking out for his children's welfare or happiness.

But it *was* little enough she could do for Ella and her children.

"Devlin Jr., don't you *dare* knock my last marble out of the circle!" Hannah warned with a laugh. "You've already won all my others. Give a girl a chance, will you?"

The carrot-red-haired boy glanced up from his position on the ground, his agate marble balanced in the crook of his index finger and thumb. He shot her a gap-toothed grin, then, with barely a moment's hesitation, shot his marble straight at Hannah's. It rapped hers smartly, sending it careening from the inner and outer circles drawn in the dirt.

Hannah threw up her hands in defeat. Devlin Jr. whooped in victory and retrieved both marbles, which he promptly dropped into his now bulging, leather marble pouch.

"Game's over," he then said, now all wide-eyed innocence. "Or, leastwise," he added with a shyly victorious little smile, "'til you can find some more marbles."

"Well, don't hold your breath," she muttered, pretending disgust. "I won't be getting to Grand View anytime soon."

The lad cocked his head. "I could loan you a few marbles. You're the most fun of all to play with, you know?"

"I'd imagine so." Affectionately, Hannah brushed a smudge of dirt off Devlin Jr.'s forehead. "Who else around here provides you with such a steady supply of new marbles?"

As if considering her question, he cocked his head, his small brow creasing in thought. "No one, I reckon," the boy finally replied. "You're the worst marble shooter in these parts."

Hannah laughed then, throwing back her head and releasing all her energy in that joyous sound. She pulled Devlin Jr. to her, engulfing him in a huge bear hug. "Oh, honey," she whispered, overcome with the realization she meant her next words with all her heart, "do you know how much I've missed playing with you children?"

"I-I've missed you, too," the little boy sniffled. "Pa's so sad most times now. He's no fun to play with. And Mrs. Ashley . . . well, she doesn't like to play."

"Then"—Hannah leaned back and smiled at him— "we'll just have to—"

"What in the Sam Hill's going on here?"

At the sound of Devlin's deep voice, taut with anger, Hannah's breath caught in her throat. She released

Devlin Jr. and scooted back, staring up at him from her spot still kneeling on the ground.

In the past week since she had finagled permission from the Widow Ashley to spend time with the children, not once had she crossed paths with their father while she was with them. She had taken the utmost care to avoid him. Until this moment, she had managed to do so with great success.

Now, though, the jig was up. There was nothing to be done but tell the truth.

"We were playing a game of marbles," Hannah replied matter-of-factly, refusing to quail before him even if his dark blue eyes did smolder now with suspicion. "You arrived too late, though, to keep your son from cleaning me out of every marble I owned."

"And who gave you permission to play with my children?" Devlin demanded, as little Mary, who had been playing nearby with Jackson and a bag of wooden blocks, rose and toddled over. "Mrs. Ashley is their caretaker now, not you."

His son stood and stuffed his marble pouch in a back pocket of his trousers. "Mrs. Ashley doesn't mind, Pa. She said so. Besides, she's always too busy to play with us."

Devlin's angry gaze never left Hannah's. "Take your sister, son, and go into the house. Hannah and I still have a bit of grown-up talking to do."

"Aw, Pa . . ."

"Do as I say, son!"

There was no ignoring the steely edge of warning in Devlin's voice. The boy shot Hannah one last, regretful look, then ambled over to his sister. Taking her by the hand, he led her into the house.

When the children were out of earshot, Devlin immediately rounded on Hannah. "Whether Mrs. Ashley," he hissed, his shoulders rigid, his hands fisted and stiff at his sides, "gave you permission or not is beside the point, and you know it! How many more ways do I have to say it? *Stay away from my children!*"

This was one battle she couldn't win, but Hannah suddenly didn't care. *Somebody* needed to set Devlin MacKay straight. She jumped to her feet.

"You've got it all mixed up, mister!" She met his glaring gaze with a defiant, unyielding one of her own. "Your son and daughters already have enough people staying away from them, including you and Mrs. Ashley. Instead of berating me, you should be *thanking* me for spending time with them. They're going through a pretty difficult time right now. You're not the only one who misses Ella."

"Blast it! Keep Ella out of this!"

"And why should I?" Hannah cried, her own anger and frustration growing. "She wouldn't want her children to be neglected, or shoved aside constantly so some silly, self-imposed schedule could be met. She would never have turned them outside all day, every day, to fend for themselves. But you wouldn't know that, would you?" she taunted. "Just as long as your house is spotless, your meals are perfect, and the children are quiet, you're content, aren't you?"

"Don't you dare lecture me—"

"Well, someone's got to. Open your eyes, Devlin. See how things really are before it's too late."

"I see plenty." Devlin grabbed her arm and jerked her to him. "For some reason, you seem intent on continuing to create havoc in my life. You're just not happy, are you, unless I'm miserable?"

"Your misery is of your own making!" Hannah twisted in his grasp, trying to break free, but his grip was like a vise. "I've never done anything on purpose to hurt you. Never!"

87

An expression of tortured anguish flashed across his face. Then, as if suddenly remembering himself, Devlin released her with a look of utter distaste. "You don't know anything about me or my misery."

"Don't I?"

Hannah's fury burned white-hot within her. She didn't care anymore about tempering the sting of her words. She didn't care what he thought, or might do. At this moment, all she knew was she was sick to death of Devlin. Did he think he was the only person in the world who had suffered and had to overcome heart-breaking obstacles?

She closed the distance between them. Standing on tip-toe, Hannah reared up right into his face. "I've learned a lot about men . . . people . . . in the past four years since I was forced into prostitution," she spat out. "I've learned about brutality and the depths of depravity the call of the flesh can lead one to. And I've kept on learning, even after coming to Culdee Creek. Learned about God, love, and forgiveness from Ella and Abby. And about cruelty, narrow-minded intolerance, and vindictiveness from you.

"Yet what have I ever done that was mean to you? Tell me that, Devlin MacKay. Did I fail to give you your money's worth when you came to me and paid me for my favors? Was I the one who, even before you called on me, threatened your marriage? And did I ever once flaunt my knowledge of your shameful secret to Ella, or anyone else on this ranch?"

"Ella wouldn't have ever known if you hadn't come here in the first place."

"So, naturally, I must have chosen sanctuary at Culdee Creek just to punish you and ruin your life, is that it?"

Devlin finally had the good grace to blush. "I don't know, or even care, why you came here. What matters is you did."

Hannah gave a shrill laugh. "Well, I'm sorry my presence here messed up your perfect, if hypocritical life! But a girl has to look out for herself, especially when she's ready to deliver a baby that Sadie and her henchmen are bound and determined to take away from her as soon as it is born. Selfish me, to think only of my child's life."

A muscle twitched in Devlin's jaw. A vein began to pulse in his neck, swelling dangerously. He loomed over her. For a fleeting instant, Hannah was afraid he might hit her.

Then, with a long, shuddering exhalation, Devlin stepped back. Wheeling about, he stalked away.

As she watched his retreat, a hysterical impulse rose in her. If he thought to run from the truth, he was sadly mistaken. Now that she had released the floodgates of her righteous fury, Hannah wasn't about to let him go until she had said it all, made him face every sad, sordid bit of truth.

"Run away then," she cried. "Sooner or later, though, even a coward has to face himself. When you do, remember that, above everything else, you failed Ella. But not in what you did with me. No, that was forgiven long ago."

The tears streamed down her cheeks; her voice went hoarse with anguish, and still Hannah forged on. "But what about her request that you forgive me? What about *that*, Devlin? What about that?"

At her words, he slid to a halt, then turned to face her. His expression, though, wasn't one of animosity or furious wrath as she had expected. His stance wasn't that of a man intent on attacking her in a murderous rage.

Instead, Devlin just stood there. He looked suddenly as if someone had beaten him, and he had nothing left to give. Yet it was his tear-bright gaze boring into hers, a gaze full of the most heart-rending anguish, that struck Hannah more forcefully than any physical blow.

The realization of what she had done seared through her, leaving a breath-grabbing ache in its passing. She gazed at him for a long moment. Then, lowering her head in shame, Hannah rushed over to where Jackson still sat with the toy blocks, gathered him up, and stumbled away.

7

All the ways of a man are clean in his own eyes; but the Lord weigheth the spirits.

Proverbs 16:2

Devlin stabbed the pitchfork deep into a pile of dung and soiled hay, lifted it high, then flung the odiferous load into a wheelbarrow. His actions were quick, angry, violent, mirroring his state of mind. But at least, he reasoned, the hard, physical labor was an acceptable outlet, unlike what he had really wanted to do.

Hannah Cutler didn't know how lucky she was that she had left him when she did.

The past hour holed up in the barn mucking stalls, however, hadn't done much to ease Devlin's tormented state of mind. His emotions had battled within him like some bucking bronco, leaping and falling, twisting and turning, until he feared he'd go mad and tear the place apart. Still, even that would've been a sight better than

91

what he yearned to do to that blond, little she-cat. He grimaced. A blond, little she cat trying to pass herself off as a lady.

At the renewed thought of Hannah, Devlin's hands gripped the pitchfork handle so tightly he drove splinters into his palms. With a low curse, Devlin flung the pitchfork aside. His legs buckled. Covering his face with his hands, he sank to his knees in the straw.

What kind of man was he becoming, he wept, to take even fleeting pleasure in such considerations? Indeed, what kind of man *had* he become to betray his wife, then deny her what she had so yearned for—a healing of his tormented soul? He was lost, and now realized he had been lost for a very long while.

Hannah's parting words just a short time ago had been harsh, cruel even, but they had also bit deeply with the sharp lash of truth. He *had* failed Ella in so many ways. He was a coward and weakling, always depending on others to hold him up. And when even that wasn't enough, when he could bear the pain of life and living no longer, there was always the bottle as his final solace.

This time, however, even the dubious oblivion of drink wouldn't erase the indisputable facts before him. Hannah cared enough about his children to stand up and challenge him. Hannah cared enough for Ella to risk his wrath and its possible consequences. Yet what did *he* dare risk for his own family in return?

"You need to make your peace with Hannah," Ella had told him that day she had confronted him about the girl. "Not just for your sake, but for the sake of me and the children."

It was hard to face the truth, especially now in his grief when he felt so utterly alone, but face it he must. The bitter truth was that his anger at Hannah had eroded more than just their relationship. It had also threatened to destroy his family.

Despair entwined about Devlin's heart, squeezing it in remorseless recrimination. No matter how hard you tried, he realized, you couldn't run away from yourself–or the truth about yourself–forever.

He lowered his hands and angrily wiped away his tears. Ella was gone. He must face the fact he was alone once more. Conor had enough worries of his own with Abby's delicate condition. He couldn't impose on his cousin yet again, especially now. Besides, he was ranch foreman. Conor depended on him to be strong and decisive.

Constantly striving to hide from all the doubts and fears that threatened to overwhelm him was hardly the most honorable or courageous way to live. Devlin sighed and shook his head. No, it was hardly honorable or courageous, and even he could–and must–do better. He must–for Ella's and his children's sake–if not for his own.

For their sake, he must face his most painful failing, even if that meant reexamining his past treatment of Hannah. Even if that meant offering her, at long last, some overture of peace. He had no other choice. To do less would be always to remember what he had been capable of becoming . . . and failed to do.

The Reverend Noah Starr arrived a week later to call on Abby. She was able to walk about a bit and sit up in a chair for an hour or so each day by then, so Conor carried her downstairs to the parlor to receive the priest. Hannah helped Conor settle Abby in one of the leather armchairs pulled up by the moss rock fireplace, then immediately excused herself and headed for the kitchen to prepare tea.

Conor paused there for a moment on his way out the back door. "Do you need help serving, once everything's ready? I'd like to check out a few things with Devlin while Abby's visiting with Noah, but I'll stay if you need me . . ."

Hannah glanced up from the task of setting the tray with teacups and a plate of freshly baked raisin scones. She smiled and shook her head. "No, I won't need any help until it's time for you to carry Abby back upstairs to bed."

"She's doing well, don't you think?"

"Yes, she certainly seems to be. When Doc visited the other day, he said another week or so and she should be out of the woods."

A look of joyous relief shone in Conor's eyes. "I know." He gave a low, almost wondering laugh. "I'm going to be a father again. God is so good."

"And I'm so happy for Abby. There were times when I'd catch her watching me and Jackson, and I knew she ached to hold her own child in her arms." Her smile faded. "Not that this one will ever take the place of her little Joshua."

"No, this one won't," he agreed with solemn emphasis, "but it'll make its own special place nonetheless. I'm just happy I can give her a child of her own."

Hannah contemplated the tall rancher with grave interest. She had never heard a man speak in such terms before. But then, she had never seen a man so in love either. God had indeed blessed Conor and Abby.

"I'm happy for the *both* of you," she said. "You give me hope that . . ." The words died in her throat. Hannah blushed and forced a smile. "Well, I'm just happy for you."

As if he had caught the true meaning behind her words, Conor's expression softened. "Be patient. Trust in the Lord, Hannah. He'll show you the man of your heart."

Hannah's face grew even hotter. What if Conor guessed she had been questioning her commitment to his son? "I-I didn't mean anything against Evan," she stammered. "I'm just so confused right now . . ."

He took her arm. "I never thought that. Besides, what's between you and Evan is private. All I meant was you should wait for God's will to be clear. Sometimes, if we're not careful, we try to convince ourselves God must want something just because *we* want it so badly." Conor smiled ruefully. "That was certainly a lesson both Abby and I had to learn."

She wanted to ask him how one knew for certain when something was God's will and when it was just selfish, misguided desire twisting things to seem so. But now, with Abby and Reverend Starr in the next room, wasn't the right time or place. So, instead, Hannah patted the hand that still held her arm and managed a wan smile.

"You're kind to talk with me like this. I'm grateful for this and everything else you've done for me."

"And I'm grateful you've been here for us during these difficult times." Conor released her arm. "I don't know what we would've done without you."

"I was happy to help."

Conor took a step closer, a sudden look of discomfiture darkening his handsome face. "I've never said this before, but I want to ask your forgiveness for my unkind behavior that night you escaped Sadie's. If it hadn't been for Abby's insistence, I'd have sent you right back to the brothel with that bodyguard of hers, Brody Gerard."

"Well," Hannah said with a wry chuckle, relieved the conversation had changed tack, "though I didn't realize it at the time, apparently you were outnumbered from the start, with both Abby and God on my side."

He grinned. "Yeah. Reckon I never had a chance, did I?"

The kettle on the cookstove began to whistle. Hannah grabbed a dishcloth and hurried to retrieve it.

"I'd best be heading on out." Conor backed toward the door where he snagged his black Stetson from a hook, and shoved it on his head. "I'll return in an hour or so to help Abby upstairs."

She watched him leave, then resumed making tea. When the tea leaves had steeped for the proper length of time, she carried the tray into the parlor, served Abby and the priest, then excused herself again.

An hour later Conor walked in, spent a few minutes visiting with Noah Starr, then politely but firmly informed him Abby needed her rest. Reverend Starr was quick to rise to leave. As his glance caught Hannah's through the open kitchen doorway, however, she saw him make what appeared to be an excuse to linger. When Conor left with Abby, the priest, a smile on his face, strode over and stuck his head into the kitchen.

"Mind if I visit with you for a few minutes, Miss Cutler?"

Hannah glanced up from the bread dough to which she had quickly lowered her gaze. A twinge of irritation flared, but she quickly tamped it down lest it show in her eyes. "Come in, Father," she said. "Don't know what we'd have to talk about, but if you haven't anything better to do with your time . . ."

"Can't see how spending a few minutes with a beautiful lady such as yourself," he said, pulling out a chair at the table to sit on, "could ever be construed as a waste of time. Even," he added with a grin, "for a man of the cloth."

She shot him a wry glance. Noah Starr was young, attractive, and unwed. In other company, his words to a former prostitute might be misinterpreted. Hannah knew, though, meeting his guileless gaze, that the priest had meant them only as a friendly compliment.

Still, there was no point served in responding in kind. If anything, Hannah wanted to discourage his interest, however well meant it might be. So she said nothing and turned her attention back to the bread dough.

Back and forth she worked the pliant mass, her actions expert, effortless. The work was soothing and hypnotic. For a few seconds, she almost forgot she wasn't alone. Finally, though, when Noah continued to sit there, silently watching her, Hannah paused. Lifting a flour-dusted hand, she pointed toward the big cookstove.

"There's water simmering in the teakettle, and some coffee left in the coffeepot. Can't guarantee the taste of the coffee this late in the morning, but you're welcome to it, if you want."

"I'm fine, but thank you anyway." The priest eyed her a moment longer, his long, strong fingers drumming a staccato beat on the tabletop. Then he grinned. "I'm heartened to see how well Abby's doing. The Lord has been good."

"Yes. Yes, He has."

She didn't look up as she formed the bread into a softly rounded rectangle and carefully lowered it into a greased loaf pan. After covering the pan with a cotton tea towel and placing it on top of the stove to rise, Hannah next directed her attention to the second half of dough still awaiting her in the bowl.

Noah Starr's eyes remained on her, but she refused to look up or ease the tense silence by making social conversation. Let *him* deal with the situation. He was the one, after all, who had insisted on this awkward and most unnecessary discourse.

"How are things going between you and Devlin?" the priest asked suddenly.

Hannah's hands stilled. She stared down at the dough as, bit by bit, her fingers arched like talons and she sank them into the soft mass. Sank them deep, clutching desperately for control while myriad emotions reeled within her.

97

Finally, from within the roiling tumult of emotions, anger rose to the surface. How dare he pry where he had no right to go? Her cheeks flamed with indignation. What business was it of his—?

"I don't mean to cause you discomfort, or to appear the nosy gossip," Noah hastened to explain. "But our conversation that day at Ella's funeral . . . well, it's been on my mind ever since."

"How so, Father?" Hannah turned the full force of her suspicious gaze on him.

Apparently unperturbed by her hostility, he cocked his head and smiled up at her. "You said that you and Devlin weren't friends. I had hoped, with time, that might change."

"Well, it hasn't. No sooner was Ella in the ground than Devlin had another housekeeper from Grand View fetched to replace me. Save for a time or two since then, we've hardly talked."

Noah sighed and shook his head. "That must have hurt you deeply."

At his softly couched statement, unexpected tears sprang to Hannah's eyes. Furious with herself—and at him for asking—she hastily blinked them away. Then, to hide her unnerving display, Hannah lowered her head as if concentrating on her task, and resumed kneading the dough.

"My feelings were never a consideration," she gritted out the admission. "It's Devlin's house and family. He can do whatever he wants."

"How can I help? It pains me to see two fine people so angry at each other, and so miserable because of it."

With rough, jerky motions, Hannah formed the dough into a loaf and all but flung it into its pan. "If you really want to help," she finally said, meeting his concerned gaze, "then go ask Devlin. He's the one who refuses to forgive. He's the one who won't give me a chance. But don't come to me and expect me to solve this problem. Face Devlin, if you dare, and then you'll understand."

She gave a shaky laugh. "On second thought, maybe you won't *want* to understand. Maybe it's safer if you *don't* dig too deeply."

"And why's that, Hannah?"

She smiled, but this time the action was totally devoid of warmth or feeling. "Don't you have enough problems to deal with, Father, without seeking out even more?"

"I can't ignore anyone I see suffering. You and Devlin are as much my brother and sister in Christ as anyone else."

Hannah gave a mocking laugh. "Perhaps Devlin is, but I was long ago separated from that particular family."

"If you ever wish to return to church, the door is always open, Hannah. Always."

She eyed him warily. Would he be surprised to learn that she had never in her entire life set foot inside a church? Indeed, she wasn't even baptized. Her parents had never put much store in religion. But to admit the truth now, Hannah feared, would only spur the Reverend Starr onto further evangelistic efforts. He was, after all, such a well-meaning, naïve fool.

"You'll be the first to know, if the day ever comes when I want to go to church," Hannah replied at last, deciding it safest to discourage him in the most direct way she could.

Noah pushed back his chair and stood. "I not only look forward to that day, but I pray for it."

Hannah met his steady gaze and saw the sincerity burning in the depths of his warm brown eyes. Remorse flooded her. She had been rude and downright hostile, yet the man didn't seem to care. He was as open and friendly now as he had been when he had first entered the kitchen.

"Well, prayer has wrought greater miracles than that, I suppose," she muttered in a sort of backhanded apology, as she carried the second loaf to the cookstove to rise. "I thank you for your concern."

"Think nothing of it." The young priest stepped back and turned toward the door. "I guess I'd best be going."

"Yes, I guess you should."

Noah gave her a farewell nod, then began to walk away.

"Uh, one thing more, Father." Hannah didn't know from whence the sudden impulse came, but nonetheless it seemed right.

He paused, glancing over his shoulder. "Yes, Hannah?"

"Please pray for Devlin, too, if you would. If anyone needs God's help right now, that man surely does."

As much as Devlin hated to admit it, Hannah had been right. So had his son, for that matter, when he had told him the Widow Ashley was too busy with other things to ever play with him and Mary. Still, Devlin could've kicked himself for the weeks that had already passed, weeks his children had been neglected save for their basic physical needs.

A bewildering mix of remorse and righteous anger roiling within him, he strode up the porch steps to his house, intent on a long overdue confrontation. She'd be surprised to see him this early in the afternoon, Martha Ashley would, but after talking with Conor and Evan, Devlin knew he couldn't ignore the problems a moment longer. They were problems even the other two men hadn't helped but notice. They were also the same problems Hannah hadn't minced any words informing him of barely two weeks ago.

All their words had been painful to hear, especially when Devlin knew he was as much to blame as the woman he had hired. Not only had he been so immersed in his grief he hardly had the energy or patience for his children, but he had all but ignored the signs of the widow's negligence.

Once again, Hannah had spoken true. He *had* been more concerned with a spotless house, meals on the table, and orderly, obedient children. Once again, Devlin admitted sadly, he had failed Ella.

There was nothing, though, to be done for what had already happened, he reminded himself as he entered the house and headed for the kitchen. All he could do now was deal with the present. A present that demanded a long overdue talk with the Widow Ashley.

She glanced up from a kettle of soup she had simmering on the cookstove. At sight of him her dark eyes widened momentarily with surprise, before a speculative look shuttered her gaze. She smiled, her cheeks dimpling prettily.

"Why, Mr. MacKay," the woman cooed, "what brings you here at this time of day? Did you come back for another slice of my luscious, fresh cherry pie?"

"No, Martha, I didn't." He motioned toward the table. "Please, have a seat. We need to talk."

"Do we now?" Her slender brows arched with coy amusement.

"Yes, we do." Once again, Devlin indicated the table.

With a toss of her head and thrust of her ample bosom, the Widow Ashley sashayed to the table. Devlin watched her go, well aware the exhibition was for his benefit. As before, though, her seductive behaviors left him cold. Did she truly imagine he could, so soon after his wife's death, look at another woman with desire?

Once the widow was settled at the table, Devlin pulled up his own chair. Folding his hands before him, he leaned toward her. "Some things have been brought to my attention. Things I hope we can mutually and satisfactorily resolve."

"And those things might be?" She made a big show of fluttering her thick, dark lashes at him.

"My children. I'd like you to spend more time with them."

A tiny frown creased her brow. "Really, Mr. MacKay. I already spend far more time than I should with them, if I'm ever to complete all the day-to-day chores you've set for me to do. I'm a hard-working woman, but two young children and two babies, plus a house to manage, isn't as easy as a man like you might imagine it to be."

"I'm not saying you're not a hard worker, Mrs. Ashley." Frustration filled Devlin. How was he to make it clear to the woman without offending her what he wanted from her? "All I'm saying is the children come first, the house second. This is a ranch, for heaven's sake. No one expects you to keep things spotless."

She inhaled a tremulous breath, and a suspicious moisture flooded her eyes. "I try, Mr. MacKay. Truly I do." She pulled out a snow-white lace hankie and dabbed delicately at her eyes. "Ah, but I feel so sorry for your dear little children, motherless and all."

"That's why I hired you. You seemed a motherly sort."

"Oh, I am. I really am." The widow straightened suddenly, the handkerchief and tears apparently forgotten. "I'm also a warm and giving woman. I could do more for you, Mr. MacKay, if only you'd let me. A man has needs just as much as do children."

Devlin went very still. Was the woman proposing what she seemed to be proposing? He considered that question briefly, then tossed it aside. No, she couldn't be.

"My needs aren't the issue here," he said, making a great effort to keep the tone of his voice cool and distant. "All I'm asking is that you mother my children."

"Yes, your poor little children do need mothering." The woman lowered her gaze, but a tiny smile tugged at the corners of her mouth. "I know it hasn't been very long since your dear wife died, but have you given any thought to taking a new wife—for the sake of your children?"

Take a new wife? Even the consideration chilled Devlin to the marrow of his bones. "No," he said flatly. "It's out of the question. Ella's been dead just six weeks. Even the thought of taking another woman to wife sickens me."

"And well it should, for a man as loving and devoted as you were," the Widow Ashley crooned. "It unsettles me, as well, to make mention of it. My dear husband only passed away just recently, too. But times are hard for us widows and widowers, Mr. MacKay, especially when there are children involved. Sometimes, for the sake of those little ones, we adults must overcome our own selfish desires."

Devlin stared at her, flabbergasted at the turn the conversation had suddenly taken. One moment they were talking about his children and her lack of attention toward them. In the next, the discussion had swung to the need for him to wed quickly for the sake of those children.

He was well aware customs out West were far more relaxed than in the East, where formal mourning lasted at least a year. The widow herself still wore dresses of black bombazine and added black gloves, and a mourning bonnet with a veil, when she went to town. Yet for some out here, such customs were considered excessive. For some out here, the harsh demands of Colorado living mandated remarrying soon—very soon—after losing a spouse.

Devlin, however, refused to consider such a thing, especially so soon after Ella's death. Still, he had the uneasy feeling the widow had not only considered it, but had set her sights specifically on him. She was just too practical and efficient not to have done so. She was also, he belatedly realized, far too practical to waste much time on such inefficient emotions as love and grief.

He could almost imagine her fulfilling her marital duties as quickly and competently as possible, then bounding out of bed to hem a tablecloth or dust the furniture. There'd be no warmth, no comfort, and certainly no love to be found in that woman's arms. Not for any man foolish enough to marry her, nor for any children trapped between them in the bargain.

Her words came back to him now, but stripped of the widow's self-serving intentions, Devlin saw them in a new light.

Sometimes, for the sake of those little ones, we adults must overcome our own selfish desires.

His selfish desires, unfair grudges, and cruel vindictiveness had been heaped on Hannah Cutler for over a year now. It had been bad enough when the battle had raged solely between them. But when he had finally sought to punish her by separating her from his children, he realized now he had gone too far.

Hannah had always treated his children as her own. She had given them love, warmth, and comfort. No matter what unresolved issues remained between them, she was the one his children needed—not Martha Ashley.

Devlin bowed his head and closed his eyes, cursing himself for his stupid, foolish pride. Then he looked up, meeting the widow's eager gaze. "You're right, ma'am," he said. "It's past time I overcame my own selfish desires for the sake of my children. I only pray it's not already too late."

8

Trust in the LORD with all thine heart; and lean not unto thine own understanding.

Proverbs 3:5

It was a beautiful early summer evening, the warm breeze a velvet whisper against the cheek, the stars bright in the night sky, the little peeper frogs down by the creek croaking in raspy chorus. As Hannah walked with Evan, she savored the sweet, strong sense of being enfolded in God's loving arms.

So much was right with her life. Jackson grew strong and healthy, safe amidst the loving community of Culdee Creek. Abby and her unborn baby now flourished. She had good, honest work, priceless friendships, and a peaceful, happy existence. She had also begun to discover, if only a little more each day, a growing relationship with and love for the Lord.

There was so much right about her life Hannah refused to allow the few problems, such as Devlin MacKay and the Widow Ashley, to unsettle her anymore. She had resolved to accept what she couldn't change and, as Abby urged, place it in God's hands. God was, after all, the only One who could truly touch Devlin MacKay's heart.

"Do you know how wonderful it is to have you all to myself again?" Evan asked softly, intruding at last into her thoughts.

As they strolled along, Hannah turned to glance up at him. He smiled at her, and she was struck once more with how handsome he was. His beauty, though, went far deeper than just his mortal frame. He was a good, kind man, a man who had weathered his own time of trial. At age seventeen, he had stolen a substantial amount of money from his father and run away to the gold mining towns of the Gunnison area. After a year of profligate living and poor investments, Evan had found himself a lot wiser but destitute.

He had come home to Culdee Creek to beg his father's forgiveness and offer to work off the money he had taken. If not for Abby's influence, Conor would've immediately turned him away. But Abby was engaged to Conor by then, and Conor's own embittered heart had begun to soften. Slowly but surely, father and son rebuilt a new, more adult relationship, one that was able to weather the trials that came their way.

"It does seem like months since we've been able to spend much time with each other," she replied finally. "I've missed our talks and walks very much."

"You're winning everyone's hearts here at Culdee Creek. What with all the sickness and tragedy that we've been through, I don't know how we would've made it without you. Even Pa can't find enough kind words to say about you nowadays."

106

"It took him a while," she admitted, "but I never faulted him for taking things slowly."

"Too bad Devlin's never come around." Evan shook his head in disgust. "You've done as much for him and his family as you've ever done for ours, and still that pig-headed—"

Hannah halted beside the base of an enormous old cottonwood and turned to face Evan. "Hush," she admonished. "Tonight's too perfect to spoil it berating Devlin. Besides, I've finally made peace with the fact he may never become my friend. I've too many wonderful things to be thankful for to bemoan something I can't seem to change."

Evan pulled her to him, then leaned back against the tree's gnarled bark. "And dare I hope I number among those wonderful things you're so thankful for?"

Hannah laughed. "Oh, Evan, you know you do. You've been a good and true—"

Before she could finish her sentence and call him a friend, the young man lowered his head and kissed her. Hannah went still. His mouth was soft, gentle, and tenderly searching. His hands clasped her arms, pulling her closer.

She knew she could pretend to respond; she certainly knew how. But to encourage him when her heart was still so conflicted wasn't right or fair. So she ended the kiss and, with a rueful sigh, smiled up at him.

"Perhaps we should be getting back to the house. I've still a bit of cleaning up to do in the kitchen, and I promised Conor I'd help Abby with her bath."

"You're always so busy caring for others." Though Evan had allowed the kiss to end, he had yet to release her. "Isn't it about time you did something for yourself?"

Unease curled within her. "Evan, I—"

This time it was Evan's turn to silence her. "Don't say another word, sweetheart," he whispered huskily. "Just

107

listen, and let me finish." As if to add emphasis to his plea, he placed a finger to her lips.

"You know how I feel about you," he continued. "You know I've wanted our relationship to grow far deeper for a long while now. Well, I think it's time, Hannah. I love you, and I want you to become my wife."

She had known this moment was inevitable. A woman would've had to be blind not to see the love and yearning growing in Evan's eyes with each passing day. But try as she might, her own emotions weren't keeping pace with his. Was there no way to put him off just a little while longer?

It was shameful to admit, but Hannah wasn't yet ready to relinquish the security and hope for the future that Evan offered. And what would happen to her current position of favor if she refused Evan's offer of marriage?

Perhaps she was wrong to doubt the goodness and sincerity of Abby and Conor MacKay. She had never known such kind and generous people. But people had turned on her, betrayed her, countless times before. Did she dare risk opening herself and Jackson to such potential pain?

With a tender touch, Hannah caressed Evan's cheek. "Ah, Evan," she breathed. "You do me great honor in asking me to become your wife. I'm the luckiest girl in the whole wide world."

Joy flared in his smoky blue eyes. "Then you will? You'll marry me?"

"I think about it a lot but"—Hannah lowered her gaze—"I'm still not ready yet." She looked back up at him. "I'm sorry. I don't mean to put you off, but there are still things unsettled, things I need to work through before I can be a good wife to anyone."

His eyes glittered. Hannah could tell he was sifting through all the possible "things" she could be talking about.

"Is it ... does your hesitation have to do with the marital act?" he ventured gently.

Of all the questions he could've asked, that particular one took Hannah by surprise. The sexual act, whether illicit or sanctified by the holy bonds of matrimony, was just that to Hannah—an act. She had learned long ago to divest any emotion from it, and to perform as expected.

"No, Evan." She smiled and shook her head. "I'm not worried about what we'd share in the marriage bed. I know you'd be kind and gentle with me."

He frowned. "Then what, Hannah? What else is still unsettled that keeps you from agreeing to become my wife?"

"Oh, excuse me, Hannah. I thought you were alone."

At the unexpected sound of Devlin's voice rising from the darkness, Hannah gasped and jerked from Evan's clasp. She whirled around.

Devlin scowled in irritation. From his front porch he had seen Hannah, dressed in a pale dress, move briefly at the edge of the cottonwoods, then disappear into the shadows. She was, he had supposed, out on a late summer's evening walk.

Immediately, an impulse to speak with her had filled him. The sooner he knew her decision about whether she would return to work for him, the sooner he would know what to do next.

Dread had held him back, though. Dread of having to humble himself to ask another favor of her for his family. Dread of the humiliation he must endure in order to apologize for how he had treated her in the past.

But Devlin also knew the only way to ease his dread was to just get it over with. Problem was, he hadn't expected to find the ever-protective and increasingly possessive Evan with Hannah. So there he stood just outside the tree's sheltering canopy of leaves, backlit by the moonlight, his face in shadows, unsure what to say or do next.

Hannah shared his dilemma. For a speechless moment, all she could do was stare up at him. He was dressed in his usual boots, denims, and white cotton work shirt rolled up at the elbows. In one hand he clutched a briar pipe that glowed red in the darkness.

"I . . . I didn't know you smoked a pipe," she choked out lamely, as the aromatic scent of burning tobacco reached her nostrils.

"This?" As if noticing it for the first time, Devlin lifted the pipe and turned it in his hand. "I rarely smoke, but every once in a while on a warm summer's night I get an urge to sit out on my front porch. A pipe just seems to fit in right nicely then."

"Well, why don't you just mosey on back to your porch and smoke that pipe then?" Evan growled, stepping out from behind Hannah. "In case you couldn't tell, we were having a private conversation."

Devlin cocked his head and eyed Evan. Standing between the two men, Hannah felt caught in a crossfire of masculine animosity. From almost her first day at Culdee Creek, she had been a bone of contention—Evan always coming to her defense, Devlin constantly berating her. Tonight, she resolved, wasn't going to become yet another battleground.

"It's all right, Evan," she murmured, reaching behind her to take his hand. "Devlin obviously came over because he had something to say. Didn't you, Devlin?"

"Yes, I do." The big foreman hesitated. "It was something I needed to talk to you about, Hannah. In private."

Evan made a sound of disgust.

Immediately, Hannah gave his hand a warning squeeze. "Well, I'm here, so talk. You can't say anything to me that Evan hasn't heard before."

"On the contrary," Devlin drawled, a twinge of wry humor softening his voice, "I'd be willing to bet he hasn't heard this. I'd still, though, rather say it to you in private." He thrust the pipe mouthpiece between his lips and gave a few deep puffs.

Exasperation filled her. She wasn't in any mood to play games tonight. "Then I guess it'll have to wait. I came out here to be with Evan, not to run off to talk with you." She turned to Evan, intent on resuming their walk.

"You're not about to make this easy on me, are you?"

Ever so slowly, Hannah turned back to Devlin. Whatever was the matter with the man? she wondered. She opened her mouth to deliver some sassy retort, then something made her think better of it.

"I don't know what you're talking about, Devlin. Truly I don't."

He took another long drag on his pipe, then exhaled. A wisp of scented smoke curled languidly up into the air. "No, I don't suppose you do," he finally said. Devlin pulled the pipe from his mouth, inhaled a ragged breath, then continued. "I know you don't particularly like or trust me. I want to apologize for what I did to cause that. I also want to ask you to come back to take care of my house and children."

In shocked disbelief, Hannah stood there, gaping at him. The night grew suddenly quiet. She could hear the blood pounding through her head, whooshing through her ears. For a frightening moment, everything spun before her.

Then Evan gave a mocking laugh, and the world righted. "What makes you think Hannah gives a hoot for your apology, or wants to commit to your slave labor again? She's not some servant, you know, to be used then cast off until you deign to need her once more."

111

"You arrogant young pup!" Fists clenched, Devlin moved toward him. "This is none of your affair. Why don't you—"

"It's my affair if I choose to make it so!" Evan snarled, stepping out in front of Hannah. "I care for Hannah, which is more than I could ever say about you!"

"Stop it. That's enough." She grabbed Evan by the arm and pulled him back beside her. "I won't have you two fighting over me, especially when this is the first apology Devlin's ever offered me."

"And why should you accept it?" her young escort hissed. "You're not some mongrel pup who needs to lick the hand of the man who's just beaten you. Besides, the only reason Devlin's swallowing his pride and apologizing is because he's unhappy with the Widow Ashley and wants you to take her place."

Hannah turned and looked at Devlin. "Is that true? That your feelings about me haven't changed, that if you weren't desperate, you'd never have come to me tonight?"

Instead of an instant protest or explanation, he stared silently down at her. The tension built as Hannah waited, stretching her nerves so tautly she thought she might scream. And then, at long last, Devlin finally answered.

"Some things don't change overnight, Hannah," he said, his voice gone low and raw. "But I know my children need you, and it's past time I be a real father to them again. If that requires me to swallow my pride and grovel, well, then so be it."

In the dim light she couldn't quite make out Devlin's expression, but she could see his eyes, burning with anguish and shame. As she gazed up at the big foreman, the wall she had built about her heart cracked a bit. Yet still Hannah hesitated. Could she finally trust Devlin? Did she dare?

"I'll have to think on your offer," she whispered. Then, taking Evan by the arm, she set out back toward the main house.

Later that evening, after the kitchen was put back in order and Abby bathed and helped to bed, Hannah sat in the rocker by her bedroom window and looked out toward Devlin's house. Even from this distance, she could see his white shirt and knew he was still sitting on his front porch. From the occasional, faint red flare of light she saw as he inhaled, she knew he was also still smoking his pipe.

She wondered what he was thinking. Had he already regretted making such a humiliating plea to her? Was he angry with her for not immediately acquiescing to his request?

One thing Hannah did know. Devlin had been correct in his assumption. After what he had put her through, she feared trusting him. That fear, if nothing else, would make things difficult between them for a long while to come.

Behind her, Jackson stirred, mumbled something in his sleep, then turned over and nodded off once more. Hannah smiled. Her son was a year old now, and had just the day before finally taken his first unaided steps. He wasn't a baby anymore.

He would need her, though, for a long while to come. Need her for love, guidance, and stability in his life. Was that, she wondered, why Devlin wanted her back in his own children's lives? If so, how would they work out their own difficulties with each other? And could he ever really come to forgive her? Indeed, could she ever truly forgive him?

It seemed too much to hope for. Yet how could she agree to his request, reenter his house, and be near him again any other way? He was such a complex, mercurial, tormented man.

Yet the children . . . Devlin Jr., Mary, and baby Bonnie . . . How could she turn her back on them—no matter how she felt about their father? Ella had begged her to care for them, to love them. But then she had also begged Hannah to forgive Devlin, and he still fought her every step of the way.

Every step of the way, that is, until this evening. Was it possible God's hand was in this? That she and Devlin were at last at a crossroads, and the next decision she made would be crucial for them both? To place such trust in a God she still felt so frequently unsure of was almost as terrifying as trusting Devlin.

Hannah halted the rocker and stood. Too many questions bombarded her, only confusing her more. There was but one way to really know, and that was to talk further with Devlin. He was still awake, still sitting outside on the porch. Hannah knew she wouldn't get much sleep until she had this settled between them.

She paused to cover Jackson with the blanket he had thrown off in his tossing and turning. Then she flung her shawl over her shoulders and left the bunkhouse. Her heart hammering in her chest, Hannah strode out across the thirty or so yards separating her little dwelling from Devlin's ranch house. At her approach, he rose and walked to the top of the porch steps.

"Had time to think about my offer, have you?"

She looked up at him. "Yes. Yes, I have."

When he made no move to step aside, Hannah glared up at him. "Well, are you going to invite me to have a seat, or must I stand here with you towering over me?"

114

A rich chuckle rose from deep within Devlin's chest. "I'm surprised you'd want to be seen keeping company with me, especially at this late hour. But, please,"–he stepped to one side and, with a gallant bow and sweep of his arm, motioned toward the porch swing–"come, sit with me."

With a caustic glance in his direction, Hannah swept past him and headed for the swing. Devlin joined her there, the sudden addition of his weight bringing the wooden bench to a jarring halt. Immediately, she scooted over as far as she could. Though there wasn't any other place for him to sit, she was suddenly uncomfortable with him so near.

"Well, what have you decided?" he asked finally when she said nothing. As he spoke, Devlin pushed off with one foot, setting the swing once more into motion. Back and forth it swayed, its movement soothing and hypnotic.

It was still a beautiful night, though a bit cooler now. Everyone was abed, save for a few hands moving about far down the hill in the large bunkhouse near the two barns. In an upstairs bedroom of the main house, a single oil lamp glowed. Hannah could see a man moving about beyond the lace curtains.

She knew it was Evan, restless and upset no doubt over their unfinished discussion. Hannah resolved to speak to him about it tomorrow. It wasn't fair to leave things hanging. Though she refused to agree to become his wife just because he thought it was time, she didn't wish Evan to view her hesitancy as a permanent rejection either.

"Well, I reckon I should take this silence," Devlin observed wryly, "as a positive sign. If you'd definitely made up your mind to refuse my offer, you surely would've told me by now."

Still preoccupied with thoughts of Evan, Hannah turned to look at him. "Whatever are you talking about?"

Devlin took a long drag on his pipe. "Correct me if I'm wrong, but you did come here to inform me whether you'd agree to care for my children and house, didn't you?"

Pipe smoke enveloped her in an aromatic, heady cloud. "Yes." She nodded, relieved to find her focus again. "First, though, I need to know your mind in this a bit more. I mean, why me?"

A frown furrowed his brow. "What do you mean, why you?"

"Even if you're displeased with Mrs. Ashley, you could always find some other woman to take on the job. Some decent, well-bred woman with respectable references."

"My children don't want a decent, well-bred woman. They want you."

Hannah didn't know what to say to that, or even how to interpret it. Was Devlin joking or just stating the bald truth? "Am I to take that as an insult or a compliment?"

He sighed, lowered his head, and paused to massage his temples. "Both, I reckon." Devlin looked up. "I'm not a man given to fancy words, Hannah. And I've said just about all I know how to say. I'm sorry for how I treated you. Sorry and ashamed for how I used you. No woman deserves to be treated like that."

"It was a business arrangement, nothing more. We both got something out of the deal."

Her flat, emotionless statement surprised him. Knowing how tight Sadie Fleming was with the money her girls made, what had Hannah truly achieved from selling her body but a bare-bones means of survival? In an attempt to shame him from his cruel attacks on her, Abby had shared part of Hannah's story with him. Yet here she now sat, speaking of her days of prostitution as if they were of little import.

"In the end, I wonder if either of us got much of anything that really mattered," he said at long last. "None

116

of that's important anymore, though. All I know or care about is that my children need you. Martha Ashley can't meet their needs. The woman's got no maternal instincts. If she were a man, she'd have made an impressive general. But my children aren't a bunch of little soldiers. They need a mother's love."

"And you think *I'm* capable of providing that? A mother's love, I mean?"

"I wouldn't have asked if I didn't think so."

Hannah rolled her eyes and leaned back in the swing. "Well, forgive my stupidity, but I still cannot fathom whatever made you change your mind about me, unless it was sheer desperation."

"My children love you, Hannah." Devlin leaped from the swing and wheeled about to sit on the porch rail, facing her. "They're a lot more important to me than my anger at you. Besides," he added grudgingly, "if the truth be told, I'm beginning to realize I haven't been giving you a fair shake."

Once again, Hannah didn't know whether to be happy or mad. Devlin MacKay could be the most infuriating, patronizing, yet surprisingly engaging of men, especially when he sat there like that, a puzzled twist to his mouth, a boyishly bewildered look in his eyes, spouting words she knew must taste as bitter as gall. Something urged her not to let him off too easily, but another part of her not only felt pity for his plight, but understood.

"You hurt me, Devlin. I don't want that to happen again." Though the admission was wrenched from her against her better judgment, she was glad she had finally said it. Now, let him deal with the real reasons for her hesitation about working for him again.

With his hands gripping the porch railing and his shoulders hunched, Devlin looked down. "I'm sorry for that, too, Hannah." He shot her a quick glance. "I'm not saying I've got it all worked out yet—my feelings about you, I mean. I can't honestly say I ever will. One thing is sure. It's going to take me more time."

"So, in the meanwhile, I should expect further snide comments and inconsiderate behavior, is that it?"

"No." He shook his head with a fierce vehemence. "You'd be doing me a big favor. This time I'm not fool enough to turn my nose up at it. All I'm saying is I still have things about us I have to work out."

She drew in a long, deep breath, then made a decision. "Well, I suppose we could give it a try. But on one condition."

"What's that?"

"This time you pay me, the same as you paid the Widow Ashley."

He grinned then. "Getting to be a regular little businesswoman, are you?"

Hannah nodded. "A woman has to look out for herself, and if *she* was worth paying, so am I. Besides, if we keep things on a purely businesslike basis, it might work out all right between us."

Devlin wasn't so sure about that, but he shrugged and replied, "Couldn't hurt to try." After all, he certainly had nothing more to lose.

9

But by the grace of God I am what I am: and his grace which was bestowed upon me was not in vain.

1 Corinthians 15:10

Two days later, fortified with a week's severance pay, the Widow Ashley was packed and ready to depart Culdee Creek. As the woman awaited a ranch hand to bring up the buckboard and load her possessions, she spared no effort spewing her pent-up bile on Hannah, who had thought to make a quick trip to her room to pick up some clean diapers before returning to Devlin's house.

"You vile, conniving little hussy!" the woman raged, shaking her fist in Hannah's face. "You meant for this to happen all along, didn't you? And after I took you into my confidence and trusted you to help me with the children! But I should've known you secretly wished to warm Devlin's bed, and couldn't dare risk a decent woman winning his heart and marrying him. How would that have made you look by comparison?"

Hannah had hoped to avoid the widow this morning. After hearing the buckboard move past the front yard of the main house, she had mistakenly thought it safe to leave Abby watching the children for a few minutes. Unfortunately, the rig had just been leaving to head around to the bunkhouse. Even now, she could hear it pulling up outside.

There was no chance of avoiding a confrontation now, though. She had all but walked into the lion's den. Still, if there was any way to prevent this from degenerating further, Hannah meant to do so.

"You're mistaken, Mrs. Ashley," she said with quiet emphasis, taking a few steps back as she spoke. "I've in no way set my cap for Devlin. I'd thought you were aware of my ongoing involvement with Evan MacKay."

"Did I say you wanted to wed Devlin?" The ebony-haired woman gave a disparaging laugh. "I hardly think so. Women like you use men to their purpose. Stupid, lust-driven beasts that they are, a smart woman of loose morals frequently has the advantage over a decent, God-fearing one."

Hannah bit her tongue lest she point out that a decent, God-fearing woman wouldn't callously use innocent children to win a husband. There was nothing she could say, at any rate, that would convince the widow otherwise. Best to fetch what she had come for and be on her way.

Martha Ashley, however, apparently wasn't finished with her yet. She followed Hannah into her bedroom and slammed the door shut behind them.

At the sound of the door closing, Hannah whirled around. "This is unseemly behavior..." Her voice faded as the other woman, rage in her eyes, advanced on her.

Then the door opened behind the widow. Devlin stood there. He took one look at Hannah's face and the way the older woman all but loomed over her, and scowled.

"Your things are loaded, Mrs. Ashley," he growled, anger glittering in his eyes. "It's time to depart."

With a gasp the woman whirled about, her hands fluttering wildly as she struggled to straighten her dress and pat down her hair. "Oh, thank you so much," she exclaimed, smiling brightly. "I was just apprising Hannah of some last minute household details and wishing her a fond farewell." She extended a hand to him. "But I wouldn't want to keep anyone waiting on the likes of little old me, so if you'd be so kind as to escort me out . . .?"

Devlin shot Hannah a final, searching look. She managed a faint smile and nod.

"After you, madam." His expression now shuttered, he offered the widow his arm.

Without a backward glance at Hannah—who assumed she was no longer of any importance now that Devlin was available—Martha Ashley flounced from the room, gathered her son from his cradle in the parlor, and stomped out of the bunkhouse. Heaving a sigh of relief, Hannah sank, weak-kneed, into her rocker. Her palms were clammy, and her heart still pounded like she had just run a race, but she was all right. She was all right, and the Widow Ashley was finally gone.

After a time the buckboard pulled away. Still, Hannah didn't move from the rocker. Then a knock tentatively sounded on the frame of her bedroom door. She looked up. Devlin had returned.

Remorse etched his rugged features. "I'm sorry about that. She had no cause to turn her anger on you. I'm the one who hired and fired her."

Hannah glanced at him, then resumed her rocking. "Most times a woman who feels she's lost a man blames it on another woman, rather than the man. I'm used to it."

"Ella never blamed you for my infidelity."

"No, she never did, did she?" Hannah smiled sadly. "But Ella wasn't like most women."

121

"No. No, she wasn't."

He looked suddenly pale beneath his tan. Hannah frowned. "Are you all right, Devlin?"

"Yeah. I've just been feeling hot and cold all morning, but it comes and goes, and then I feel all right for a spell again." He raked an unsteady hand through his hair. "Maybe, once I get the men started on the calf branding, I'll go lay down for a spell."

Hannah shot him a dubious look. "Well, I'll be back up to the house in a few minutes."

"Yeah, sure. You do that." Devlin nodded vaguely, then turned and walked away.

Once Devlin finally lay down after the noon meal, he found he couldn't get back up. He could barely even find the strength to pull off his boots. His head swam; his whole body ached so badly he felt as if someone was trying to wring him dry, and he became hot with fever. By the time Hannah looked in on him after nursing and changing Bonnie, he knew he was sick.

As she leaned over him and put the back of her hand to his forehead, he licked his lips. "I . . . I don't know why . . . but I feel like I've wrestled with some steer and got . . . the short end of it."

Hannah straightened, a tiny furrow forming between her brows. "You're really hot, Devlin. Let me get you something cool to drink."

He made a motion as if to wave her away. "Yeah, get me some water. I'll be fine . . . once I sleep this off."

As she stepped back from the bed, his lids grew heavy. The next thing he knew, she was back with a cup of water.

"Here, take a drink," she said.

Greedily, Devlin swallowed the entire contents of the cup, then pushed it aside. "I . . . I need to get up. There's work to do."

Hannah placed a firm hand on his shoulder, pinning him to the bed. "Oh no you don't. You're in no condition to be going anywhere."

Any other time Devlin would've set her straight about her high-handed manner. Just because they had agreed on a business arrangement didn't mean she was suddenly queen of the roost. But the thought of talking, much less arguing, was suddenly more than he could contemplate. His lids were just too heavy to keep open . . .

Sometime that evening, Devlin awoke to someone pulling off his shirt. His vision was foggy, but he could make out the form of a slender, blond woman hovering above him.

"H-Hannah?" he croaked, his throat dry and raw.

"Yes, it's me, Devlin," a soft voice replied.

"W-water."

A cool hand slid beneath his neck and lifted his head. A pottery mug was pressed to his lips. "Swallow this," a soothing voice urged. "It's willow bark tea. It'll help bring down your fever."

The brew was bitter, but Hannah kept at him until he had drained it all. Then, with a shuddering sigh, Devlin fell back into a semi-stupor.

It was still night when he next awakened. Something cool and wet moved across his forehead, then down his neck and across his bare chest. He moaned, grasped blindly, and captured a hand. Ever so slowly his gaze fixed on it, then focused.

A small, delicate hand clasped a damp cloth. Confusion filled him. "E-Ella?" he rasped. "Is that you?"

"No." The hand pulled away. There was movement, the sound of water in a pan, and then the cool cloth was pressed once again to his forehead, cheeks, neck, and chest. "It's not Ella," the sweet voice replied. "It's Hannah."

Hannah . . . Devlin struggled to say something–anything–but he was too weak to fight the strength-sapping illness raging through him. Darkness beckoned once more, dragging him down into the welcome oblivion of sleep.

For that night and into the next day, Devlin tossed and turned, caught up in the throes of a particularly virulent strain of influenza. When he seemed even worse the next morning, Doc Childress was called. After examining him, the doctor smiled reassuringly.

"He's young and strong," he informed Hannah. "Keep cooling him with the willow bark tea and cold compresses. Whenever he's awake, get him to drink. If all goes well, he should start feeling better by tomorrow."

"And if he doesn't?" Anxiously, Hannah watched Doc wash his hands at the kitchen pitcher pump, then dry them and sit at the kitchen table to put his stethoscope and other equipment into his black bag. "What then?"

"Well, he could catch pneumonia. It's always a possible complication of the influenza." He glanced up, his dark eyes and brows a startling contrast to his silver-white hair and beard. "You're a good nurse, though, Hannah. Devlin should do fine."

She forced a smile. "The children are scared, especially Devlin Jr. He remembers this was how his mother got sick and died."

Doc nodded in sympathy. "You've got your hands full, don't you, what with caring not only for his children, but now Devlin, too."

Hannah felt her cheeks redden. "Beth helps me with the children during the day, and even cooks part of the meals. She's growing up into a wonderful young lady."

"Yes, yes, she is," Doc agreed with a nod. He shoved his hat on his head, picked up his bag and jacket, and stood to leave. "Well, I'd best be on my way. Take good care of our patient, will you?"

"Oh, I will. Have no doubts about that." Hannah walked him to the door, and watched as he climbed into his buggy and drove away. Then, with a sigh, she headed back to check on Devlin.

Late that night, Devlin's moaning roused Hannah from her spot in the rocker beside his bed. She yawned, rubbed her gritty eyes, then glanced down at him. He was bathed in sweat. Still, though his face was flushed, it had lost the hectic color of the past two days.

She moistened a cloth in the pan of water sitting nearby, wrung it loosely, then began blotting him with it. As she worked her way down to his hair-roughened chest, Devlin moaned again. His lids fluttered open. He struggled to his elbows, trying to sit up.

"Lie back down." Hannah scooted from the chair and dropped to her knees to push gently at his chest. "You're too weak to go anywhere. What do you need?"

"Work," Devlin mumbled. "Time . . . to get . . . to work." He strained against the hand still pressing against his chest.

His strength, however, wasn't sufficient to fight Hannah for long. He soon fell back, panting. His gaze, though, never left hers.

It was anguished, confused, and Hannah knew he was still caught in the throes of his fever. "It'll be all right," she crooned, taking up a mug of fresh willow bark tea.

125

She turned back to him. Sliding her hand beneath his neck, she lifted his head and brought the mug to his lips. "Here, drink this. It'll make you feel better."

He swallowed half the mug's contents, then lay back and closed his eyes. Hannah watched him for a few minutes. Watched his broad chest rise and fall, watched him gradually slip into a peaceful, quiet slumber. Then, once again, she wet the cloth, wrung it, and lightly wiped him with it.

Devlin was getting better. He *had* to get better. What would his children do without him? What would Conor do, if he lost his cousin and ranch foreman?

Her gaze moved to his face. His ruggedly handsome features appeared peaceful now, his mouth relaxed beneath his lush, dark mustache. As she looked at his strong if slightly irregular nose, Hannah wondered if Devlin's father, during one of his many brutal beatings, had been the one to break it.

The consideration filled her with sadness. Devlin had suffered so much in the past, and suffered still. The more she came to know and understand him, the harder it was to hate him—and the easier it became to forgive him.

Still, Hannah knew her forgiveness of him was incomplete. Some small part of her held back, remembering the countless times he had hurt her, and fearing what he might yet do.

It was a failing she was ashamed to face, but face it she must. Face it and hope in time, with the Lord's help, she would find some good and honorable solution.

A day later, Devlin felt well enough to sit up in bed and try his first bowl of broth. His muscles, though, were still so weak he quickly gave up hope of feeding himself, and was forced to endure yet another humiliation at Hannah's hands—being fed by her. For her part, he had to admit as he opened his mouth for yet another spoonful of savory chicken broth, she hadn't yet teased him about it or acted put out about squandering valuable time doing so.

He watched her as she intently scooped yet another spoonful of the liquid from the bowl. Funny, he mused, how he had never noticed before the aura of quiet dignity that surrounded Hannah, or the resolute determination and strength that lay beneath her delicate features. Perhaps in the past he had been waylaid by her glowing beauty and womanly form, and not cared to look any deeper. After all, he had never desired anything more of her but what was needed to meet his carnal desires.

The realization shamed him now, as he patiently awaited her gentle ministrations. He had never treated Hannah with the consideration and respect she deserved—not when he had used her body, and not when he had hounded her after she had come to Culdee Creek. Yet still, here she was, tenderly caring for him through his illness and recovery.

Devlin well knew he wasn't worthy of such kindness. He never had been. Not from Hannah, or Ella, or anyone else. No, he wasn't worthy, but he meant to try harder to be so, starting with Hannah.

"This broth," Devlin said between mouthfuls, "is delicious. Where'd you learn to cook so well?"

She smiled. Momentarily, Devlin was caught up by how delicately the color washed her elegant cheekbones, how tenderly the corners of her mouth curved upwards. He stared, fascinated, for several seconds, then remembered himself. Hot color shot up his neck and warmed his own cheeks.

Blast, but he was acting like some love-besotted schoolboy! The influenza must have weakened more than just his body. It must have addled his brain, too.

127

"Abby taught me, of course," Hannah replied before bringing another spoonful of broth to his lips. "Whatever good I have accomplished or know, I owe it all to Abby."

Obediently, Devlin accepted the broth and swallowed it down. "Abby's a good woman and fine example, but don't shortchange yourself, Hannah."

At his words, her head jerked up in surprise, and she almost dropped the spoon. "Why . . . why thank you, Devlin," she managed finally to respond. "That's very kind of you to say that."

He gave a disparaging laugh. "After all you've done for me and my children, guess it's about time I started treating you with a little more kindness."

She scooped up yet another spoonful of soup. "I'm just thankful you don't seem so angry at me anymore."

"I think you deserve more than that from me, Hannah."

Her eyes widened, but she said nothing.

Devlin inwardly cursed. Now he had *really* gone and done it, tripping all over himself in his awkward attempt to make amends. "I just meant maybe we could work at being friends."

Relief brightened her eyes. "Friends. Oh my, yes . . . friends." She smiled and offered him more soup. "Ella will be so pleased."

Frowning, Devlin put up his hand to forestall the spoon directed at him. "I see Abby's been pushing her religious beliefs on you, too. You think Ella's in heaven, don't you?"

"Don't you?" Hannah laid the spoon back in the bowl.

He shrugged. "A part of me would like to think that. Ella put a lot of store in God. But then another part of me can't quite swallow all those well-meant, but make-believe, stories about God and heaven."

Hannah laughed. "Can't say as how it was all that easy for me at first either. I was hard on Abby, demanding she show me, prove to me that God existed and truly loved me."

"What changed your mind?" In spite of himself, Devlin wanted to know. He told himself he was just curious about Hannah, but even as he did something deep within called him a liar. He quickly, savagely, quashed that tiny voice.

She smiled. "Not long after I came to Culdee Creek, Abby told me the story of the woman who was found and taken in the act of adultery, then brought before Jesus. She told me how Jesus not only silenced the woman's accusers by daring any of them who were without sin to cast the first stone at her, but then refused even to condemn her himself. He didn't let her off easily, though. He challenged her to a new life."

Suddenly, Devlin didn't care much anymore for the turn of the conversation. Talk of God and the implied need to reform his life made him uncomfortable, plucking at long-buried emotions he had no intention of ever reexamining. Why should he? What had God—if He truly *did* exist—ever given him but a bucketload of pain and problems?

"Well," he growled, "if it makes you happy to believe all that, I wouldn't want to be the one to take it from you. Me, though, . . . I reckon I'll just go on leaning on myself to get by. That way there are no games, and no unpleasant surprises."

She appeared to consider his pronouncement for a long moment, then sighed. "Yes, I suppose you're right—about there being no surprises that way. I don't imagine I'm the one to convince you otherwise at any rate. One thing I do know, though. You've got to meet God halfway, and if you don't ever try, you won't ever find Him."

"So, you've found Him then, have you, Hannah?"

"Yes," she murmured, her eyes glowing now with a quiet joy, "I think I'm beginning to."

10

Being reviled, we bless; being persecuted, we suffer it.
1 Corinthians 4:12

As the days passed Devlin regained his strength. By the end of the week he was able to get around the house and even walk to Abby and Conor's place for a short visit. By the end of the next week, he was back at work.

The third of July dawned bright and hot. Hannah rose early to help Abby make the bread and pies they planned to serve for the next day's Fourth of July feast. Then, after nursing Bonnie, she left the baby and the other children in Beth's care. Grabbing her pocketbook and a large wicker basket, she tied on her sunbonnet and hurried out just as Devlin drove up with the buggy.

"Ready for our trip to Grand View?" he asked as he tied the reins to the carriage's front railing and jumped down. "Can't spend all day there, mind you, but Conor was willing enough as long as it's only for a few hours."

He walked up to her and grasped Hannah by the arm. She hadn't been this close to him since his illness, she realized. As imposing a man as Devlin MacKay was flat on his back, he was positively breath-grabbing when standing upright. She didn't at all like the way his nearness made her heart race.

With a quick step up and Devlin's assistance, Hannah climbed into the buggy. Already, though she had quite a few items that needed replenishing, she was beginning to regret mentioning those needs to Devlin. Evan would've jumped at the chance to take her to town. And as dashing and handsome as he was, Evan had never unsettled her like Devlin could.

By the time Devlin joined her in the little two-seater, Hannah had managed to settle herself both emotionally and physically. As he untied and lifted the reins, she gave him a quick nod, then turned her gaze down the long road leading out of Culdee Creek's main gate. With a cluck of his tongue and smart snap of the reins, Devlin urged the horse forward.

It was a beautiful summer day, the sky a deep azure blue, the billowing clouds an equally sharp contrast of white. Grass grew tall and green in the large, open meadows. Ponderosa pines, like dark sentinels, jutted high in the rapidly increasing distance behind them, a looming mass of forest and shade. Above it all towered Pikes Peak's craggy summit, hours away yet still overshadowing the region with its majestic splendor.

Happy and content, Hannah settled back in her seat. Her confused feelings for Devlin notwithstanding, she couldn't believe she was back in his house—at his express request no less—and that he was finally even attempting to treat her with civility. Indeed, if the truth were told, Devlin was actually beginning to ask her advice and talk to her as if she was worthy of respect. It was a dream come true, and it seemed the last obstacle to her continued security at Culdee Creek had all but disappeared.

"You look quite pleased with yourself," the man of her thoughts interjected. "You should do that more often."

Hannah glanced at him. Devlin drove the carriage with a practiced ease, sitting straight and tall in his seat. A dark brown Stetson shaded his eyes, worn leather gloves covered his hands, and he had donned a rich nut-meg-colored leather vest atop his usual denims and blue chambray shirt. Though his tan had faded a bit with his illness and extended stay indoors, his face and forearms still possessed a healthy–and most attractive–color.

"I'm pleased with this beautiful day, and with my life," Hannah replied, jerking her gaze from him before he began to notice she had been staring, "but I wouldn't say I yet presume to be pleased with myself."

"And why not?" He shot her an inquisitive glance. "You've got just about everyone at Culdee Creek wrapped around your little finger, not to mention a respectable, paying job. What more could anyone possibly want?"

"Not much, I suppose." She grinned.

"Except maybe a formal proposal of marriage from Evan?"

Her grin faded. Whatever had possessed him to bring up that subject? "Evan and I are taking things slow. Marriage isn't anything anyone should rush into."

"Funny, but I got the impression you two were all but engaged. Evan sure makes it clear to anyone who'll listen that you're hands off."

Hannah sighed in exasperation. Not that again! Another talk with Evan was definitely in order. "We're not engaged. I'm not ready to commit to any man. Even a man as good and decent as Evan." She turned in her seat to face him. "Is that so wrong? To hold off a while, I mean? I don't wish to lead Evan on but–"

"But you're also not ready to run him off yet either," Devlin finished for her. "It's been over a year since you came to Culdee Creek, Hannah. Evan's been all but courting you since the very beginning."

"So, what you're saying is I should agree to marry him or tell him it's over. Is that it?"

"Pretty much."

That wasn't what she had wanted to hear, though, for the life of her, Hannah couldn't say what she *did* want to hear. "And who suddenly appointed you Evan's spokesman?"

Devlin shrugged. "No one, I reckon. But he's Conor's son and I care about him. He's been through enough. I don't want to see him hurt."

"So, now you think I'm the right woman for Evan?"

The question apparently gave him pause. He scowled; his mouth tightened. "I've no objections anymore, if that's what you're asking," he finally growled, an edge now in his voice.

She should never have allowed this particular subject to come up, much less discuss it with the likes of Devlin. What Evan and she eventually decided was between them, and no one else. It was none of Devlin MacKay's business.

"I don't mean this to sound rude," Hannah gritted, now strangely upset with him, "but I think we should change the subject."

"So you're saying I blundered into something I shouldn't have, is that it?"

"Pretty much," she said, mimicking his earlier reply.

Devlin paused, then nodded. "Fine. So, what are you needing to buy in town today?"

Just as he finished speaking, the whistle of the Union Pacific, Denver, and Gulf locomotive shrieked in the distance as it pulled out of Grand View's train depot. Then the carriage topped the last hill separating them from sight of Grand View. Below them spread gently undulating grasslands. Among those grassy hills nestled the little town.

Grand View's prosperity had always depended on the surrounding farms, which produced mostly potatoes and wheat, cattle ranches such as Culdee Creek, and the timber from the thick ponderosa pine forest to the west that was known as the Pinery. It was blessed with two churches, one Presbyterian and the other Episcopal, which the MacKays attended and where Noah Starr served as assistant pastor. Besides the churches, the town boasted the basic amenities such as a mercantile store, icehouse, post office, blacksmith and livery stable, school, hotel, town hall, rooming house, and saloon. Doc Childress also kept an office on the main street, as did the sheriff.

However, as Devlin headed the buggy down the hill, it was the large, two-story frame house standing about a quarter mile outside town that caught Hannah's eye. She had never ridden past Sadie's bordello with Devlin at her side. Suddenly, all the old memories swamped her again.

Memories of the long, horrible nights. Memories of the beatings when she refused to obey Sadie or one of her bodyguards, or when she failed to earn the minimum quota for the night. Overshadowing them all right now, though, was the recollection of that night she first saw Devlin there.

From the corner of her eye, she watched him. He looked straight ahead, his expression inscrutable. A muscle, however, jumped wildly in his jaw, and a flush crept up his neck and face. Devlin was, Hannah decided, just as unsettled about passing Sadie Fleming's as was she.

Grasping wildly for anything to distract him, she recalled his question about what she needed to buy. "All sorts of things," she blurted out of the blue. "Flour, sugar, lard, dried beans, coffee, and tea, just for starters. And then there's a bag of marbles, because I promised Devlin Jr. another game and he's fresh cleaned me out of marbles. And I'd also like to buy some calico to make Mary a dress, and–"

"Whoa, hold on there." Devlin laughed, the tension easing from him. "What in the Sam Hill are you talking about?"

"You asked me what I needed to buy. I was just telling you."

He frowned. "You don't need to make Mary any dresses. They take too much work. Just buy some ready-made ones. Mr. Gates carries them now."

"I know. But I've had a hankering for a long while now to learn to use Abby's sewing machine, and she's agreed to teach me. So, one way or another I need fabric, and since Mary needs a few new dresses . . ."

Devlin shrugged. "Suit yourself."

Their conversation died as they entered the outskirts of town. They passed the Prancing Pronghorn saloon, Nealy's smithy, where the anvil rang with each blow the brawny blacksmith struck, then the rooming house and newspaper office on their left. Across from the newspaper office sat Gates' Mercantile on the corner of Winona and Russell Streets. Devlin turned there and halted the buggy. He jumped down, tied the horse to a hitching rail, and walked around to help Hannah step down.

"I need to stop by the newspaper office and place an ad for Conor," he said, once he had settled her on the wooden boardwalk fronting the building. "Then I've got to visit the feed lot and order more corn for the cattle. How long do you think you'll be needing for your shopping?"

"A half hour or so." Hannah removed her sunbonnet and laid it on the seat, then turned and pulled the large

135

wicker basket from behind it. "If I finish before you, I'll wait for you here."

"Same goes for me, if I finish first." He hesitated. "Are you sure you feel okay going it alone? If you're worried about anyone bothering you—"

She cut him off with a laugh. "I can manage just fine. After all, it's not like we're out in the middle of nowhere, or that you'll be all that long getting back here."

"Okay then. See you soon." Devlin stepped back, tipped his hat to her, then turned and strode down the boardwalk.

Hannah watched him go, admiring, for a fleeting moment, his manly silhouette of broad shoulders, powerful chest, trim hips, and long legs. He was indeed impressive and—

With a sudden, dismayed gasp, she caught herself. As much as Devlin might have changed since that night he had apologized and asked her to come back to work for him, he was still a man to step lightly around. Besides, it wasn't decent to be lusting after Ella's husband. Why, the poor woman had only been dead a little over two months! Whatever was the matter with her?

She clutched her basket and pocketbook to her and hurried around the corner and into Gates' Mercantile. After the brightness and heat of the midday sun, the store's interior seemed cool and dark. Once her eyes adjusted to the diminished light, Hannah glanced around.

Mrs. Edgerton, stern of countenance and rail thin, stood at one of the two long counters flanking the room, talking with Russell Gates, the proprietor, as he measured out flour and other staples for her. Her daughter, nineteen-year-old Mary Sue, stood nearby, painstakingly sorting through a display of colorful satin ribbons. At sight of the pretty, ebony-haired girl, Hannah stiffened.

There had never been any love lost between them. Mary Sue, ever on the prowl for a husband to suit her apparently lofty station as daughter of the town butcher, had always treated Hannah with disdain. The girl had once set her sights on Conor MacKay, only to have Abby whisk him right out from beneath her regal little nose. Then, not long afterwards, she had tried to capture Evan's attention. That attempt had been even more quickly doomed to failure, when he soon made it clear he had eyes only for Hannah.

Hannah couldn't help but wonder how long it would be before Mary Sue began to consider Devlin as potential husband material.

Well, one way or another, she lectured herself as she made her way to the bolts of fabric stacked at the end of the other long counter, it wasn't any of her business. She had come to do her shopping, not speculate on Mary Sue's marital prospects.

After finally settling on a bolt of checkered green and white gingham and another of blue and orange-flowered calico for dress material, Hannah next busied herself picking out lace trims and colored buttons. Mr. Gates finished wrapping Mrs. Edgerton's packages, measured and cut several lengths of ribbon for Mary Sue, then ambled over to Hannah.

"Haven't seen you in a month of Sundays," the gray-haired, bespeckled man said. "The MacKays been keeping you busy, have they?"

Hannah smiled up at him. Mr. Gates had always treated her kindly, even when she used to come into his store in her days working at Sadie's. "Yes, as a matter of fact, they have. I'm now taking care of Devlin's children and house again, too."

The older man grinned. "I heard about that. Mrs. Ashley spared no words—or kindness—in telling everyone how you'd undermined and usurped her position at Culdee Creek." He rolled his eyes and shook his head. "Whooee, but how that woman went on."

Hannah could well imagine how the Widow Ashley had gone on, and that none of it had been charitable. But no purpose was served adding fuel to the fire by joining in the gossip, so she just chuckled softly, then held up the first bolt of fabric.

"Could you cut me three yards of this one, Mr. Gates?" she asked. "And I'd also like the same amount of this color—"

"Well, I declare," a familiar female voice rose from behind her. "And if it isn't the backstabbing little tart who stole my position. Didn't think I'd so soon see you showing your fancy little behind in town."

Hannah whirled around and came face to face with Martha Ashley. The woman must have entered the mercantile without her even hearing the door open.

Before she could gather her wits, much less formulate some sort of reply, Mr. Gates paused from cutting the last piece of fabric and cleared his throat. "That was uncalled for, Martha. Hannah has as much right to shop here as anyone else."

The ebony-haired woman turned to him. "I suppose she does, if you wish to encourage riffraff in your establishment. Personally, though, I don't know of any decent ladies who'd care to associate with her."

Anger flared in Hannah. It was one thing to insult her. It was quite another to besmirch Abby's and Ella's reputations.

"Then, Mrs. Ashley, your definition of 'decent,'" Hannah said, fixing her with a piercing stare, "must not imply 'godly' or 'God-fearing,' for you've forgotten Mrs. Conor MacKay and the late Mrs. Devlin MacKay, both of whom have happily associated with me."

Well aware of the high esteem in which townsfolk held the two MacKay women, the widow mottled beet red. "Well, it was only because they *were* so God-fearing that they took you in. But look at how you've rewarded them for their kindness, leading Evan MacKay around by the nose and flirting with his cousin so outrageously he finally succumbed to your low-class feminine wiles."

Hannah nearly choked on her outrage. "I never flirted with Devlin," she cried, balling her hands into fists and advancing on the woman. "If anyone flirted, it was you . . . you no account, conniving—"

"Whoa! Hang on there, ladies." Mr. Gates stepped between the two women. "I can't be allowing any fisticuffs in my store. Especially between two fine women like yourselves."

Mortified that she had lost her temper, Hannah flushed crimson. She inhaled a shuddering breath, then nodded. "You're right, of course, Mr. Gates. I beg pardon for my unseemly behavior." She then forced herself to turn to the Widow Ashley. "I also beg your pardon, madam, for my unkind words."

The shop's proprietor turned to the other woman and arched a shaggy, graying brow. Mrs. Ashley glared at Hannah for a moment. Then, without further comment or apology, she turned and stomped over to join the two Edgerton women, who had been watching the altercation with barely disguised glee. The three formed a tight little circle and began whispering furiously amongst themselves.

With a sigh, Mr. Gates glanced at Hannah. "Things don't improve too quickly around here, do they?"

"No," she agreed tautly, "and neither do most people."

Suddenly, the day's heat seemed to permeate the store. Hannah felt hot, stifled. She gathered up the cloth Mr. Gates had cut for her, added the buttons and lace trim she had picked out earlier, and gestured to the food-stuffs stacked in shelves behind the other counter. "If you don't mind, I'd like to get the rest of the items I came for and be on my way."

139

He cast another look in the direction of the three women, still whispering and occasionally glaring in their direction, and nodded. "I almost wish I could join you," he muttered, then headed across the store.

Fifteen minutes later, Hannah had all her parcels packed in her basket and the bill for them credited to the Culdee Creek account. After thanking Mr. Gates once more for his help, she strode from the mercantile without a backward glance. Momentarily, bright sunshine blinded her. Turning to head down the boardwalk and around the corner to the buggy, she almost tripped over old Jeremiah Walker, half asleep on a bench outside the mercantile, his legs stretched full length before him.

"Hey, watch yer step there, missy," the old man yelped, jerking back his long, bony legs. "Glory be, but it ain't safe for a body to sit outside anymore."

"I-I'm so sorry, Mr. Walker," Hannah stammered. "I was just . . ."

Hot tears stung her eyes. She blinked them back, furious with herself. She refused to let those mean, narrow-minded, self-righteous biddies get the best of her. And she absolutely, positively wasn't going to let them make her cry.

"Oh," she finally sputtered in frustration, "I'm just sorry!" With that, Hannah gathered her skirts and hurried away. By the time she reached the buggy on the now deserted side street, she craved the haven wherein to hide.

She put her parcel-laden basket behind the seat, threw her pocketbook onto it, then climbed in. Luckily, this side of the street was shaded, but even so it was warm. Hannah pulled out her fan and began to fan herself, her movements as quick and sharp as her thoughts.

The nerve, the bald-faced nerve of the Widow Ashley to dare accuse her of flirting with Devlin! Ella had been her friend. She would never dishonor her memory by chasing after her husband so soon after her death, if she *ever* considered such a thing anyway. True, she had noted Devlin's physical appeal of late, something that had left her cold when he had been her enemy. Yet now, as he began to treat her with kindness and consideration, a surprising and most disturbing attraction seemed slowly to be emerging.

But that's all it was or would ever be, she fiercely reminded herself, a simple physical awareness that Devlin MacKay was a virile, good-looking man. She had and would never flirt with him. Just like Evan, he surely wasn't the man for her.

At the thought of Evan, a twinge of guilt assailed her. What had been the widow's words–leading Evan around by the nose? Was it common knowledge then that she purposely kept the adoring Evan at arm's length?

Hannah closed her eyes. Ah, what was she to do? Was it her fault Evan had always tried to force the pace of their relationship faster than she was comfortable? If only he would back off, give her some breathing space!

The very next chance she had, Hannah vowed to broach that subject yet again with him. It was past time she face her fears and not allow herself to take advantage of Evan in any way. He deserved better than that.

"Waiting for someone special, or just waiting?" a deep male voice asked silkily.

With a horrified gasp, Hannah opened her eyes. There, only inches from her, stood Brody Gerard. As he stared up at her his handsome, swarthy face crinkled into a smile, but that was as far as the look of greeting went.

Terrifying memories flashed before her. Memories of that night he had tracked her through the streets of Grand View like some animal, nearly succeeding in bringing her back to the bordello. Memories of other nights, of him leaning over her with a belt clutched in his hand, lifting it high, then lowering the belt forcefully on her naked flesh.

She cursed herself for not hearing his approach. If she had, she could've climbed from the buggy and avoided him. But now it was too late. Now there was no hope of escape as he reached out and clamped a big, strong hand around her upper arm.

"Yes, I *am* waiting for someone who should be returning any moment," Hannah said, struggling to regain her composure and keep a tremor from her voice. "I assume you know him? Devlin MacKay?"

He smirked, and only tightened his grip. "Oh, I reckon I know him. He's Culdee Creek's foreman. He hired me to work there once."

Brody's unsavory reputation had preceded him even before he had taken the job at Sadie's as bodyguard and bouncer. He had held a job at Culdee Creek for a few weeks around Thanksgiving, the year Abby had first come to work for Conor. After Brody tried to rape Abby in the barn one evening, Conor had thrown him off the ranch. It was then Hannah had first met the brutal, arrogant man, when he had quickly been hired on at Sadie's.

"Well, then, if you know Devlin, you should also know he'll be none too pleased to see you hanging around me." She twisted in his grip, trying to free herself, but to no avail. "Please, Mr. Gerard. Let me go."

"Mr. Gerard, is it now?" He leaned close and Hannah could smell the whiskey on his breath. "I remember a time when we weren't on such formal terms, Hannah, honey. You were always one of my favorites." His lips stretched into a leer. "I'll bet if we hurried, we could have a little fun down that alley over there, and you'd be back, all prim and proper, in this buggy before MacKay even showed up."

Revulsion filled her. She slapped him hard across the face. Gerard reared back, releasing her, a startled look in his eyes. However, as his hand lifted to the reddening

142

handprint on his cheek, growing fury rapidly replaced his look of surprise.

"Why, you uppity little–!" He grabbed her arm again, this time viciously, and jerked her to him until Hannah was suspended half in the buggy and half out of it. "Quit putting on airs with me. We both know what you are, and will always be. Your little hideaway at Culdee Creek won't last for much longer, and then what will you do? You'd better watch out then, when you have to come crawling back to me."

"I'll never crawl back to you!" Hannah cried, her fury lending her courage. "I'd rather die first!"

"Oh, you're too fine a piece for me to ever let that happen." A hard, speculative look darkened his eyes. "In fact, you're too fine a piece to waste on that ranch. I think I just may have to do something about that."

A chill rippled through Hannah. Brody Gerard never thought of anyone but himself. Even here, in broad daylight, if he set his mind to something . . .

Her courage fled. Panic engulfed her. "Let me go! Let me go!" She struck out at him with her free hand, fighting all the while to break away. Her blows, though, fell on him like a gentle rain on parched ground, leaving no mark.

With a low, throaty chuckle, Brody clamped a hand over her mouth and pulled her from the buggy. Terror exploded in Hannah's brain. She fought like a wildcat as he dragged her down the boardwalk toward the nearest alley.

Suddenly, he gave a hard jerk. His arms released her just before he plummeted to the ground.

Hannah staggered backward, almost losing her balance before she caught herself against a building. Then she looked up, and met Devlin MacKay's furious gaze.

143

11

When thou art converted, strengthen thy brethren.
Luke 22:32

Devlin stood there, fist still raised, staring down at a disheveled, ashen-faced Hannah. A multitude of emotions flooded him—relief she was all right, confusion as to why she had been with Brody Gerard, and a murderous anger at the man.

"What in the Sam Hill were you doing?" he rasped, pointing to the prone form of Sadie Fleming's hireling. "Have you lost your mind, associating with a man like him?"

Hannah's face reddened, but she met his gaze with a resolute one of her own. "No, I haven't lost my mind," she gritted out tautly. "And I wasn't *doing* anything with him, except trying to get away. I thought that was obvious."

"Well, I kind of figured that after a few seconds." Devlin pulled off his Stetson and ran a hand through his hair. "Or at least I didn't see much point in waiting around to ask." He shot Brody a considering glance.

"Wonder how long he'll be out." He squatted, pulled Gerard's limp form to a sitting position, then leaned down and slung him over his shoulder.

"What are you going to do"—Hannah quickly rose and helped him stagger to his feet with his awkward burden—"take him to Doc Childress's?"

Devlin grimaced under the weight. "Hardly. I'm taking him to jail. Sheriff Whitmore can deal with him." He paused to eye Hannah. "Why don't you tag along? No telling what kind of trouble you might get into again while I'm gone. Besides, I may need a witness to verify my underhanded attack on the poor man."

She shot him a jaundiced look. "Poor man, indeed."

"Kind of my thought." He shifted Brody's body to a more comfortable position higher on his shoulder, then strode off.

As he headed back down Russell Street and out onto the more populated Winona with Hannah following close behind, people paused to stare. The wind began to pick up and dark clouds furled overhead, threatening rain. Women gathered on the boardwalk to whisper to each other; men joined the procession quickly forming behind the trio.

Sheriff Jake Whitmore walked from his office just then, the Reverend Noah Starr with him. Both men frowned when they saw the crowd, Devlin at its head, bearing down on them. Jake hitched his gun belt a little higher on his hips, then hurried over to meet Devlin.

"What have we here? Brody been hitting the bottle a mite too early in the day again?" The tall, chestnut-haired sheriff helped Devlin unload Brody from his shoulder and carry the unconscious man across the street to his office.

Devlin halted on the boardwalk outside the jail. "Help me get him inside," he demanded tersely. "Then we can talk."

Hannah hurried up onto the boardwalk to join the men, then followed as they hefted their inert burden into the jail. After laying Brody on a nearby cot, Devlin walked back to close the door on the curious onlookers. When they continued to stare inside, he also pulled the roller blinds on the two windows fronting the door.

"Nosy old coots and biddies," Devlin muttered as he rejoined Hannah and the two men standing by the cot, removed his Stetson, and wiped his brow.

"Can't much blame 'em," Jake said with a chuckle. "It isn't often Grand View sees such excitement, especially in broad daylight." His expression sobered. "So, tell me, Devlin. What happened for you to end up with Brody Gerard slung over your shoulder?"

The foreman scowled. "Found him trying to drag Hannah down some alley. Did the first thing that came to mind. I knocked him out."

"Well, don't that beat all?" Scratching his beard-shadowed jaw, Jake stared down at Brody for a long moment.

"Why was he trying to drag you off, Hannah?" Noah Starr asked, meeting her gaze with a concerned look.

Devlin's gaze swung to his housekeeper. In all the confusion, he had failed to ask that question. "Yeah, why, Hannah?"

She swallowed hard, then met the three men's inquiring glances. "I'm not absolutely certain," she began hesitantly, "but I think he meant to take me back to Sadie's. He said,"—she blushed crimson—"he said I was too fine a piece to waste on Culdee Creek, and that he was just going to have to do something about that."

Renewed anger, mixed with a strange possessiveness, filled Devlin. "Well, that does it," he snarled. "Gerard is either going to be run out on a rail or stand trial. We don't need his kind in these parts."

Jake Whitmore cleared his throat. "It's not that easy, Devlin. I can't legally hold him without formal charges."

146

He looked at Hannah. "Is that what you'd like to do, Miss Cutler? Press charges?"

Before she could reply, Devlin cut in. "Of course she wants to press charges. Didn't I already all but say that?"

The sheriff didn't even look at Devlin, but instead exchanged a troubled glance with Noah. "The decision is Miss Cutler's, Devlin, not yours." As he spoke, his gaze skittered off Devlin's then came to rest, once more, on Hannah. "Before you answer," Jake said, "I think you should consider all the aspects of pressing charges."

"Go on," she urged uneasily.

"I can't hold Brody for more than a few hours, unless you want me to charge him. Then I can jail him until he can be brought to trial for assault and attempted kidnapping." A decidedly uncomfortable expression crossed his face. "However, considering your past . . . er . . . profession and history of involvement with Brody Gerard, those charges might be thrown out when it does come to trial. And in the meanwhile, town sentiment might be stirred up even worse than it already is . . ."

When Hannah's shoulders slumped in defeat, something snapped in Devlin. "So what you're saying," he said, his voice gone low and husky in his anger, "is that Hannah's past will be held against her for the rest of her life. That no matter what, she's never going to be believed or protected from scum like Gerard? That she's fair game for any lowlife who wants to attack her?"

An irritated look flared in Jake's eyes. "You're jumping to some mighty high-handed conclusions, MacKay. I don't like it any more than you do, but it's the truth of things. You're a fool if you can't see it."

"Gentlemen, gentlemen." Noah stepped quickly between the two men. "Both of you have brought up valid points but, in the end, the decision must lie with Hannah." He turned to her. "Whatever you decide, I'll stand by you."

147

"I will, too," Devlin offered gruffly, feeling a bit miffed that Noah had beaten him to the punch.

Hannah managed a tremulous smile. "Thank you both for your support. It's deeply appreciated." Her gaze swung to Jake's. "Sheriff Whitmore, however, has made a valid if painful point. Perhaps, Sheriff, if you could just have a long, hard talk with Brody, it'd be enough to make him stay clear of me from now on. And tell him," she added with firm emphasis, "that next time I *will* press charges."

Devlin moved to stand beside her. "Yeah, and tell Gerard that next time *I* won't go so easy on him either."

"Can't say as how I'd blame you." Jake Whitmore's mouth quirked wryly. "Not that I'm condoning violence, of course," he hastened to add when Noah shot him a reproachful look. "I was just meaning to say that I'd understand."

"Well,"—Devlin grasped Hannah's elbow—"guess we'll be heading on out then. Looks like a storm's brewing. We need to get back to the ranch before it breaks."

Jake nodded to Hannah. "Nice to see you again, ma'am, even if it couldn't be under more pleasant circumstances."

"Good-bye, Hannah," Noah added, smiling gently. "If you ever need to talk . . ."

As Hannah nodded and turned to Devlin, thunder rumbled in the distance. "I think we'd better be on our way."

Devlin quickly bid his farewells, then slapped his Stetson on his head and escorted Hannah from the jail. With nothing left to gawk at and the weather changing rapidly, most folk had dispersed and headed elsewhere. The few still lingering outside eyed them with frank curiosity, but said nothing.

Devlin soon had Hannah back at the buggy and seated inside. As she tied her sunbonnet snugly, he climbed in, gathered up the reins, then paused to gaze at the sky.

"It's going to be close, but I think we can make it home in time."

At his comment, Hannah looked up. While they had been in the jailhouse, the clouds had turned gunmetal gray and were now churning furiously. Fitful gusts of wind blew through the streets, kicking up miniature dust cyclones. It suddenly seemed cold, and the scent of rain was in the air.

"Well, we'd better head on out, then." She grabbed hold of the buggy seat arm. "Can't say as how I want to spend anymore time in town today anyway."

Devlin shot her a quick, searching glance then clucked at the horse to set out. As they drove out of town, neither spoke. Hannah supposed Devlin was intent on controlling the horse in the increasingly windy weather. And she didn't know what to say, or how to say it. Her emotions confused, she once again hovered on the verge of tears.

"You know"—Devlin's voice pierced the tumultuous muddle in her mind—"I meant what I said back there."

Puzzled, Hannah twisted in her seat to face him more fully. "What? I'm sorry, but I didn't quite get that."

"I meant it when I said I'd stand by you. It's not fair that some folk hold your past against you, while Brody Gerard can do whatever he likes and get away scot-free." His mouth tightened; a muscle leaped in his jaw. "The man is spoiling for trouble. And if he doesn't watch himself, I just might be the one to give him a good dose of it."

The wind swirled down then, sending Devlin's Stetson flying. With a disgusted oath, he halted the buggy, handed the reins to Hannah, and climbed down to chase the runaway hat. She cast a nervous glance at the ominously blackening clouds overhead. If the weather hadn't been worsening so rapidly, she would've almost laughed at Devlin's comical efforts.

A trace of moisture grazed her cheek, then another and another. Thunder sounded increasingly nearer. She prepared to yell at Devlin to forget the hat, when he finally lurched forward and grabbed it. "Hurry up," she called to him. "The storm's about to break!"

He jumped into the buggy, wedged his hat on the floor between his legs, and grabbed the reins. Slapping the leather lines hard over the horse's back, he urged the animal into a gallop. They rolled down the hard-packed road leading to Culdee Creek at a breakneck pace and, for a time, Hannah imagined they might make it.

Then the heavens seemed to open. Rain fell, harder and heavier by the second. The torrential downpour quickly drenched them. Lightning arced from cloud to cloud in a deadly display of brilliant energy before reaching downward to strike the earth. As the lightning bursts grew nearer, the cracks of thunder became almost deafening. The horse began to shy and rear in fright, fighting its traces.

Her bonnet now limp around her face, and her dress plastered to her, Hannah grabbed Devlin by the arm. He shot her a taut, worried look. "What?" he yelled over the rushing wind and bedlam of thunderous sound.

"Shouldn't we stop . . . somewhere . . . and find shelter?" she shouted.

He nodded and pointed to a low rock overhang jutting from the side of a hill just thirty yards away. "Over there. We'll take shelter over there."

Once more lightning crackled, this time in a stand of cottonwoods less than a hundred yards away. The air sizzled with static, making Hannah's skin crawl. The horse reared in terror, then slipped in the mud, losing its footing. For a horrible moment, Hannah watched the animal struggle to keep its balance. Then, almost in slow motion, it toppled backward, falling straight toward them.

150

"Get out! Jump!"

Even as he shouted the command, Devlin pushed her from the carriage. Hannah's right foot caught on the edge of the buggy, and she felt it twist painfully. There was no opportunity to consider her ankle, though, as she threw out her hands to break her fall. She hit the ground hard.

With a terrified squeal, the horse slammed into the carriage. In its wild thrashing, the animal managed to tip over the conveyance. Hannah was on the side opposite where the horse hit, but as she climbed to her knees in the rain and mud, she realized Devlin had jumped from the other side.

Panic seized her. She started to stand, only to have her right ankle give way. "D-Devlin!" Hannah choked back a gasp of pain as she tried once more to test her ankle. "Devlin, where are you?"

She took a faltering step forward. Again her ankle buckled, and a sharp pain lanced through it. She dropped to her hands and knees.

"H-Hannah?" With a groan, Devlin scrabbled around from the backside of the overturned buggy and stood. Aside from a bloody gash on his forehead and his now mud-soaked clothes, he looked in one piece.

Overhead, thunder rolled, and the rain poured down. She pushed to her knees and lifted her hands to him. "Help me. I twisted my ankle jumping from the carriage."

At Hannah's entreaty, Devlin hurried over and helped her to stand. Even with his assistance, though, she quickly discovered she couldn't walk. With her first pained inhalation, he swung her up into his arms and carried her to the rock overhang.

Hannah closed her eyes and silently willed her heart's pounding rhythm to ease, her body to cease its trembling. She was but shivering from the cold, she told herself. Her painful ankle combined with the storm's fury

151

were the sole reasons for her racing pulse. Still, she couldn't help but clasp her arms about Devlin's neck a little tighter and lay her head on his shoulder.

"We're here." Hannah's eyes snapped open. They had reached the rocky shelter. Squatting, Devlin laid her down gently. "Can you scoot in there yourself?"

"Y-yes, I think so."

Gingerly, Hannah crawled in beneath the overhang. It was dry and padded with old leaves and moss. She moved as far inside as she could, then turned.

Even then, Devlin was hurrying away. "Where are you going?" she cried, her fright swelling anew. "The storm . . . get in here!"

"In a minute," he called back. "I've got to check on the horse."

An interminable amount of time passed. Repeatedly, lightning struck not very far away. Each strike made Hannah jump, filling her with renewed fear for Devlin's safety. At long last, though, he returned.

Crawling in beneath the overhang, Devlin scooted close and began to place a blanket around her.

"Luckily, it was wedged between the seat and floor and didn't get too wet," he said. "You're soaked to the skin. The blanket will warm you."

Until he mentioned it, Hannah hadn't realized she was still shivering. Already the blanket felt good. "A-and what about y-you?" she asked through chattering teeth. "You n-need to get w-warm, too."

"I-I'll be all right."

Though his voice sounded gruff, Hannah could detect Devlin's efforts to hide his own shivering. "W-we can sh-share this blanket, you know," she said.

"No . . . that wouldn't be pr-proper."

Exasperation filled her. "Oh, h-hang propriety! I'm not going to let you freeze to death for the sake of some silly social customs." She lifted the edge of the blanket closest to him. "Now, get over here, before I th-throw the whole blanket at you!"

He hesitated just an instant, then moved toward her and pulled the blanket over him. Hannah scooted closer to him. "There, that should give you more blanket. You need it more than I, to protect you from the rain and wind."

He pulled the extra amount of blanket she had provided more snugly over him. "Good thing no one can see us right now," Devlin whispered. "The tongues would wag and never stop."

At the image his words stimulated, Hannah giggled. "I know it's mean of me to laugh, but I couldn't help seeing Mrs. Ashley's face, or Mary Sue's either, for that matter. They'd be so jealous."

"Don't know why. I'm no prize."

Her laughter faded. "Why do you say that? You're hardworking, honest, and loyal. You're a good father, and you were a loving husband to Ella."

"Was I really?" His voice dipped low, resonating with pain. "You, of all people, know what kind of a husband I really was. Not a very good one."

"So all the love and devotion you gave Ella count for nothing, in light of a short time of unfaithfulness? You now mourn her wholly from guilt, and nothing else?"

"You know it's not just guilt," he muttered. "I loved Ella with all my heart. I just didn't love her enough, or in the way she deserved. If I'd been a better, stronger man, I never would've cheated on her."

"But you did, and she forgave you," Hannah said softly. "That's a gift she gave you, Devlin. Because she loved you." She expelled a long, thoughtful breath. "You were blessed to have had a wife as wonderful as Ella. But she counted you a blessing, too. Her love for you would never have stayed so true and steadfast if you weren't good to her."

"I wish I could believe that, Hannah."

His voice rose from the darkness, deep, rich, but anguished. His sadness plucked at her heart, and that tightly guarded fortress crumbled a bit more.

"Oh, Devlin . . ." Hannah turned to face him. She lifted her hand and touched his cheek.

He jerked, then went very still. "Hannah . . ." Devlin's voice dropped to a low, rough rasp. Then he took her hand and lowered it, imprisoning it between them. "I don't know what got into me to tell you the things I did, but I shouldn't have." Suddenly, he seemed unable to meet her gaze. "I wasn't looking for sympathy or comforting, and I sure didn't mean for you to get the wrong idea."

Each word stabbed at her heart. "I *didn't* get the wrong idea," she whispered, the warmth flooding her face. "I just felt . . . well, I just . . . *understood.* So much of what you said reminded me of my own journey." She cocked her head, smiling sadly. "A lot of folk think if I'd been a better, stronger person, I'd never have let myself be forced into prostitution. After all, wouldn't a decent woman kill herself, rather than let such a horrible thing happen to her?"

Devlin nodded in careful, cautious agreement. "Some folk might think that. I've certainly believed that about you. But I'm starting to see I was wrong. It's easy to judge when you're not actually faced with a life-and-death decision. Besides, what you did is over and done with. Folk need to judge you for who you are now, not then."

"As must I, wouldn't you say? Judge myself for how I am and act now, rather than for what I once was and did?"

Slowly, a smile tugged at the corner of Devlin's mouth. "Okay, you've made your point. Easier said than done, though."

She laughed. "Don't I know!"

He paused then, as if listening for something. "Sounds like the storm's passing. Haven't heard any thunder for the past few minutes."

"You're right." Hannah pulled her hand free of Devlin's clasp. "Come on, let's go see."

"Don't reckon you'll be going anywhere fast, what with that twisted ankle of yours," he observed dryly, "but you can at least scoot out to the edge of this overhang."

At the reminder of her ankle, Hannah's face fell. "Oh, I'd almost forgotten . . ."

Devlin turned and crawled out. "Let me check the buggy and weather, then I'll come back for you. Okay?"

"All right," Hannah said, gingerly following in his wake. From the vantage of the overhang, she watched Devlin climb to his feet and stride to the buggy. It was still tipped on its side, but Devlin was able to right it. The horse, however, was nowhere to be seen.

Hannah glanced up at the sky. Though gray clouds still roiled overhead, patches of blue and a few sunbeams peeked through several rents in the turbulent canopy. East of them, thunder rumbled weakly, punctuated only occasionally now by jagged flashes of lightning.

She smiled. Soon the sky would clear. Save for the raindrops sparkling on the foliage and the damp scent of the earth, one would never know they'd had a storm. But *she* would, Hannah thought, as she awkwardly struggled to her feet and grabbed the rocky outcropping for support. Her ankle, if nothing else, would remind her for a while to come.

Just then the sound of hoof beats from the direction of Culdee Creek caught her attention. Sure enough, she realized as she turned in the direction of the rhythmic pounding, it was Conor, Evan, and three hands. Most likely, their buggy horse had hightailed it straight back to the ranch.

155

Devlin walked over, smiling. "Looks like we've got ourselves a search party."

"Yes," Hannah agreed, reaching out to grasp his arm for support, and smiling back up at him, "looks like we have."

12

What shall it profit a man, if he shall gain the whole world, and lose his own soul?

Mark 8:36

She walked in a grassy meadow, sunlight sparkling off the knee-high, windblown grass. Her long red hair was unbound, curling then unfurling about her face in the warm breeze. She wore a simple dress of green calico, and her feet were bare.

Terrified she'd disappear before he reached her, Devlin ran down the hill after Ella. She turned to him as he drew up beside her, an impish grin lifting her lips.

"I-I've missed you so." He gazed down at her with tender affection.

Her grin softened into a loving smile. "Walk with me."

There was nothing that Devlin would've rather done. He moved close, his arm encircling her shoulders, and shortened his stride to match hers. She felt good, solid, and surprisingly real against him.

"I love you," he said, his voice husky with pent-up longing.

"I know." Ella glanced at him. "I've always known."

Though her answer did little to ease his pain, he was nonetheless happy to hear it.

"Don't lose hope, my love." Ella's look of understanding was ample proof she knew what he had been thinking. "This time of mourning will pass, and you'll find joy again." She clasped his arm, halting him. "But first you must face your grief and anger, and look past it to God's eternal plan. Only then will you become a whole man, a man of God."

Devlin gazed down at her, his heart so full of yearning he thought it might rip in two. "I don't care about God or His plan," he rasped finally, pulling her into his arms. "Part of His plan was to take you from me. All I know is I want you back. Oh, Ella, I need you so badly!"

"You need far more than I could ever give, my love." As she spoke her face blurred, began to fade. Devlin's sense of flesh and bone in his hands seemed to melt away. "Look to the Lord," she whispered in farewell. "Look to the Lord . . ."

With that, Devlin awoke with a start. It was morning, the first rays of sun kissing the windowsill and wooden floor, the lace curtains—curtains Ella had made—wafting gently in the warming breeze. From force of habit, he turned to the spot where his wife always laid. It was empty.

In a rush of mind-numbing emotion it all came back. The dream . . . his precious time with Ella . . . her words. *Look to the Lord.*

Cursing savagely, Devlin swung out of bed. In the aftermath of his dream, freshened anguish filled him. The dream had seemed almost as real as actually having her present and alive. The all but tangible sensation of holding his wife and talking with her, even now, seemed unnervingly authentic.

Frustrated despair warred with Devlin's growing anger. Blast it all! What a cruel trick his mind had played on him! He didn't need God. He needed Ella!

By dint of a superhuman effort and several deep breaths, he regained an iron grip on his emotions. Devlin washed, dressed, and stalked from his bedroom. A couple of strong cups of coffee, he thought as he headed for the kitchen, should drown this crazy tumult in his head. And, after the coffee, Devlin resolved, grimly making plans, a morning of hard work should banish whatever was left of the empty ache in the middle of his chest.

Hannah wasn't about yet, he noted as he entered the kitchen. After having sprained her ankle yesterday, she'd most likely need help even making it over from her bunkhouse. Just as soon as he got some coffee into him, he would fetch her.

Devlin quickly stoked the cookstove and set water on to heat. When his restless, unsettled feelings wouldn't ease, he paced the room with clenched hands and stiff strides. Eventually, the water began to boil. Devlin made himself a pot of coffee, then carried the pot to the table where he poured himself his first cup.

The coffee was black and gullet searing—just how he liked it. He sipped deeply of the bitter brew, willing it to warm his belly and soothe his mind. It did neither, however, serving instead to irritate his empty stomach.

He leaned over his mug, gripping it tightly with both hands. Closing his eyes, Devlin fought to block out the memories, the heart-deep ache. Yet, time and again, the dream returned to haunt him.

"I-I can't stand it," he finally choked out, tears stinging his eyes. "Ah, Ella, Ella. Why must I dream of you?

It gives me no peace, no comfort. All it does is lay open my heart to bleed anew."

Another swig of coffee did little to assuage his torment. Devlin shoved the mug aside and stared down at the flowered tablecloth, watching as its colorful images blurred then swam before his tear-filled eyes. Why, he wondered, every time he thought he was beginning to come to terms with his wife's death, did something always happen to blindside him and bring him back to his knees? He buried his face in his hands. Would the pain never end?

"Oh, Ella, Ella." The tears brimmed over at last, coursing down his cheeks.

From a distance he heard himself endlessly repeat her name. It seemed so unreal, though, as if he were disembodied and hearing himself from some place far away. It couldn't be him, yet it was.

Then there was a movement behind him, a halting shuffle. A small, uncertain voice called his name.

"Papa?"

With a groan, Devlin turned and gathered his son to him. They remained that way for a time, silent tears running down Devlin's face. Though one part of him screamed out in shame at weeping, another part yielded, knowing his sorrow was right and good, and that his son needed to share this with him.

The moment Devlin ceased his interior battle, surrendered his pride, an incredible sense of peace engulfed him. Peace . . . In his mind, he pulled back to examine the strange sensation from a safer distance. When had he last felt such a wondrous, healing emotion? But then, when had he ever deserved it?

Words teased the edges of his memory. Words Hannah had spoken not long after he had begun to recover from his bout of influenza. Words about God's grace, and that no one ever deserved it.

Was this sudden sense of peace a small token of God's grace, of His love for him? Devlin wondered. If so, why now? Why not all the other times he had called out to the Lord, screamed and cursed and raged at Him?

It made no sense. He was crazy even to consider such a thing. God had better things to do than waste time on him.

But then nothing made much sense right now. Devlin sighed. His life, however unsettled it might have been, seemed on the verge of becoming even more so.

Devlin hadn't known she was there. Only a half hour earlier, Evan had helped both Hannah and Jackson make the short trek up the hill to the ranch house, depositing them on the front porch before taking his reluctant leave. She had paused only a moment to gaze down at his retreating form before grasping the cane Evan had made for her, taking her son by the hand, and entering the house.

No one had been up but Devlin Jr., who was playing quietly in his room. After leaving Jackson in his temporary care, Hannah headed down to the cellar to retrieve some sausages stored there for their breakfast. As she climbed back up the stairs, however, she heard Devlin's voice, low and hoarse with anguish.

Concern filled her. Hannah hurried up the last few steps. There, from the darkness of the cellar doorway across from the kitchen, she saw him, seated at the table, his face buried in his hands. She heard him whisper Ella's name, and knew he was weeping.

Myriad emotions engulfed Hannah. She wanted to rush to Devlin's side, take him in her arms, and comfort him. Yet fear made her hesitate. What if he rejected her overtures, or became angry at being discovered in this moment of weakness? Maybe it was better just to steal away, and give him the private time he needed.

Yet even as Hannah wavered, Devlin Jr. moved past her and entered the kitchen. At the sight of his father, the boy hesitated for an instant, then walked up to stand beside him. He spoke his father's name. Devlin went still, then groaned and pulled his son to him.

Watching the pair, the large, dark head bent over the smaller red one, Hannah's heart swelled. It touched her that the son loved his father enough to reach out to him. But it stirred her even more profoundly that the father loved his son enough to open himself to him, to expose his vulnerability, and share their common grief. Such an act took courage and trust and so very, very much love. Such an act revealed a depth–and compelling quality–to Devlin that she had never seen before.

Hannah stood there in the shadows for a few seconds more, then quietly headed down the hall to where she could now hear her son playing. The tender moment she had witnessed, however, lingered in her heart and mind for a long, long time to come.

"So, what do you think of my latest creation?" Hannah asked one rainy October morning nearly four months later.

Abby, eight months pregnant and now very obviously in a family way, held the little dress Hannah had just handed her up to view. "I've seen a lot worse," she replied finally, after examining it critically. "But, I must admit," she added, her mouth curving into a grin, "I haven't seen many better."

162

Hannah smiled and leaned back from the double lockstitch sewing machine. "Well, I did have a very good teacher."

"Humph," Abby countered with a disbelieving snort. "I'd say, rather, you've already equaled and bested your teacher." She lifted the dress's skirt and examined the hemming and seams. "You really should consider making several more dresses like this one and putting them out on consignment in Gates' Mercantile."

"Oh, I couldn't do that." Hannah flushed and shook her head. "No one in Grand View would buy the dresses, once they learned who'd made them."

Her friend paused to consider that for a moment. "You have a point," she admitted finally. "And aside from lying and saying I made the dresses—which wouldn't be right to do—that leaves only one other solution."

Hannah eyed her warily. "What would that be?"

"Why, take the dresses to Colorado Springs, of course! I know a lady—Mrs. Waters—who runs a fine millinery shop just off Cascade Avenue there. All the wealthiest ladies of society frequent her shop. It would be the perfect place to sell your dresses."

Misgiving filled Hannah. She couldn't help, though, feel a tiny spark of hope flare. "Well, I don't know about that. My dresses are far too plain—"

"It would be a simple matter to add extra lace and trimmings, and to use a better quality material." With a casual wave of her hand, Abby dismissed Hannah's protests. "Besides, what the fine ladies look for in children's clothing is as much quality of workmanship as opulent fabric. Mark my words." She handed the dress back to Hannah. "You'll soon create a demand you'll never begin to fill."

Hannah knew Abby had experience in the millinery business, having worked at the highly respected Mrs. Waters's Millinery shop for a time. But to consider sell-

163

ing any of her own creations . . . It was the answer to all Hannah's problems, a dream come true!

If she could succeed at sewing clothes people would pay good money for, comfortably supporting herself and Jackson in a respectable manner was a real possibility. A world of opportunities and options would be hers. Above all, though, she would never again have to depend on the charity of others. She could stay or leave Culdee Creek as she wished, and not have to worry about ever returning to a life of prostitution.

Glancing up at Abby's beaming face, a twinge of guilt shot through her. If Abby could guess her thoughts right now, Hannah knew it would hurt her friend's feelings. And it wasn't as if she wanted to leave Culdee Creek or the life she had made here. It was just that a smart woman always had a backup plan.

Besides, Christmas was only two months away. There was a bite to the air at night now, and they had even had a couple of brief, light snowfalls. It was never too soon to begin thinking about holiday gifts—gifts she might be able to buy, instead of just make this year, if some of her dresses sold in time.

There would even be an additional gift to buy, Hannah thought with happy anticipation, if Abby's baby arrived on time. Doc Childress had estimated the baby's due date at around the 14th or 15th of December. If all went well, there'd be a Christmas baby at Culdee Creek this year.

Yes, Hannah mused as she took up the little dress and began to pin a gathered ruffle to the end of the puffed, royal blue batiste sleeve, this Christmas promised to be a most wondrously joyous celebration. Jackson was nearly eighteen months old, and a more happy, healthy, bright little boy she had yet to see. Abby's pregnancy, now that she was well past the threat of a miscarriage, was progressing well. Baby Bonnie, Devlin Jr., and little Mary seemed to be thriving now that a loving rou-

164

tine had once more been established. And their father . . . well, suffice it to say Devlin's and her friendship appeared to grow with each passing day.

As her thoughts harked back to the past few months, Hannah's lips curved in pleasant memory. Not only had Devlin asked her to make Bonnie's christening gown, but he had also invited her to attend his daughter's baptism in St. Mary's Church in Colorado Springs, the closest Roman Catholic Church. Devlin wouldn't have cared one way or another if Bonnie had ever been christened. But he had still done so, because he knew it was something Ella would've wanted.

Hannah had never been in such a large, impressive building. The neo-Gothic church of red, pressed brick and cut limestone, though still under construction, was complete enough for services to be held in the basement. Its little chapel was quite tasteful and reverently inspiring in its own right. Beth and Evan served as Bonnie's godparents. Watching the touching ceremony, Hannah was struck by an intense longing to be baptized.

Since that day over a month ago, she had prayed over that desire, and had finally resolved to approach Noah Starr about the possibility of taking instruction in the Episcopal faith. Gathering up the necessary courage to approach him about the subject, however, was another matter entirely. She knew that if she asked, Abby would've gladly helped her. But Hannah wanted the news of her baptism to be a special surprise for her friend. So she bided her time and awaited the right moment to speak with Noah.

"How have things been going with you and Evan?" Abby asked, tugging Hannah back to the present. "I mean, since you had that talk with him and told him to back off a bit and give you some breathing room?"

Hannah glanced up from the second sleeve she was now pinning. She considered her friend's question for a moment, then sighed. "He seemed to accept it pretty well for a while, but the past few weeks . . ." She shook her head. "It almost seems as if Evan's decided he's allowed me enough time, and now things should go back to the way they were."

Abby studied her gravely. "He's young. His intentions are good, but he's not always the most patient man in the world." She grinned and began slowly to rub her distended belly. "He gets that from his father, I'm afraid."

"I know that, Abby." Frustration filled Hannah. "It's just the more he pushes me, the more I want to pull back. Sometimes, Evan's love is so smothering!"

"Are you just not ready to marry? Or is Evan just not the man for you?"

Her friend's words echoed Hannah's own questions, questions she had repeatedly asked herself in the past months. Perhaps it was time to face her doubts.

"I'm not sure I know what kind of man is the man for me." Hannah lowered her head. "I'm not sure if I should even dare hope that there *is* one out there for me. But, until I'm certain, is it so wrong to cling to Evan? He makes me feel cherished and loved."

Awkwardly, Abby rose from her chair and walked to Hannah's side. "You *deserve* to be cherished and loved, but it isn't fair to lead Evan on. He loves you. The longer you keep him waiting and hoping, the harder the eventual parting will be on him."

"I'm just so afraid," Hannah whispered, feeling ashamed but even more scared. "For such a long time after I came to Culdee Creek, he was my whole future."

"God is the only one you should ever fully depend upon." Her friend's hand settled supportively on her shoulder. "He will lead you toward the future *He* has always intended for you."

Hannah glanced up through tear-blurred eyes. "And will He also lead me to the man I am truly meant for?"

"Yes," Abby agreed with a smile. "If that's part of His plan for you, He'll lead you to the man who has always been meant for you. The man who will love you with a true and holy love."

Two hours later, just as Hannah had finished the dress and was putting away the sewing supplies, Conor walked into the room. At the sight of her husband—whom she hadn't expected back from town quite so soon—Abby's face brightened with pleasure. That expression quickly faded, though, as she took note of his worried frown. Hannah hurried over to stand at her side.

"What's wrong, Conor?" Apprehension threaded his wife's voice. "Is someone hurt? Should I get out the bandages and such?"

"Won't do him any good." Culdee Creek's owner raked a hand through his windblown hair. "Sam Starr's dead. Died of a sudden heart seizure yesterday evening."

Hannah exchanged a shocked look with Abby. Samuel Starr was Noah's uncle and Grand View's Episcopal Church rector. Hannah felt a stab of sympathy for the younger man. Overnight, he had become the leader of the town's Episcopal community. He must also now take on the support and comfort of Mildred Starr, Samuel's widow.

"How soon . . . will the funeral be?" Abby whispered and began stroking her abdomen in an almost unconscious, soothing gesture. "We should attend . . . pay our respects."

"Two days from now, on Friday."

"Is there anything we can do in the meanwhile?" Though she had hardly known the older Reverend Starr or his wife, Hannah felt compelled to offer her help.

"Perhaps send some food? And will there be a reception after the burial? We could offer to cook something for that, too."

Conor shrugged, his own feelings of confusion and sorrow etched plainly on his face. "I forgot to ask. Guess I can send a hand back to see what else might need doing for them."

Abby nodded in agreement. "That would be best. In the meanwhile"–she shot Hannah a resolute look–"we'll start cooking."

The funeral and burial at Grand View's forested cemetery was well attended by most folk in town, as well as by those from outlying farms and ranches. Though Hannah had to endure caustic looks from some of the local women–Mary Sue Edgerton and the Widow Ashley included–Evan and Devlin stood protectively on either side of her, with Conor and Abby bringing up the rear. It felt good to have such loyal friends.

After the ceremony, they all reassembled in the town hall for a communal meal. Hannah watched from across the room as others solemnly paid their respects to Noah and his aunt. She hesitated to join in the receiving line. Already the day had dragged on interminably, laden with unspoken but eloquent censure. The thought of subjecting herself to it yet again was almost more than she could bear. But then, if she hadn't wished to endure it, she lectured herself, she shouldn't have insisted on coming along.

Yet she had, and the gesture had been motivated by the memory of all the kindness Noah had shown her. It was past time–and the decent thing to do–to offer him compassion in return. It was also past time, she decided, that she broach the subject of joining his church.

Finally, as the receiving line began to dwindle, Hannah gathered her courage, rose, and walked over to wait her turn. A woman she didn't know, standing just ahead of her, cast her a sour look and immediately sidled closer to her husband. From across the room near the punch bowl, Mary Sue gave a disdainful snort and met Hannah's gaze with a narrowed one of her own.

Evan immediately strode over to join Hannah. "Looks like you're needing an escort again."

Bless dear, loyal Evan. "It's all right, really it is." She managed a weak, lopsided grin. "Besides, if it came to blows, I think I could handle the likes of Mary Sue."

He shot the dark-haired girl an appraising look. "Yeah, I reckon you could at that. But I like being with you any chance I get. I don't mind standing in this line again."

Despite her talk with Abby two days ago, Hannah still hadn't summoned the courage to speak with Evan. If the truth be told, finding the right words to tell him it was over between them had been even harder than finding the resolve. But she would soon enough, she knew. She had to.

Evan deserved that much. And so did the Lord, if she was ever to cast all her trust upon Him. Right now, though, she must deal with Noah Starr and his aunt.

Her turn finally came. Evan, by then apparently satisfied it was safe to leave her, rejoined his father and cousin at the punch bowl across the room. Hannah walked up to stand before Noah. His face haggard in his grief and weariness, he stood there for a long moment, staring in surprise. Then, apparently remembering himself, he accepted her proffered hand.

169

"I just wanted to tell you how sorry I am for the loss of your uncle," Hannah forced herself to say. "I know it must have come as quite a shock to you and your aunt."

"Uncle Samuel had been ailing for some time," the young priest admitted, "though he kept the truth about his infirmities hidden. He didn't wish to cause concern or allow it to diminish his ability to serve his people."

"He was a good man," was her simple reply.

The Reverend Samuel Starr had indeed been a good-hearted if sometimes officious man. Hannah wondered now if he wouldn't have welcomed her into his little congregation if she had ever dared ask. It was too late now, though, to find out. What she could do, however, was ask his nephew.

She noticed, then, that Noah had yet to release her hand. She glanced down at it, clasped as it still was in his larger one, and flushed. Somehow, some way, Hannah sensed Noah had already guessed she had come just now for more than the offering of condolences.

Lifting her head, she met his gentle, questioning gaze. Here goes, Lord, she whispered silently. "When things settle down a bit," Hannah began, her voice sounding surprisingly husky all of a sudden, "would you consider accepting me for instruction? I'd like"–she swallowed hard, then forged on–"I'd like to be baptized and join your church."

For the longest time Noah stared down at her, almost as if he couldn't believe what he had just heard. Then, like the morning sun bursting forth over the horizon to gild a new day, a joyous smile brightened his face. He gripped her hand all the tighter and gave it a small shake of confirmation.

"Yes," Noah breathed in quiet conviction. "Yes, I'd be happy–no, *privileged*–to accept you for instruction."

13

The LORD is the strength of my life; of whom shall I be afraid?

Psalm 27:1

Two weeks later, under Noah Starr's patient tutelage, Hannah began her instruction in the Episcopal faith. To keep the secret from Abby, she arranged to spend the necessary time with Noah during her trips to town for supplies. Though those trips occurred a bit more frequently than usual—and required Devlin's, Evan's, or some hand's escort—Abby never appeared to catch on.

But then, nearing the last month of her pregnancy, Abby didn't seem to notice nearly as much as she once had. Her face took on a dreamy quality; she slept more, and her activity level gradually lessened. "Settling into her nest" or some such phrase was what Conor called it. For his part, Devlin, father of three himself, could only chuckle and second his cousin's observation.

While Abby nearly floated through the days, Hannah agonized about how best to tell Evan their "engagement" was over. Numerous times she rehearsed the words and phrases she would use. Then, numerous times, she just as quickly discarded them. Finally, Hannah decided she would simply spit out the truth, choosing her next words based on what Evan said.

Two days before Thanksgiving she gathered her courage and, after getting Beth to watch the children for a short while, sought him out. It was a bitterly cold, windy afternoon when Hannah managed to track Evan down in one of the barns. He was cleaning a stall and, fortunately, was alone.

A blast of cold air followed her through the side door as she slipped into the barn, alerting Evan to his visitor. An armful of clean, dry straw in his arms, he paused to glance over the stall divider. At sight of Hannah, dressed in her usual blue wool jacket, a multicolored knit scarf over her head, and mittens on her hands, he grinned in unabashed delight.

Throwing his load onto the stall floor, Evan quickly wiped his hands on his denims, swiped at any stray pieces of straw that might be clinging to his dark hair, and hurried over. "What a pleasant diversion," he exclaimed, his smoky blue eyes bright with gladness. "How did you know that, just this moment, I'd been thinking of you and wishing you were here?"

As if to punctuate his declaration, Evan took her by the arms and pulled her to him. Before Hannah could respond, he lowered his head and kissed her.

This wasn't, she thought in dismay, at all how she had intended her talk with Evan to begin. Drawing up her hands against his chest, Hannah pushed back as gently as she could.

Always the perfect gentleman, Evan immediately released her. The look of puzzlement–and even a tinge of hurt–in his eyes, though, revealed his confusion. In Evan's mind, Hannah realized, nothing had changed between them.

"Evan, there's something we need to talk about." She busied herself with the task of pulling off her mittens and headscarf, then glanced up and found a load of hay bales, yet to be stacked, in one of the empty stalls. She gestured to them. "Can we sit for a spell?"

"Suit yourself," he muttered, but complied.

When they were both seated, Hannah gathered her rapidly waning courage and launched into the purpose of her visit. "It's about us, Evan." She gazed earnestly up at him. "I've thought long and hard about it, and I don't think I can ever be the kind of wife you want me to be. I'd like to go back to being friends–permanently."

He stared at her for a long moment, and Hannah could see the emotions flash by in his eyes. Shock, hurt, then briefly, a spark of anger he quickly damped.

"If I'm pushing you too hard, I can back off more," Evan offered finally. "If it's more time you need–"

"No." She raised her hand to halt him. "It's not that. It's . . . us. We're not right for each other. At least not," she hurried to amend, "as husband and wife anyway. I love you dearly, Evan, but as a brother, a friend. And that's no way to come to you in marriage."

He looked away. "Plenty of folk marry for reasons other than love. And a lot of them still manage to find it eventually." His gaze swung back to lock with hers. "You have to work at a marriage, Hannah. It isn't all flowers and high emotion."

Frustration filled her. Oh, how could she make him understand without hurting him even further? More than anything, she didn't want to hurt Evan.

Yet it seemed more and more apparent the only way to avoid hurting him was to acquiesce to his request that they marry. There was no guarantee, though, that her heart would change once they were wed. Indeed, if she trusted her instincts in this matter, Hannah felt certain things would only worsen between them.

"Yes, you do have to work at marriage," she forced herself to reply, "but there has to be something there to begin with. Something to build upon. Though you seem convinced something already exists, I'm not. It's over between us, Evan. You've got to accept that and go on."

"Accept that? Go on?"

The young man leaped to his feet so quickly it startled Hannah. She reared back, her hands lifting instinctively as if to ward off a blow. Her action only deepened the anguish burning in Evan's eyes.

"Why now, Hannah?" he demanded, towering over her with clenched hands and rigid shoulders. "Ever since you went to work for Devlin, things have changed between us. It's almost as if . . . as if he's put ideas into your head. Ideas about him!"

Hannah blinked in confusion. Gradually but inexorably, the meaning behind his words trickled into her mind. Horror filled her. She blushed furiously.

"No." Hannah shook her head with vehemence. "Devlin has never, ever shown any romantic interest in me. Not before Ella died, or after. At best, we're becoming friends. But that's all, Evan. I swear it!"

Her response appeared to mollify him. "Good thing," he muttered, his handsome face mottling with anger. "If I thought for a moment Devlin was horning in where he had no right, especially so soon after losing Ella . . . well, I don't know what I'd do. He's always been too big for his britches. A little too high and mighty, especially considering all his own failings."

"Well, let me assure you one of his failings isn't running after other women so soon after Ella's death. He still mourns her deeply."

"Maybe so," was Evan's grudging reply. "You can't blame me for wondering, though. It did seem like you started changing toward me after you took up house-keeping for him and taking care of his kids. Why, I hardly see you nowadays!"

"I've been very busy with the children," she countered defensively. "Besides, I'd begun to have my doubts about us long before I first started working for Devlin."

As much as she hated to admit that to him, Hannah felt compelled now to do so. All she needed, atop Evan getting angry at her for breaking things off, was for him to take out that anger on Devlin.

A look of stubborn determination flared in Evan's eyes. "Doubts or no, you could still give me a chance. A man can change a lot about himself, if the right woman is willing to give him a chance."

Hannah drew in a deep breath, then slowly let it out. "Evan, it's over between us. And you certainly don't need to change for my sake. Better you just wait for the right woman to come along." She stood, pulled her mittens from her pocket, and put them on.

"Where do you think you're going?" He took her by the arm. "I'm not done talking."

"Yes, you are." She tried to free herself, but his grip only tightened. "Let me go, Evan. Just let me go."

For an instant he looked as if, for once, he intended to refuse. Hannah could see the warring emotions in his eyes, the muscles in his jaw clenching, and the rigid way he held himself.

Terror washed over her. Then she recalled whom she was with. Evan wasn't like the other men. No matter how angry he might become, she knew him, trusted him. He'd never hurt her.

"Let me go, Evan. Please," she repeated, this time gently.

He released her then and stepped back, breathing heavily as if it had taken all the strength within him to do so. Hannah turned and walked toward the door. Just as she reached it, his voice, hoarse with determination, reached her.

"I'll let you go, for now," he cried. "But I'm not giving up. Not by a long shot. You're still searching, Hannah. And as long as you are, there's still a chance for us. Just remember that. There's still a chance!"

Hannah gripped the door latch and pushed down hard, then walked out. Immediately, the wind caught her in its icy grip, buffeting and slapping at her as if to chastise her for treating Evan so cruelly. She gritted her teeth, lowered her head, and plowed onward.

The wind hadn't anymore right than Evan to berate or doubt her. It was her life, her decision, and no one else's.

She hadn't fought so long and hard to escape the horrible, denigrating life of the bordello to have someone else attempt to control her now. Anger swelled within her; her heart pounded, and frustrated tears filled her eyes. It didn't matter if Evan's love made him think that what he wanted was right for her.

The wind began to howl, the noise giving expression to Hannah's pain and confusion. Sleet started to fall, pelting the earth, pricking her tender skin—and equally tender conscience. Hannah's face and ears grew cold—she had forgotten to tie on the knit scarf she had earlier stuffed into her pocket. She pulled it out now, flinging it over her head.

Just then a particularly brutal gust surged down and whipped it from her, sending the scarf soaring. "No!" Hannah screamed. She ran after it, racing back down the hill.

The sleet came harder now, coating the ground with an icy layer. Hannah slipped and fell, hitting the cold-hardened earth with a surprising impact. Far down the hill, the brightly colored scarf danced out of sight.

The tears came then, coursing down her cheeks. The frustration and anger at Evan—for not listening to her, not accepting what she had told him, and for having to hurt him—swelled in her throat, threatening to choke her. For the life of her, she couldn't get up, couldn't compel her limbs to carry her onward. That sudden lack of strength terrified her.

Then there were footsteps and hands—strong hands—grasping her and pulling her to her feet. A voice—Devlin's voice—beckoned, calling her from her downward spiral of confused emotions. He pulled her into his arms, where he sheltered her within the warm bulk of his body.

"Hannah, what's wrong?" Devlin's words, fraught with concern, washed over her like a soothing balm. "Did you hurt yourself somehow when you fell?"

For a brief, blessed instant, Hannah savored the sweet protection of his body and the sense of safety and comfort it seemed to provide. Then, on the downdraft of yet another frigid gust, reality returned. She couldn't trust Devlin in such a matter.

She pushed back from him and hastily swiped away her tears. "I'm okay." She forced what she hoped was a reassuring smile. "I just slipped chasing after my scarf."

Devlin turned in the direction Hannah gestured. Far down the hill, the knit scarf had blown back in the opposite direction and was now snagged in a low-growing pine tree.

"If you'll excuse me," she said, "I need to go after it."

Devlin halted her. "No, you don't. It's freezing out here, and you're not dressed for this weather."

His frowning gaze took in her cotton dress and lightweight shoes beneath her short wool jacket. "I'll fetch your scarf. You head to the house and fix us both a hot cup of coffee."

Devlin turned then and strode down the hill. Still somewhat dazed by all that had transpired in the past minutes, Hannah could only stand there and watch him go.

He was dressed for the weather. His Stetson snugly covered his head; his thick canvas jacket was layered over a wool shirt and neck scarf. Stout leather gloves covered his hands. Yet despite Devlin's warm attire, his cheeks and nose were already wind-chafed. In comparison, she could only imagine how she must look.

With an exasperated sigh, Hannah headed up to the house. At this particular moment, she wasn't in any mood for a talk with Devlin, or for a chivalrous rescue. Right now she was so tired of men she didn't want anything to do with any of them. Somehow, though, recalling the look on Devlin's face, she doubted she would be given that option.

The kitchen was a cozy haven after the cold outdoors. She hurried to stand by the big cookstove, savoring its radiant heat. After a time, Hannah began to feel warm again.

Pulling off her mittens, she tucked them into her jacket pocket, then shrugged off her jacket and hung it on a peg by the back door. Luckily, she had earlier set a coffeepot of fresh water on a back burner. Tendrils of steam now wafted gently from its spout. By the time Devlin walked in, her scarf clenched in his hand, Hannah had coffee ready.

As he hung her scarf atop her jacket and pulled off his own outer clothing, she poured him a mug. Hannah filled her own mug as he stirred several spoonfuls of sugar into his coffee. She remained standing, however, giving a fierce shake of refusal, when he pulled out a chair for her.

With a shrug, he took his own seat at the kitchen table, then looked up at her. "Why won't you sit down?"

178

She took a tentative sip of her steaming brew. "I've got too much work to do."

"Work can wait a few minutes." He gestured to the chair on his right. "Come on. Sit for a spell."

Irritation flooded her. She didn't want to talk to him, especially after what she had just gone through with Evan. Indeed, her thoughts were still so jumbled she didn't know what to think about it all herself.

"Devlin, I don't want–"

"Hannah, what's wrong?" He cut her off, a look of concern darkening his rich brown eyes. "It takes more than a fall or lost scarf to make you cry."

Her lips tightened mutinously. "It's really none of your business."

"No, it's not, if you don't want to tell me." He leaned back in his chair and locked gazes with her. "But you've been good to me and my children, and I owe you a lot. I was just trying to offer my help, if you needed it."

Oh, what was the point of keeping the truth from him anyway? she thought in defeat. One way or another, he'd find out soon enough. With a sigh, Hannah walked over and sank into the chair Devlin had offered earlier.

"I just talked with Evan," she said. "I finally decided to tell him I didn't want to marry him. He didn't take the news well . . ."

Devlin didn't comment. He just sat there, sipping his coffee and listening.

Hannah leaned on the table, her forearms embracing her mug, and lowered her head. "I feel so guilty for hurting him. Yet I'm angry, too, that he won't listen or hear me. I've been trying now for several months to do this, but Evan refuses to believe I really mean it."

"Why, Hannah?" Devlin asked softly. As he spoke, he stroked the sides of his mug. "Why *are* you doing this? It makes no sense."

179

Startled, she jerked her head up and stared at him. "Why?" she echoed his question. "Why else, Devlin?" With a great effort, she struggled to contain her indignation. "I don't love him, or at least not like a woman should love the man she's to marry."

Devlin didn't say anything right away. Rather, he just sat there, appearing to find a sudden interest in intently swirling his coffee. "What caused you to come to this decision?" he asked finally, glancing up at her.

She forced herself to meet his piercing gaze. It hadn't been all that long, less than six months at best, since she and Devlin had at last come to a truce. In that time, their relationship had gradually improved. But could their fledgling friendship withstand the truth of her cowardly insistence on clinging to Evan, and the security his love had offered?

Hannah wasn't so sure. And, to expose that weak, grasping side of herself . . . She shivered, filled with self-revulsion at facing up to yet another of her secret shames.

When she had first come to Culdee Creek, all she had wanted, all she had known was to survive in any way possible. There had been no self-respect, no moral code to draw upon. She had been willing to do anything, use anyone, to keep from having to return to Sadie Fleming's.

Evan had so eagerly offered his help, then his heart. A heart—a man's heart—Hannah had learned long ago how to maneuver to her best advantage.

No, she resolved fiercely, she couldn't admit the brutal truth to Devlin. He wouldn't understand. And it might well shatter the fragile bond beginning to build between them.

"I realize now Evan caught me at a time when I was confused, lonely, and very vulnerable," she said finally. "He was so kind and attentive. He treated me with respect." Hannah sighed and lowered her gaze to finger the tablecloth. "I guess I convinced myself, at least at first, that I was in love with him."

"That's understandable, I suppose. But I repeat, what caused you finally to decide you weren't in love with him?"

What indeed? Hannah asked herself. She shrugged. "I don't know . . . maybe coming to know myself better. Maybe getting to know Evan better, too. I'm sure finding God and striving to live in a more honest, loving way also had an influence. I finally realized prolonging this charade would only hurt Evan worse in the end. And I didn't want to do that. Not ever."

Devlin lifted his mug to his lips and took a deep swallow. "Well," he observed as he set the mug back down, "you have the right to change your mind and admit you made a mistake. I just hate to see Evan hurt. And he will be hurt, no matter that you did your best to end this as soon as you could. The repercussions, though, could cause some pretty nasty tension around here for a while to come."

Hannah stared at him, puzzled. Repercussions? What kind of repercussions?

Why now, Hannah? Evan's words in the barn slowly filtered back through her mind. *Ever since you went to work for Devlin, things have begun to change between us. It's almost as if . . . as if he's put ideas into your head. Ideas about him!*

Was that what Devlin was getting at, when he had spoken just now of repercussions? Did he think . . . did he imagine she had decided to turn her wiles to winning him, rather than Evan?

She must, she decided, lay to rest once and for all any doubts Devlin might have about her and her motives. If not, she'd never be able to look him in the face again, much less work for him.

181

"I made it clear to Evan my reasons for breaking our engagement were entirely personal, and had nothing to do with any other person. You have my word on that."

A look of relief softened his features. "Good." Devlin exhaled a deep breath, and shrugged in an apparent effort to ease the tension from his shoulders. "Forgive my bluntness, but I was afraid Evan would misinterpret our friendship. He and I have had a rather stormy relationship over the years, and probably will for some time to come. I don't ever want to put Conor in the position of having to choose between us, though. That, I'm afraid, would near to break his heart."

"I wouldn't want such a thing to happen either." For the first time since they had come inside, Hannah smiled. "Thank you for your honesty, Devlin. I know it must have been difficult to say, but I'm glad you trusted me enough to say it anyway."

He downed the rest of his coffee, then grinned. "It's been hard, picking my way back with you. But you've always met me more than halfway, and that made it a sight easier. You're a good woman, Hannah. I mean that in all sincerity."

Once more, tears prickled in her eyes. She was certainly getting awfully emotional of late. But then, a lot of wonderful things seemed to be happening, too.

"Thank you, Devlin," she said. "That's just about the nicest thing anyone's ever said to me."

14

Except a man be born of water and of the Spirit, he cannot enter into the kingdom of God.

John 3:5

Abby's labor began early on the morning of December 2nd during a freak rainstorm that quickly turned to sleet, then snow. Unlike Ella's, it was an easy delivery, and a black-haired, squalling baby boy soon arrived into the world. The proud parents promptly named him Sean, in honor of Conor and Devlin's grandfather, the brave Scots immigrant who had first come to the United States. Also, as Abby joyfully put it, because their son was truly a gift from God.

Though Conor tried to keep his energetic wife confined to bed for the next couple of weeks, Abby felt too well to lay around for long. By the middle of the week she was already coming downstairs for a few hours in the morning and afternoon while her son napped, and by the beginning of the next she was back to doing all her usual chores. The cradle both Hannah and Ella had used for their newborns was soon set up in a quiet spot in the parlor where Abby could frequently check on her baby.

Soon thereafter, preparations for Christmas began in earnest. The main house's kitchen was filled with the spicy scents of cookies and fruitcakes baking. Children's laughter floated through the parlor as they helped string popcorn and make paper garlands to trim Christmas trees. In no time both houses were well-stocked with goodies, and each pungent pine tree embellished by the gaily wrapped and extravagantly bedecked gifts set beneath them.

On Christmas Day, both MacKay families as well as the unmarried hands gathered in the main house for a fine Christmas feast. Afterwards, the children congregated upstairs in Beth's room to play with their new toys. As Hannah and Abby started to clean up in the kitchen, all the men suddenly discovered the need for a long walk to, as they claimed, "wake them up" after such a filling meal.

"Just another excuse to avoid helping with the dishes, I'd say," Abby grumbled good-naturedly after the last man departed.

"Well,"–Hannah filled the wash pan with hot water and soap–"did you really want the mess their lumbering about in your kitchen, dropping dishes and tripping all over themselves, would create, if such an unheard of event were ever actually to occur?"

Her friend grinned. "No, can't say as I would. But it would be nice if, for a change, they all weren't quite so quick to skedaddle every time it came to doing some kitchen work."

"Or to changing a baby's messy diaper."

At that, both women laughed. The next few minutes were filled with companionable silence as Hannah washed and rinsed, and Abby dried the dishes. It was a blessed time, Hannah mused, filled with a peace and contentment such as she had never known before.

This was the kind of life she had always yearned for, she realized, even when she couldn't put words to what she needed. God was good. She knew that to the depths of her being more and more with each passing day. And, with each passing day, as she studied the lessons and biblical passages Noah Starr had set her to learn in preparation for her baptism, she grew in her knowledge and love of the Lord. There didn't seem to be much of anything more that Hannah could wish for from life.

"How soon will you have the next set of dresses ready for Mrs. Waters?" Abby asked, breaking into Hannah's thoughts. "Conor's planning an overnight trip to the Springs next week. He promised me a night in the Antler's Hotel, with dining and dancing on New Year's Eve. If you'd like, I could take your dresses to Mrs. Waters then."

"They should all be finished well before New Year's." Hannah handed Abby another dish to dry. "I still can't believe how well the first two consignments sold. Or that those fine ladies in the Springs liked them." She shook her head in disbelief. "Well, it plum boggles the mind."

"Maybe so, but I never doubted that you'd do well. You've a gift, Hannah." Abby set the dried dish aside and reached for another. "Whatever will you do with all the money you're bound to make?"

Hannah shrugged. "Save most of it, I'd imagine. Right now, Jackson and I don't need much. But it never hurts to have something set aside for a rainy day. The best part of all, though, is that I'll now have that security if I ever need it. It's a wonderful feeling."

"Yes, I suppose it is." The chestnut-haired woman grinned. "Why, just think. At the rate you're going with your dresses, you'll soon be a woman of means. If that doesn't bring the young swains around, nothing will."

"That'll be a sight for sure." Hannah laughed. "Since I first came here, the only man who has ever shown any real interest in me has been Evan. I hardly think that's going to change any time soon."

"Oh, don't be so certain of that." Abby cocked her head and pursed her lips. "I've seen a few of the hands gaze admiringly at you when you weren't looking."

Hannah laughed. "Well, if you say so." She handed Abby the last dish, then turned to the glasses and silverware. Less than fifteen minutes later, as if by cue, the men stomped onto the back porch. Hannah and Abby removed their aprons and greeted the men as they entered the kitchen.

"So, what's next on this glorious eve?" Conor, his cheeks rosy from the brisk time outdoors, smiled down at his wife. "Knowing you two women, I'd bet there's all sorts of fun still planned."

Abby grinned up at him. "Well, there's Christmas carols in the parlor, then fruitcake and pie." She tilted her head impishly. "First, though, I recall a sprig of mistletoe hanging over the parlor door that, so far, has been sadly neglected."

"Oh, it has, has it?" He took Abby by one arm, and Hannah by the other. "Well, let's see what we can do about that."

Hannah cast Conor, then Abby, an uncertain glance. "Er, I don't recall voicing any complaints about the mistletoe."

"Maybe not," Culdee Creek's owner amicably agreed, pulling her along all the same. "But it's Christmas, and I aim to make the most of the chance to kiss the two prettiest ladies in these parts."

At that, Hannah giggled, but without further protest decided to join in the fun. As they drew up beneath the mistletoe, Conor first pulled Abby to him. He gave her a resounding kiss, then turned to Hannah. Grasping her by both arms, he leaned down for a quick kiss. As he raised up, however, Conor paused and grinned again.

"Can't see hoarding all the fun for myself," he said, speaking to the rest of the men who had come up behind them. "I'm sure you ladies would be willing to get a bit of further use out of this mistletoe, wouldn't you?"

Abby rolled her eyes. "Do you know, Conor MacKay, that you're the biggest troublemaker on the entire Front Range?"

"Well, you did say the mistletoe had been sadly neglected, didn't you?"

"Yes," she nodded in smiling affirmation, "yes, I did." Abby glanced at Hannah. "Are you up to a few more kisses then? I'm sure the rest of the men wouldn't mind."

Hannah chuckled softly. "Of course not. It's Christmas, after all."

With that, Conor stepped into the parlor, and the hands—Evan among them—quickly lined up. Soon Hannah was so involved in the laughter and kissing she didn't notice Devlin standing back from the rest.

Her glance finally met his. Something dark and shuttered passed between them. Her smile faded.

Behind her, Abby caught sight of Devlin. "Come on, Devlin," she called. "There's no backing out now. All the others have run the gauntlet, and so must you."

He hesitated a moment more, then smiled. "I hope you two ladies have saved your best kisses for last then, because a little peck on the cheek won't do me." As he spoke, he strode forward, slipped a hand around Hannah's waist, and pulled her to him. "You did save me your best kiss, didn't you?"

Though his words were light and full of fun, the look in his eyes swiftly changed from a teasing one to something more intent and searching. Hannah's heart gave a leap and hung in her throat. "I-I can't promise you that," she stammered. "I'm almost fresh out of kisses."

"Well, guess that's what I get, coming last and all." With that Devlin's head lowered and his lips met hers.

It began as a chaste kiss, gentle and warm. At best, Hannah supposed it lasted a few seconds. But it was long enough for the kiss to deepen into something more ardent, for her eyes to close, and for a shiver of pleasure to ripple through her.

Then Devlin pulled back, releasing her.

She blushed and lowered her head. She couldn't help it. Though the kiss might not have meant much to Devlin, it had ripped open her tightly locked heart. It had stirred something deep within her, something she was terrified to examine too closely.

But that realization wasn't something she could allow Devlin, or anyone else, to discover. With a gay little laugh, Hannah tossed her head and, with a sweep of her skirt, stepped aside. "Come along, now," she said. "Abby's waiting, and you haven't finished until you kiss her, too. Then it's Christmas carols, isn't it, Abby?"

She turned to glance back at her friend.

Abby nodded. "Yes, we still have to sing the Christmas carols." Her gaze took in Devlin, then Hannah once more.

Hannah's heart sank. The look in Abby's eyes was troubled, thoughtful.

Her stomach clenching, Hannah looked past her to where Evan stood. It took only one glance at him to fill her with a sick foreboding. A muscle twitching erratically in his jaw, Evan's furious gaze was fixed on Devlin.

For the next few weeks, Devlin mentally kicked himself time and again for his handling of Hannah's innocent kiss under the mistletoe. Not only had he all but seized her and forced his kiss on her, but he had embarrassed her and angered Evan in the bargain. He didn't know what had come over him at that moment he had first seen her, standing there in the doorway, her eyes laughing and bright, her face luminous, her lips soft and inviting.

He felt ashamed, dirty, like he had betrayed both Ella and Hannah. Trouble was, he didn't know what to do about it. With that kiss, something had definitely changed between them. Their relationship was no longer lighthearted and friendly. He was surprised to discover how much he missed that.

Yet if he apologized, Devlin feared he might make matters worse by saying the wrong thing, only aggravating the offense. If Hannah had thought nothing of the kiss, his obvious discomfort with it would make her feel uncomfortable. But if he didn't mention it, and she *had* found the kiss unsettling, Hannah might wonder at what his true intentions had been. And that could even be worse than no words at all.

In his dilemma, there was little Devlin could do but procrastinate. He worked long hours each day to avoid Hannah as much as possible, most times coming in late in the evening. Time passed, and still relations between them didn't improve. Where once Hannah was happy and comfortable around him, now she rarely spoke unless absolutely necessary, and her gaze constantly skittered away from his. The situation became increasingly intolerable.

Finally, one cold, bright mid-January day, Devlin gathered his courage and broached the subject with Hannah. "About Christmas Day," he said as he guided the buggy down the road to Grand View for Hannah's biweekly lessons with Noah Starr. "I've been very unhappy for a while now about how I handled kissing you under the mistletoe. My behavior was unseemly, not to mention un-gentlemanly. I wish to apologize."

"You didn't do anything wrong, Devlin." She shot him a bright, understanding smile. "It was all in good fun."

Devlin knew Hannah was just being kind. It might have all been in good fun for everyone else, but the way he had kissed her had been far more than simply friendly. And the feelings she had stirred in him, when he had pulled her close and covered her mouth with his . . .

"Yes, I did do something wrong," he gritted out the admission. "I kissed you hard and hungry, and you know it."

Hannah's smile faded. She turned to gaze out on the winter-browned countryside. "So why *did* you kiss me the way you did?" she demanded tautly. "Did you do it to anger Evan?"

Like talons clawing down his spine, Devlin could feel his irritation rise. Obviously, the kiss hadn't had the same effect on her as it had on him. "And why the Sam Hill would I want to make Evan angry?"

"How am I to know?" She shrugged. "You said your-self you two don't get along all that well."

"I didn't kiss you to spite Evan!"

"Then you just thought to humiliate me in front of the others, is that it?"

"Humiliate you?" Devlin couldn't believe his ears. Here he was all but confessing to his lustful feelings for her, and she didn't appear to have any inkling—or even care—how she had affected him! "I just finished saying I humiliated *myself!* You're turning my words around." With a quick tug of the reins, he halted the horse. "Why is it women are always so good at twisting a man's words?"

"I didn't twist a thing, Devlin MacKay! You started this, so don't go changing the subject now."

His brows rose in surprise, and he stared at her, mouth agape. Well, now he had done it, he supposed. Despite his best efforts to the contrary, he had gone and made Hannah angry.

"Look," he muttered, trying a different tack, "all I'm saying is that it was my fault. You looked so pretty and happy standing there, that I forgot myself. I didn't mean you any disrespect, and I didn't do it to spite anyone. I just plain wanted to kiss you."

The color drained from Hannah's face. "You . . . you *wanted* to kiss me?"

Devlin rolled his eyes. "Haven't I just spent the last five minutes trying to explain that to you?"

She didn't answer for a long moment. "It's not fitting . . . so soon after Ella's death."

He flung back his head and exhaled a breath of pent-up frustration. "I know that, Hannah. I did something on impulse I now regret. For Ella's sake, *and* yours." He turned toward her. "Can you forgive me?"

"Yes," she said softly. "I suppose I can. I must. But it can't happen again, Devlin. It just can't."

Relief washed over him. He turned back to the horse and, clucking his tongue, urged it on. "No, it can't happen again," he said and meant it with all his heart.

Fifteen minutes later, on the far side of Grand View, Devlin dropped Hannah off at the church rectory, then headed down Sweet Road back into town. She stood outside for a few minutes, watching as he drove down the length of the main street, passing the stone building that served as the town saloon before pulling up at the livery stable a short ways past and across from it. Devlin planned to wait there while Simon Nealy mended two

191

broken harness buckles, a harness ring, and three bridle bits. If all went as planned, her hour-long appointment with Noah Starr should be just enough time for the smithy to complete the repairs.

Gradually, Hannah became aware of the cold. To warm herself, she stomped her feet and clapped together her mitten-covered hands. Then, with a pensive sigh, she turned and hurried up the little gravel-strewn path to the rectory's front door. Hannah knocked smartly. A few seconds later Mildred Starr came to the door.

A pleasant looking, matronly woman, Millie–as she preferred to be called–always wore her heavily silvered brown hair plaited into a single braid, and twisted at the base of her neck to form a neat, tight bun. Her eyes were a bright blue, her cheeks plump and rosy, and what seemed a perpetual smile was always on her lips. At sight of Hannah standing there, Millie's smile broadened.

"Well, if it isn't Miss Cutler, and right on time!" She swung the door wide, stepped back, and motioned for her to enter.

The scent of something sweet and spice-laden filled the air. Hannah smiled. If she didn't miss her guess, Noah's aunt had some treat baking. Millie was always commenting on what she viewed as Hannah's too thin frame, saying that she needed "a little fattening up."

"Smells good." Hannah removed her wool jacket, knit headscarf, and mittens.

"Apple spice cake." Her hostess took her things and hung them on the oak hall tree standing by the front door. "You'll stay a bit after your instructions, won't you? A hot cup of tea and warm piece of cake will fortify you for the cold trip back to Culdee Creek."

"I'd love some of your cake," Hannah said, loathe to disappoint Millie in any way. "But if Devlin is ready for me early–"

"Then he can just come on in and also have cake while he waits," the older woman finished firmly.

Behind them, a door opened. "Ah, Hannah," a deep male voice said, "I hadn't realized you were here." Noah walked up to stand before them. "I hope I haven't kept you waiting long?"

She met his welcoming smile with a warm one of her own. "I just arrived. Your aunt and I were discussing plans for after my lessons."

He shot his aunt a quizzical glance. "Let me guess. Do these plans have anything to do with food?"

Millie laughed, then shooed them away. "Now you stop that right now, Noah Starr," she chided with mock severity. "Hannah's not the only person who could use a little extra meat on her bones."

Chuckling, Noah took Hannah by the arm and led her into his study. It was a room she would've expected of a preacher, she thought, surveying it yet again with ever curious eyes. Two walls, from floor to ceiling, were filled with shelves stuffed with books. In the center of the room, facing the door, was a huge, oak desk, centered on a blue-, red-, and green-fringed Aubusson rug. Before the only window, hung with thick, dark green velvet drapes that stood open to brighten the pine-trimmed interior, sat two blue damask-covered wing chairs.

From her earlier visits, Hannah knew to head for the chairs. As she settled herself, Noah walked to his desk and picked up his Book of Common Prayer, then joined her. After taking the seat opposite Hannah, he leafed through the book until he found the spot he wanted, slipped a bookmark between the pages, and then closed it.

"So, how have things been for you of late?" His brown eyes warmed with interest. "I haven't seen you since just before Christmas. That makes it"–he crinkled his brow in thought–"that makes it almost three weeks, doesn't it?"

"Yes." Hannah nodded. "Almost three weeks since my last instructions."

"And how have you been?" he repeated.

She looked away, directing her glance to the window. The view outside was one of flattened, dry grass where the relentless Colorado wind had scoured the snow away, and small, shriveled mounds of white where it hadn't. A few desiccated, drooping stalks still stood within the picket fence enclosure of what remained of Millie's lush, summer flower garden. And in the yard's far corner, a skeletal cottonwood, its gray, gnarled bark and limbs providing a stark backdrop, presided like some ancient behemoth.

Still, the bleak scene was a peaceful contrast to the tumult raging within her. Should she tell Noah about her and Devlin's Christmas kiss? Would he be scandalized to learn how much Devlin's kiss had aroused her? And did she dare reveal to him Devlin's belated admission of his own guilty desire?

It was all so confusing. Still, Hannah needed someone to talk to who wasn't part of the MacKay clan. And she needed to know what path the Lord would wish her to take with this.

She sighed, turned back from the window, and met the priest's questioning gaze. "Christmas Day provided a bit more excitement than I'd bargained for. Abby and I ended up standing under the mistletoe, and kissing all the men there after they returned from their walk." Hannah hung her head. "I'd told you, the last time we talked, that I had ended my relationship with Evan. And it wasn't as if I was truly trying to entice anyone. Abby and I were just feeling high-spirited with the holidays and all. But it got out of hand."

Noah leaned forward, his gaze now serious, concerned. "What happened, Hannah?"

"Everything was okay, until I Devlin kissed me." As she spoke, she could feel the blood heat her face. "He pulled me close and kissed me full on the lips, not at all like how the others had kissed me. And I . . . I liked it. I liked it very much."

The priest straightened, then settled back in his chair. He propped his elbow on one armrest, cradling his chin in the fork of his thumb and forefinger. "And now you feel guilty about it. Because Ella's been dead less than a year."

"Yes." Hannah swallowed hard. "But there's more. On the way here today, Devlin finally confessed he had wanted to kiss me. We almost ended up in an argument, and now he's feeling so guilty I'm afraid the friendship we've built over the past months may well be over." Her hands clenched, and she pounded a fist on her thigh. "I'm afraid I've ruined everything, and all in one moment of silly, thoughtless fun!"

"There's no harm in a friendly kiss. And it wasn't as if you singled one man out on purpose." Noah considered her thoughtfully. "There's also nothing wrong with you being attracted to Devlin, or he to you."

"But what about Ella?" Hannah wailed. "What kind of people does that make us, not even to pay her the proper respect of a decent mourning period?"

"Have you or Devlin done anything untoward before or after this Christmas kiss?"

The blood drained from Hannah's face. No, she thought, unless you count Devlin's calling on me at Sadie's as untoward. But she knew Noah meant since Ella's death, and she wasn't about to drag that other time back into the light. That was in the past. Nothing could be done about it.

"Since I came to Culdee Creek, Devlin has never talked to me or tried to touch me in an unseemly way. That's why the way he kissed me came as such a surprise."

195

"So lay aside the memory of the kiss, allow the proper time to pass, and see where this newfound attraction leads." Noah smiled gently. "There's no rush, is there? No reason why you can't allow things to take their natural course."

Hannah shook her head. Noah didn't understand, but then, how could he? She hadn't told him the whole story. "It's not as simple as that."

"Do you perhaps imagine, because of the life you once led, that you don't ever deserve to find happiness with a man? Or is it you fear you now can never have a normal relationship?"

Mortified at what she imagined he was implying, Hannah jerked her gaze back to his. "I-I don't know if we should be talking about such carnal things. You being a man of the cloth, and all, I mean."

The young priest chuckled. "As if I haven't ever had such thoughts myself, or wondered how it would be with the woman I might someday wed. But I wasn't speaking of the intimate aspects of a marital union, Hannah, but of the more spiritual, emotional relationship."

"I don't understand."

"Let me phrase it another way then." For a long moment, Noah was silent, his brow furrowed in thought. "Do you still harbor guilt over your past life? Feel unclean, even damned? And does that make you wonder how you can ever bring a joyous, sanctified heart to a marriage? How you will ever feel worthy enough of a man you come to love and wish to wed?"

Tears stung her eyes. She lowered her head quickly to hide them. "I don't know if I ever will, but in coming to the Lord, I have hope . . ."

"As well you should." The priest opened his book and began to thumb through it. "There's a passage I want you to hear, one that can be used for baptism. Ah, here

196

it is." He looked up and met Hannah's gaze, then lowered his once more.

"Heavenly Father," he read, "we thank You that by water and the Holy Spirit You have bestowed upon this your servant the forgiveness of sin and have raised her to the new life of grace. Strengthen her, O Lord, with your presence, enfold her in the arms of Your mercy, and keep her safe forever."

Slowly, reverently, Noah closed the Book of Common Prayer. Once again, he looked up and locked gazes with Hannah. "Do you understand what that means, Hannah?"

"I think so." She hesitated, then forged on. "It means that with my baptism, with my turning to the Lord with all my heart, all my sins are forgiven. And my life begins anew."

"Yes. That's exactly what that prayer means. What an astounding gift baptism is." He smiled. "To start anew, free from sin . . . What a wondrous blessing!"

Even the barest consideration of such a miraculous offering overwhelmed her. "It's a gift I'm almost afraid to accept," she admitted, suddenly pensive and unsure. "What if, even after I'm forgiven and cleansed, I weaken and fall back into sin?"

"Conversion to the Lord is a firm determination to live for God, Hannah. Not a certainty that you'll never sin again. Even if you fall—and we all do, time and again—you must never take your eyes off the Lord. Your trust in Him must be so strong that you're convinced of His forgiveness if only you ask. And you must be equally convinced that God will always help you, and pick you up no matter when or if you should fall.

"In my mind, that is the greatest gift of baptism," the young priest said, his eyes glowing with a glorious light. "It marks the beginning of a journey that will take us to God, a journey that will make us one with Christ, a com-

197

pletely new person and a child of God—washed clean and white as snow."

"A child of God," Hannah breathed in an awestruck whisper. "What a wondrous gift. It fills me so full of happiness, my heart feels near to bursting."

She had come home at last, she realized, to the only home that truly mattered.

"And it's only the beginning."

"Yes." She laughed in delight. "But, oh, what a beginning it is!"

15

But we believe that through the grace of the Lord Jesus Christ we shall be saved, even as they.

Acts 15:11

On April 9th, the eve before Easter Sunday, Hannah was finally baptized in Grand View's Episcopal Church. A small group of MacKays–Devlin included–joined the townspeople attending the Easter Vigil service. Dressed in her own creation–a high-necked gown of rose-colored spotted silk lavishly trimmed in cream Venetian lace and sporting a flared full skirt, puffed sleeves, and big bow tied to the front side of her waist–Hannah was a dazzling sight.

Her physical accoutrements were nothing, however, in comparison to the radiant glow in her eyes and her luminous expression. Try as he might, Devlin couldn't keep his eyes off her. He had dressed up for the occasion himself, wearing a plain black sack suit with a crisp, white shirt and black four-in-hand tie. Although he had avoided church and anything religious since Ella's death, he made an exception this once, knowing how important his presence at the baptism was for Hannah.

Funny thing was, the prayers and readings touched him. He felt downright comfortable sitting in the pews with the rest of the MacKays. Too comfortable, Devlin realized. A man like him didn't deserve to be in church, much less almost enjoy it.

Yet he did enjoy it, and that admission stirred an ache deep within him. To put a name to that yearning, though, was still more than Devlin would dare do. So he tucked the feelings deep inside his heart and tried to forget . . . like all the times before.

After the service, Noah and his aunt opened the rectory for a social hour to honor their newest church member. Several families—including the Edgertons, Nealys, and the Widow Ashley—politely begged off, citing other obligations. Enough stopped by to visit, however, to allay some of Hannah's fears about her acceptance into the congregation.

"This hasn't been so bad, now, has it?" Devlin asked as he joined her with two cups of ginger punch clutched in one hand, and a plate laden with almond macaroons, velvet cake, and two crème horns balanced in the other. After setting the plate on a nearby windowsill, he handed one cup of the chilled drink to Hannah, then took a sip of his own before popping a macaroon into his mouth. "I mean, a good two-thirds of the congregation turned out for the social," he added, after chewing and swallowing the nut-laden treat.

"It was very kind of them," Hannah murmured, scanning the room with a gratified smile. "I'm especially happy for Noah's and Millie's sakes."

Devlin frowned. "And what about for your sake, Hannah? You count, too."

She nodded. "Yes, but I'm used to the scorn and rejection. I'm more concerned that all Millie's work for the

200

social wasn't for naught, and that Noah doesn't lose most of his congregation because he has taken me in."

"Well, from the looks of it tonight, I'd say he has most of his congregation still with him."

"Yes, so it seems." Hannah took a sip of her punch. "Noah was right when he insisted Grand View's filled with more good Christians than you might imagine. But then, the longer I know him, the more I realize what an insightful, God-filled man he is."

The tone of admiring affection in Hannah's voice whenever she spoke of Noah Starr nowadays was beginning to rankle Devlin. He knew he shouldn't let it get to him, that he should be happy that she kept making new friends. But it did bother him. Indeed, it made him downright jealous.

Noah Starr was one of the town's most eligible bachelors. Even if Hannah, with her checkered past, would never be accepted as a serious possibility for the preacher's wife, Devlin couldn't help fretting over her unabashed enthusiasm for the handsome, young priest.

Since that mid-January day, now three months ago, he and Hannah hadn't spoken again of the kiss they had shared. Everything had eventually settled back to its usual routine–he working ten to twelve hours a day, she taking care of his house, children, and meals before retiring to her own little bunkhouse each night. Problem was, that Christmas kiss had reminded Devlin just how desirable Hannah really was.

His growing awareness, however honorable it was this time, didn't set well with his conscience, or his intention to remain true to Ella's memory. The resultant jumble of emotions left him frequently drained and angry.

Hannah had never once, in any way, indicated she wished him to kiss her again. Unfortunately, her apparent disinterest in him only unsettled Devlin all the more. It stung his pride, even as he knew he shouldn't even be wishing she saw him as anything other than her employer. It was torture of the cruelest kind to want a woman who apparently didn't want him, then feel guilty about it to boot.

"Will you be seeing Noah regularly anymore?" he gritted out the words. "Now that you're officially accepted into the church and your instructions are finished, I mean?"

"I shouldn't think so. Besides, it would be inconsiderate to impose on his time. Noah's a very busy man, what with the responsibility for the entire congregation now on his shoulders."

"He's up to the challenge," Devlin muttered, then grabbed a crème horn and bit into it.

"Oh, I'm sure he is." Hannah took the other crème horn he offered. "He's such a wonderful pastor."

Devlin almost choked on his sweet. "So, how are things between you and Evan now?" he asked, deciding it was time to change the subject. "He doesn't say much to me, unless he absolutely has to, but we never were much for small talk anyway."

Her happy expression faded, and Devlin almost regretted asking.

"He doesn't say much to me anymore either." Hannah sighed. "But sometimes, when I think he doesn't realize it, I catch him staring at me with the saddest eyes. I think I've hurt him badly, Devlin."

"The boy needs to let go. It's not healthy to hang onto a hopeless situation."

She turned to look more fully at him. "It's not easy for most people to recover from a loss. And you MacKays, you don't do anything halfway. Why, I've never seen a more passionate, headstrong folk. Problem is, such passion and determination can serve equally to one's disadvantage as advantage."

"Well, if those failings of ours don't run you off sooner or later," he said with a wry laugh, "nothing will."

"I think, rather, those passions–good and bad–are what attract me. They're what I've always admired in Conor and Evan, and even in you." Hannah angled her head and studied him. "I like people who aren't afraid to live life to the fullest, even if in the doing they risk great pain as well as great joy. I've missed so much of that in my past years, that it has made me hungry for everything I can now have."

Listening to her impassioned words and watching her face come alive with ardent longing, Devlin felt an answering fire spring to life within him. A fire that burned, searing him with the same fierce desires Hannah seemed to feel.

But to what purpose? he asked himself. Hannah wasn't yet even twenty. Despite her rocky start in life, she still had many good years ahead of her. Despite her lingering self-doubts, she *would* succeed. She was too resilient, too much a fighter, not to do so.

He, on the other hand, was sixteen years her senior. He'd be a fool to pin any hopes on ever having a life with her. Indeed, it would be selfish even to seriously consider it. She deserved better than him.

With a shake of his head, Devlin flung aside the futile thoughts. Hannah had said she was hungry for life. But that life could never include him.

"Then *be* hungry," Devlin rasped, his voice rough with suppressed emotion. "Be brave and pursue your heart's desire. This time is yours now, Hannah. Don't ever let *anyone* try to take it from you. Not ever, ever again."

The same people who snubbed Hannah's baptismal social continued to treat her with aloofness and disdain every Sunday thereafter. In time, several families no longer regularly attended Grand View's Episcopal Church. Hannah had to admit she didn't particularly miss them, especially the Widow Ashley and the Edgertons. Still, she worried Noah might suffer from the repercussions.

The young priest, however, continued to maintain a resolute front, welcoming Hannah as heartily as he did any other parishioner. His sermons, however, suddenly began to take on a new theme—the problems in the early church.

"He's trying to make a point, Abby," Hannah said one hot mid-July day as they sat on the front porch of the main house preparing freshly picked green beans for canning. "I mean, if that reading from chapter fifteen of Acts wasn't a challenge to all of us, nothing was."

Her friend glanced up from the bowl of beans she was snapping, and smiled. "And God, which knoweth the hearts," she quoted, "bare them witness, giving them the Holy Ghost even as He did unto us . . ."

"And put no difference between us and them, purifying their hearts by faith," Hannah finished the passage for her. She leaned back in the wicker rocker and heaved a deep, frustrated breath. "I only hope Noah can touch all our hearts with those words about all people being equal in God's eyes. I know I continue to struggle with my pain and anger when people judge me. I even find myself judging them in return."

She sighed. "It can be so hard at times, and I fear instead of being seen as a lost lamb who has returned to the fold, in the end I'll just be remembered for Noah's ruination."

"Oh, I wouldn't say it's as bad as all that. It's not *that* many families, at any rate, who've left. Besides, Noah's an eloquent, passionate preacher. And who can truly fault him? He only speaks the truth. *God's* truth."

"I know. But it's so hard to forgive, especially where sins of the flesh are concerned."

Abby nodded. "And especially when those sins frequently strike so close to home."

"Yes, indeed," Hannah agreed. "Funny, though, how the wives find it so much easier to blame the prostitutes, than the husbands who sought them out." She straightened in her rocker. "I don't blame the women for feeling hurt and angry at me, though. I just want them, in the name of Christ's love, to forgive me."

Abby finished filling one bowl of beans, leaned down, placed it on the floor beside her, and took up another empty one. "That may well come, in God's own time. Meanwhile, *you* must forgive them, and pray for them."

"I'm trying, Abby. Truly I am." Once more Hannah reached into her own bowl of green beans and, with a little paring knife, began to slice off the ends.

"I can see that. And you've had such a wonderful influence on Devlin's children. They all adore you. Why, I'm certain our young Bonnie even thinks you're her mother."

At the mention of the auburn-haired toddler, Hannah's lips curved with pride. Now fifteen months old, the toddler was already moving about the house with great alacrity, and constantly getting into everything. She was also, Hannah thought, becoming quite attached to her own two-year-old son, Jackson.

"There are times," she admitted, "when I do almost feel like the mother of my own little family of four. Devlin's been very tolerant of his children's attachment to me. Even those times when they turn to me for advice, with him sitting right there at the table with them."

"How does he treat Jackson?"

Hannah shrugged. "Pretty much like one of his own. Why?"

Abby set aside her bowl and rose. "Give me a moment. There's something I'd like to show you."

She walked into the house. Through the porch window, its lace curtains swaying in the gentle breeze, Hannah could hear her opening a drawer in the parlor's large, oak cupboard. A few minutes later her friend returned, handing her a faded old daguerreotype.

It was an image of two young boys who appeared to be very close to Jackson's age. One, the taller and apparently older of the two, stood beside a wooden wagon holding the younger boy. They both, Hannah realized the longer she studied the daguerreotype, resembled her son in many ways—the dark wavy hair, deep, piercing eyes, stubborn set of their chins, and small, curved mouths. If Hannah hadn't known better, she would've sworn they were all brothers.

"Who are these two boys?" she asked quietly, even as unease curled within her.

"I think you know."

Her friend's blunt statement confirmed her growing fears. "Conor and Devlin?"

"Yes."

Struggling to contain the sudden swell of hope that she might have found her son's father, Hannah handed the daguerreotype back to Abby. "I've always wondered if Devlin might have been Jackson's father, but considering all the men I'd been with . . . Well, it seemed fruitless to dwell on it, and was nothing I would've ever confronted Devlin about at any rate." She gave a short, disparaging laugh. "It would only have caused more problems between us."

"But now, now that you've seen this"—Abby held up the daguerreotype—"what will you do? It wasn't I who first noticed the startling similarity. Conor did, when he asked me to help him sort through some family belongings the other day."

For a long moment, Hannah considered her options. Then she sighed and shook her head. "I'm not going to do anything. Devlin has his hands full as it is with three children. He doesn't need to know he might have to take on responsibility for yet another."

"But is that fair, Hannah? To deny him his right to know, to make his own decision about his son . . . and you?"

"And me?" She stared at her friend, puzzled. "How do I enter into this?"

"If Jackson's his son, the decent thing for Devlin to do would be to marry his son's mother."

Hannah stared at Abby, too shocked to reply. Could Abby be serious? Use Jackson to manipulate Devlin into marrying her?

She shook her head firmly. "No. I'd never do that to Devlin. Never. It would destroy everything we've managed to build between us so far. And it would bring us full circle back to where we began. This time, though, instead of taking his money in payment for my body, I'd be asking to take his name."

"I never meant it like that," Abby protested. "I just thought the possibility of Jackson being Devlin's son might, in time, lead you two to face other things, like your true feelings for each other."

Hannah blushed and averted her gaze. "I don't know what you're talking about."

"Don't you, Hannah? I saw the effect that Christmas kiss had on the both of you. And I've been watching you two ever since." She reached over and touched Hannah's hand. "I saw the way Devlin looked at you at your baptism. I've never seen a man so full of yearning in my whole life. I can tell how deeply you care for him, too, from just the little things you say and do for him each day."

"I don't love him, if that's what you're implying." In spite of her efforts to control it, her voice quavered. "I don't know how to love. Evan would vouch for that."

"Just because you weren't in love with Evan is no reason to decide you're incapable of love." Abby rose, walked to her, and knelt before her. "There couldn't be anything further from the truth than that." She placed her hands on Hannah's knees. "Since you first came to Culdee Creek, you've never shown anyone anything less than love. Even Devlin, when he treated you so abysmally, received only kindness and compassion in return."

"That wasn't due to any love for him, though." Hannah couldn't meet her friend's gaze. "I don't know if I can ever truly love a man, or be the kind of wife he'd expect of me. Not after . . . after what I've suffered at the hands of men."

"You lost respect for men. You found you couldn't trust them anymore. And without respect and trust, there can never be love. But you *are* coming to respect and trust Devlin, aren't you, Hannah?"

"I also respect and trust Evan," Hannah countered, "but I don't love him enough to marry him."

"No, you don't," her friend agreed. "But it's different with Devlin, isn't it? Still, I get the feeling it's something more than a fear of that love that's holding you back."

Hannah buried her face in her hands. The floodgates holding back her deepest, secret fear broke open, and all the pain spilled out. "I don't know if I can ever, *ever* find pleasure in that act, no matter how much I love a man," she wept.

Immediately, Abby rose and pulled her into the comforting circle of her arms. "Hush, sweetheart. Hush," she crooned, stroking her hair. "I always wondered, but I didn't know how to ask. Ah, curse them all for doing this to you! They've taken so much from you, crippling

208

your beautiful heart and generous nature. But the Lord *can* heal all, if only you let Him. He can heal even this."

"How, Abby?" she sobbed. "How can God heal this?"

"Perhaps by bringing you to the man who was always meant for you. He uses us to help each other, you know?"

Was it possible? Hannah wondered. Could the Lord heal even this most grievous of wounds? Oh, if it could only be!

She hadn't told Abby the full truth, when she said she feared she would never be able to find pleasure in the act of physical union with a man. She *had* felt pleasure, even desire, in Devlin's Christmas kiss. That realization, though, had frightened her. How *could* she suddenly find something heretofore so revolting and degrading even remotely pleasurable?

Hannah didn't understand, and what she didn't understand she feared.

He uses us to help each other . . .

Abby's words, like honey flowing onto the tongue and down one's throat, filled Hannah with a warm, comforting feeling. Perhaps she and Devlin *could* help each other. Maybe they could, with the Lord's help, eventually heal the terrible wounds life had inflicted upon them both.

"So, what do I say to Devlin?" she asked finally. "I've no real proof, other than what this picture suggests, that Jackson's his son. And how do I convince him my love for him is separate from the fact he's Jackson's father?"

"Perhaps it would be best to broach one subject at a time." Abby grinned, then released her and walked back to her seat. "Men, poor dears, don't deal well with too much good news all at once."

"Well, of the two, I'm guessing he'll take the news about Jackson best. I think I'll try that first." She extended her hand. "Could I borrow the daguerreotype for a day or two, and think on it a bit more?"

Her friend picked up the little print and handed it to her. "If you need some help . . ." Abby took up her bowl, and began snapping the beans in two with renewed determination.

Hannah watched the chestnut-haired woman for a moment, then pocketed the daguerreotype. In thoughtful silence, she turned her attention to her own bowl, pondering all the while how she could possibly tell Devlin the truth about their son.

16

The LORD is good, a strong hold in the day of trouble; and he knoweth them that trust in him.

                                                    Nahum 1:7

She knew if she thought about it long enough, she'd find some way to avoid ever doing it. Hannah couldn't help herself. She feared Devlin's reaction to hearing the news about Jackson, feared the possible repercussions. And feared, most of all, losing his friendship.

But Abby was right. Devlin had the right to know. All she could do, she resolved, was tell him, then make it clear she expected nothing that he didn't wish to freely give. Nothing need change between them, nothing save that he accept Jackson as his son. If he wished it so, life could go on just as it had before.

Still, it took another two days for Hannah to muster up the courage to approach Devlin. That evening, she lingered in Devlin's kitchen rather than head immediately back to her bunkhouse. She'd had the foresight to plan ahead, and had asked Beth to watch Jackson in the bunkhouse after supper. By now, the little boy was probably already snug in bed himself.

One way or another, he didn't need to be present when his father finally learned the truth about him. If there were problems, if Devlin took the news badly, Hannah didn't want Jackson in the middle of it. He was totally innocent in the matter.

Devlin finally sauntered into the kitchen after tucking his children into bed. At the sight of her, sitting at the table, a dark brow arched in surprise. "So, what's the occasion?" He walked to the cookstove and poured himself a cup of coffee. "Is there a problem with one of the children?"

She waited until he came to the table, sat, and finished stirring two spoonfuls of sugar into his coffee before replying. "Yes, it's one of the children," Hannah then forced herself to say. "It's about Jackson."

"Oh?" Tentatively, Devlin sipped his coffee, apparently found it cool enough to drink, and took a longer, deeper swallow. "What's wrong with the lad? He seemed fine at supper."

Pulling the daguerreotype from her shirtwaist pocket, Hannah slid it across to him. "There's nothing wrong with Jackson. It's just that it's been brought to my attention that he looks an awful lot like these two boys."

Devlin frowned, picked up the daguerreotype, and studied it. "But this is a picture of Conor and . . ."

His voice faded. His eyes widened. From her vantage point across from him, Hannah could see his face blanch beneath his tan. Then, ever so slowly, he dragged his gaze up to meet hers.

"What are you trying to tell me, Hannah?" Devlin demanded, an edge of wariness in his voice.

She inhaled a steadying breath. *Here it comes now.* "This wasn't my idea, or even something I finally faced until it was brought to my attention. But even you must see the striking resemblance between Jackson, and you and Conor as young boys."

"Abby's in the middle of this, isn't she? She's bound and determined to keep you here at Culdee Creek, and now that you've gone and broken off with Evan—"

"No." Her worst fears were materializing. Devlin didn't want to hear this and was seeking to cast blame where it wasn't deserved. "You're wrong, Devlin. Conor was the one who first noticed the resemblance, and *he* mentioned it to Abby. Abby then told me, because she thought I should be the one to tell you. Because you had the right to know."

He shoved his mug of coffee aside so violently its contents sloshed over the sides. "Why now, Hannah?" Devlin snarled, leaning forward on the table. "Why, over two years since Jackson's birth, do you suddenly feel it's now necessary to tell me?"

"I didn't really know until two days ago, when I saw the daguerreotype. I'd wondered at times, noticing the features you and Jackson shared. But I also realized that another dark-haired, brown-eyed man could've easily fathered him. Now,"—she gestured to the print he still held in his hand—"now I can't so easily pretend or make excuses."

As if burned, Devlin flung the daguerreotype on the table and buried his face in his hands. "I'm only glad Ella didn't live to see this day. This would've destroyed her, broken her heart."

Hannah shook her head. "I think Ella would've handled this better than you, Devlin. It's you it would've destroyed, because you would have had to endure yet another living example of your transgressions. And you couldn't have handled that."

At her words, he jerked his head up and glared at her. "What makes you think you know about me? Just because you think you've got your proof to dangle in my face for the rest of my days? Well, I'm sorry if this sounds harsh, but I'm sick to death of feeling guilty. You're not going to get me to accept that child as my own!"

That child. Sweet Lord, how it hurt to hear Devlin speak of Jackson in such a way! But why should she be surprised? she asked herself. Whenever Devlin was threatened, he closed himself off from others and lashed out.

"I never said I expected you to accept Jackson as your own," Hannah said, a sad smile hovering on her lips. "I hoped you would, but I didn't expect it. I can take care of him just fine all by myself. And no one—aside from Conor and Abby, of course—need ever know. It's up to you, Devlin. But at least I gave you a choice, rather than hid something you might someday have wanted to know."

"How kind."

His sarcasm, after all this time and all they had been through, cut her to the quick. Hannah scooted back her chair and stood.

"I'm sorry, Devlin, that this isn't what you want to hear. I guess I hoped that we'd be able to deal with this together, to help each other become better people through it."

"I don't need your help, or anyone's, to make me a better person!"

"We all need one another, Devlin."

"Well, I don't need you!"

All Hannah's hopes crumbled beneath the onslaught of those cruel words. She had been a fool to imagine this could've turned out any other way.

"Do you still want me to work for you?" Hannah asked softly.

He stared up at her for so long, Hannah began to wonder if he had even heard her question. Then, just as she opened her mouth to repeat her words, she saw something crumble, go bleak and hopeless in his eyes.

"I don't know," he mumbled, lowering his head. "This isn't the best time to ask me anything. You've handed me a big wad to chew on tonight. It's best you just leave me be."

"I didn't tell you this to punish or manipulate you, Devlin. I did it because I respect and care for you, because I couldn't bear to be less than honest with you anymore. And I did it because I wanted Jackson to have his father in his life." Her voice caught, and it was a moment before she could go on. "What else would you have had me do? What else, Devlin?"

"I reckon I don't know, leastwise not right now." Devlin took his mug and drank from it deeply, before finally looking back up at her. "Look, I'm sorry, Hannah. I don't mean to hurt you. But I'm going to need some time to work through all this." He set aside his mug and met her gaze. "Will you give it to me?"

It wasn't what she really wanted to hear, but she knew the request came hard for him nonetheless. Considering how things had gone tonight, Hannah supposed she could content herself with that. She *had* given him a big wad to chew. What man wouldn't be overwhelmed by such news?

"Yes," was her ragged but resolute reply, "I'll give it to you."

After Hannah left, Devlin pondered the contents of his coffee mug for a long while, the memory of her words running through his mind like a fast-moving stream. She had said Jackson was living proof of his transgressions. But then she had also said it was his choice what he chose to do about it.

215

His choice . . . yet when had he ever truly had a choice about anything? Devlin smiled grimly. Well, he supposed he had made a choice when he had decided to visit Sadie Fleming's. And he had also made a choice when he had chosen Hannah over all the other girls there.

It didn't matter that prostitutes weren't supposed to get in the family way. But why, oh why, had it fallen to his lot to father her child? And would he never, ever be able to put all this behind him?

Footsteps sounded on the front porch. For an instant, Devlin thought Hannah must have returned. Then he realized the footsteps were heavy, as was the knock on the door.

With a weary sigh, he pushed back his chair and rose. After what he had just learned, he really wasn't in the mood to deal with any more visitors tonight. Being ranch foreman, though, sometimes demanded twenty-four-hour service.

To his surprise, Evan stood at the door. Devlin scowled. "What can I do for you?"

"Can I come in? We need to talk."

A premonition prickled down Devlin's spine. "Does this have to do with the ranch? If not, it can wait until tomorrow."

The young man took a step closer. "No, it can't. I've got something that's been rubbing me raw for a long time now. Tonight, hearing the angry voices and knowing you were riled up with Hannah was just about the last straw. We need to talk, get things out in the open once and for all."

An impulse to slam the door in Evan's face filled Devlin, but he resisted it. This was Conor's son and his cousin. Evan was family.

He swung wide the door and motioned him in. "Suit yourself." Without another word, Evan strode in. "Want a cup of coffee?" Devlin asked as he closed the door behind him and followed the young man to the kitchen table.

"No, thanks." Evan took the chair recently vacated by Hannah. "What were you two fighting about this evening?" he demanded. "I saw her leave, and she didn't look any too happy."

"None of your business." Devlin, coffeepot in hand, returned to the table, refilled his mug, then set the pot on a sun-dried, clay trivet Devlin Jr. had made him for Christmas. Flipping his chair around, he straddled it and faced Evan. "Any other questions?"

"She's going through some difficult times right now," Evan said through gritted teeth. "She's got a lot on her mind. You don't need to add to her confusion."

Where was this heading? Devlin arched a brow. "And what confusion would that be? Her confusion over you?"

Crimson crept up the young man's neck and face. "Hannah cares for me. Your interference–"

"And how exactly have I interfered, Evan?" Despite his best efforts to contain it, Devlin could feel his anger rising. First Hannah showed up and dropped the biggest surprise of his life in his lap. Now Evan was sitting here–in his own house no less–and trying to tell him what he could and couldn't do in regards to Hannah! "It was never my choice that my wife die so that I needed to hire Hannah to take care of my children and home!"

"She's a fool to keep coming here so you can find new ways to hurt her!" His face livid, Evan jumped to his feet. "She's too fine, too good for the likes of you. Sooner or later, you'll break her heart."

"I'd never do that to Hannah!" Devlin leaped up, swept his chair aside, and came to stand face-to-face with Evan. The memory of how he had just finished hurting Hannah flooded back with a vengeance, making him

217

even angrier. "You're not the only one who cares about her, you know."

"Yeah, I kind of figured that," his cousin snarled, refusing to back down. "But tell me, Devlin. What exactly do you have to offer her? You're nearly old enough to be her father. You've got three kids and a house you basically rent from my pa. Sure, you're Culdee Creek's foreman, but that's a dead-end job because you'll never own this ranch."

He gave a disdainful snort. "A fine husband you'd make for Hannah."

"I never said I wanted to marry her!" Devlin's hands fisted at his side. More than anything, he wanted to knock that sneer off Evan's face. That sneer of contempt that he should ever aspire to a woman as good and beautiful as Hannah.

"Well, then we understand each other, don't we?"

The sad thing was, Devlin did. In one debilitating rush, he felt the anger drain from him. "Just because I'm not the man for Hannah doesn't mean you are, Evan," he said with quiet but deliberate emphasis. "You can't make that decision for her. After all she's been through, she deserves better than that."

"I'm not trying to force her to do anything. I want her to take all the time she needs. But I also don't want you muddying the waters."

Devlin rolled his eyes. "You worry too much, Evan. Hannah's not interested in me."

"That's not the impression I got at Christmas when you kissed her."

"That was a mistake that hasn't happened again. And it won't."

"Do I have your word on that?"

Automatically, Devlin opened his mouth to give it, then snapped it shut again. He didn't owe Evan any promises.

Despite what he had said to her earlier, the longer he talked with Evan, the less convinced Devlin was that he wanted Hannah and her son out of his life. *Their* son, he corrected himself with a jolt of surprise, whether he ultimately chose to accept the boy or not. The threads that seemed to draw them inexorably closer with each passing day, he realized, had pulled just a bit tighter this evening.

No, Devlin decided, he couldn't promise Evan anything. It was enough he followed his own conscience when it came to Hannah. Besides, he didn't particularly like being pushed around by a jealous kid.

"Sorry," he growled finally, "but you don't have my word. I'll try to do what's best for Hannah, but I'm not going to box myself into some corner in the process, just to please you. You'll just have to trust me when I say I'll always try to place her interests above mine."

Evan eyed him narrowly, then nodded. "Fair enough, just as long as you stick to those intentions." He pushed back his chair and, without a backward glance, walked across the kitchen and out the back door.

The next morning, Hannah had already arrived and was preparing breakfast in the kitchen when Devlin finally dragged himself out of bed and made his way down for some coffee. At his entrance, she shot him a quick glance over her shoulder, then returned her attention to the bacon she was frying.

"Morning," she said.

The fortifying aroma of freshly brewed coffee mingled with the mouthwatering scent of bacon and biscuits. "Morning," Devlin replied, then immediately headed for the cupboard where he took down two mugs and returned to the table.

Walking to the stove, he grabbed a towel and picked up the steaming coffeepot. "Want some?"

She didn't look at him. "Yes, please."

He poured them both a mug full of the dark, rich brew, set the coffeepot on the table trivet, then took a seat and prepared his coffee. The first few sips banished the remaining cobwebs from his sleep-deprived mind. From the looks of the dark smudges beneath Hannah's eyes, he noted, casting her a surreptitious glance, it didn't appear as if she had slept too well last night, either.

On the heels of that realization rushed yet another surge of guilt. It was his fault, his cruel words, which had once again caused her pain. He was lucky she hadn't finally chucked it all and walked out on him and the children.

A clatter of blocks tumbling to the floor rose from the corner. Devlin looked up and met Jackson's contrite gaze. He stared at the little boy for so long—and he guessed too sternly—that Jackson's eyes filled with tears and his lower lip began to wobble.

Devlin sighed in exasperation. That was all he needed. On top of what had transpired last night, if Jackson started bawling now, Hannah would think he had caused it. He put down his coffee mug and held out his arms. "Come here, Jackson."

The boy jumped up and toddled to him, throwing himself into Devlin's arms. In the next instant, he had climbed up and happily settled himself in Devlin's lap.

Devlin's face flushed with his embarrassment. "That was quite a tower of blocks you were trying to build," he said, choosing to focus his attention on a far easier topic to address. "Pretty soon, we'll have to start teaching you how to build things with a real hammer and nails. Would you like that?"

Jackson's head bobbed in joyful assent. "Uh huh. Like Dev . . . win." With a chubby finger, he poked him in the chest.

Devlin smiled. The boy was quite bright and endearing.

"Want . . . to pwaay." Jackson suddenly began to squirm against him. "Down."

"Okay." Devlin released the restless little boy, who immediately slid off his lap and hurried back to his corner full of blocks.

He watched him for a time, myriad emotions roiling within him, until Hannah jerked open the warming oven door to place a platter of fried bacon inside. Distracted, his gaze moved then to the cookstove, where she was pouring a bowl filled with beaten eggs into the frying pan. Her slender arm moving in a rhythmic, circular fashion, she began to scramble them.

The morning sun, glinting through the lace-curtained kitchen window, caught in her hair. Shades of flax and winter wheat sparkled in her pale tresses. Light kissed her smooth, flawless cheek and shimmered on her long neck and delicately curved shoulder. Sitting there in the food-fragrant, already summer-warm kitchen, Devlin thought he could watch her forever.

Like a mist rising from a night-cooled lake, sadness filled him. He wanted Hannah to belong here, in this house, in this kitchen, with him and his children. But he knew it could never be. He could never atone for what he had done to her. There was no chance of happiness and redemption for him anymore.

Still, life went on. And he owed Hannah an apology. It seemed, Devlin thought wryly, he was having to do a lot of that of late. A smart man would've learned his lesson a long time ago.

"Hannah?"

For a fleeting instant, she stiffened. She was exhausted after a sleepless night; Devlin's silent and staring presence in the kitchen had only made her more tense.

She was on the verge of tears, and she didn't like feeling so out of control. The closer she drew to Devlin, the easier it seemed for him to hurt her. If she were a smart woman, she would turn and run as fast and far away as she could from him.

For the moment, though, that wasn't an option. Indeed, Hannah wondered if she'd ever be able to leave. Her heart and life had long ago become entwined with those of Devlin's children. She didn't know if she could turn her back on those dear little ones.

"Hannah, please talk to me, listen to what I have to say."

She scraped the cooked eggs onto a large plate, then shoved them into the warmer beside the bacon. Finally, after checking the biscuits in the oven and moving the frying pan into the sink, Hannah walked to the table and took a seat.

"I'm listening, Devlin."

He stared at her for a long moment, his glance sweeping her face with concern. She felt her defenses begin to weaken and forced herself to recall his harsh words of the previous night. Freshened pain swept through her. Her resolve hardened in renewed self-protection.

"Where and how do I begin?" Briefly, Devlin lowered his gaze, then lifted it to meet hers. In his eyes she saw shame and remorse. "I'm sorry for what I said to you last night. I was wrong to speak to you in such a manner. You didn't deserve it." He paused to inhale a deep breath, then forged on. "I still need time to work through my feelings about Jackson and what I want to do about him, but in the meanwhile I want you to know I won't change how I've always treated him. He's a fine little boy. I won't do anything in any way to hurt or punish him for what we've done."

"That's good to know," Hannah replied evenly, maintaining rigid control of her emotions. "If I ever suspected for an instant you'd take out your anger at me on him . . . well, I'd never go near you or this house again."

Fleetingly, a smile quirked the corners of Devlin's mouth. "That's good to hear. I wouldn't want the mother of any child of mine to act any other way." He leaned forward, resting his forearms on the table, and clasped his hands together before him. "I know I've hurt you time and again, Hannah. But the news you shared with me last night . . . well, let's just say you scared me near witless."

"Hence your wretched, thoughtless words," she offered with bitter sarcasm. "I'm not your enemy, Devlin. I don't hate you or wish you ill. When will you finally get that into your head?"

He straightened and ran a hand roughly through his hair. "I'm trying, Hannah. Really, I am. And the fault's not yours. It's mine."

She sighed. "That doesn't make these outbursts any easier to take. I do the best I can to be your friend, to treat you honestly. But I don't know how much longer I can tolerate how you treat me when–"

"It's been a long while now since we first made our peace with each other. Over a year, if I'm not mistaken." He managed a weak, lopsided, little grin. "Isn't a man allowed to make a stupid, brainless fool out of himself once a year?"

She eyed him warily, but said nothing.

Devlin stood, came around to where she sat, and took both of her hands in his. Pulling her to her feet, he gazed down with an expression of heartfelt entreaty. "Please, Hannah. Forgive me. I don't mean to make light of the cruel things I said to you. It breaks my heart to see you hurting and know I was the cause of it."

He hesitated, chewing on his lower lip in a gesture of tortured indecision the like of which she had never seen before. "I . . . I care about you," he ground out finally, his voice low, his words halting. "You've given me so much, and never asked hardly anything in return. I know I don't deserve it and am ungrateful most of the time to boot, but I do recognize how much you do for me and the children."

"Devlin, I–"

"Hush, let me finish." He released one of her hands and grasped her shoulder. "It's always been hard for me to let myself trust others, to allow myself to care about them or come to need them. Too many times to count, I've lost someone I loved, or been betrayed by them. After a while, it just seemed safer not to let anyone get too close."

"You let Ella get close, and your children."

He smiled sadly. "Yeah, well I didn't say some folk didn't manage to slip past my guard. But the few times I've let that happen, it seems I've always had to pay a price. Gets kind of tough to lower your guard after a while."

"But that's part and parcel of life, Devlin." She moved closer, drawn by the fascinating glimpse he offered of his wounded heart. "You have to trust–trust in God and in your fellow man. From that trust comes the ability to love and accept love. But there cannot be one without the other."

"Ah, Hannah, Hannah." Devlin smiled down at her. "You're so full of love, it surrounds you like some shining aura. I think that's why I'm so drawn to you, hoping some of that glorious light might somehow fall my way."

"We all need each other," she said, suddenly concerned he might see her as more than she really was. "I need your light as much as you need mine."

"Do you, Hannah?" He lifted his hand and touched her, tenderly stroking the side of her face from temple to cheek. "Do you really?"

As he spoke, his eyes went dark, smoldering. His voice turned rich and husky.

His unexpected reaction stirred something deep within Hannah. Excitement raced through her. Desire flared, scorching her with its sudden surge of power.

They had come to another crossroads. Devlin was a grown man in his prime, and not one to be trifled with or put off as she had managed to do with Evan for so many months. Whatever she next said he would hold her to.

Yet what else was there but the truth? She loved Devlin. That meant he possessed the power to hurt her. But he also, if he wished to use it, possessed the power to bring her great joy. The choice for or against him—frightening as it was—was hers.

She lifted her arms and encircled his neck. Pressing close, Hannah laid her head over his heart. "Yes, Devlin," she whispered achingly, "I *do* need you. I need you so very, very much."

17

Eye hath not seen, nor ear heard, neither have entered into the heart of man, the things which God hath prepared for them that love him.

1 Corinthians 2:9

The summer days wore on, hot and sunny until late afternoons when the thunderclouds building over the Rockies would move eastward. Then the rains would come.

The heavier-than-normal rainfall that year kept Culdee Creek's ponds full. Abby and Hannah took to accompanying the children down to their favorite swimming holes several times a week. Occasionally, if the day got too hot and ranch work drew to a temporary halt, some of the hands even joined them. It was a good time, a bountiful summer, and everyone savored it to its fullest.

Late one particularly warm, still morning in mid-August, Hannah was storing away the last loaf of bread she had baked earlier when Devlin walked in. In his hands he held a colorful assortment of wildflowers mixed with some strategically placed garden blooms. With a shy grin, he held them out to her.

"Here, these are for you."

Bemused, Hannah accepted the bouquet. The large handful, she noted as she looked them over, included wild white yarrow, blue penstemon, milkweed, and the last few flowering, lavender-hued dame's rockets as well as pink hollyhocks, several shades of blue delphiniums, cornflowers, and two red roses. "Why, th-thank you," she stammered, meeting Devlin's glance again. "What's the occasion? You've never given me flowers before."

"Actually, you need to thank Beth and Devlin Jr. They picked the flowers. I happened to pass by and, since the hands and I had just finished putting up another cutting of hay, I decided to take the rest of today off to spend with the children. It was my idea to fix a picnic lunch and head down to the swimming hole. They thought some flowers might entice you to come with us." He paused, an eager look in his eyes. "Did it work?"

She was surprised at the momentary twinge of disappointment she felt as she realized the flowers hadn't been Devlin's own doing. Then Hannah schooled her features, pasting on a happy smile. "It would've worked even without the flowers. Of course I'd be glad to accompany you all down to the swimming hole." She cocked her head. "Am I to assume my services are also required to prepare the picnic?"

He grinned. "Well, you didn't think those flowers came without a price, did you?"

Hannah laughed. "I think I've been had, Devlin MacKay!"

"Oh, you have," he agreed, laughing in turn, "but I'll be glad to help you get it all together."

They spent the next fifteen minutes slicing bread and making cheese sandwiches, which soon joined a mess of cloth-wrapped gingerbread cookies and a jar of pickles. To the rest of the food she had placed in the large picnic hamper, Hannah added some leftover potato salad, fried sausages, and a jug of apple cider she sent Devlin to retrieve from the springhouse.

"Well, that should be enough to fill the stomachs of an army," she said at last, surveying the basket's contents.

Devlin joined her to peer inside. "Yeah, should be just about enough to feed me. So what are you and the children eating?"

She elbowed him in the side and laughed again. He graced her with a wry smile.

A half hour later, Beth, Devlin Jr., and now nearly four-year-old Mary were playing in the deeper water of one of the larger ponds, while Jackson and Bonnie happily splashed in the shallows at the pond's edge. Beneath the cool shade of a nearby cottonwood, Hannah and Devlin lay on an old quilt and watched. For a while they said nothing, preferring the comfortable, contented silence.

Finally Devlin stirred. "Are you thirsty? I've got a sudden hankering for some of that springhouse cooled cider."

Hannah considered his offer, then nodded. "Yes, that does sound good." She sat up and turned to the picnic basket, when Devlin's hand settled on her arm.

"You just lay back and enjoy yourself. I'll get the cider."

Surprised but pleased, Hannah did as ordered. From a stout rope hung on an overhanging branch of another cottonwood, Beth, dressed in a ruffled, red-and-white bathing dress, swung out over the pond and let go not far from where Mary stood. With a wild Indian whoop, Devlin Jr., attired in his own navy-striped, one-piece bathing suit took a running start, grabbed for the rope, and sailed out even farther before letting go and cannonballing into the water. At the resounding splash he made, both girls squealed in outraged delight.

Devlin chuckled. "Leave it to my son to outdo everyone else."

Hannah, her attention turned at that moment to Jackson, who had just dumped a small pailful of water on Bonnie's head, nodded in distraction. "Seems like it runs in the family."

At Bonnie's indignant wail, Devlin glanced in his daughter's direction just in time to see her smack Jackson in the head. "Two of a kind, I'd say."

Their glances met and locked. Hannah searched his eyes for some sign of his feelings about their son, some sign, after all these weeks, that he had finally come to a decision about him. For the life of her, though, she couldn't discern a thing.

Nonetheless, Devlin must have seen her unspoken question. "About Jackson." He swung his gaze back out to the pond and children. "I've given a lot of thought as to what to do about him. Problem is, publicly claiming him as my own puts us both in an awkward position. Actually, it puts *you* in more of an awkward position. I don't give a hoot what folk say or think of me."

His eyes went dark with some indefinable emotion. "But it might make any future suitors for your hand a bit uncomfortable, not knowing where we stand with each other."

"I'm willing to take my chances," Hannah replied softly. "One way or another, I'm still the mother of an illegitimate child."

"There's also the problem of my other children. Devlin Jr.'s getting old enough to understand, ask questions. And sooner or later Mary and Bonnie will be old enough to do the same."

"Don't you think, whether you accept Jackson or not, that folk–including your children–are eventually going to notice the resemblance? How long do you think you can hide the truth?"

"I just don't want to put my children through this right now, that's all."

"So what you're saying," Hannah muttered, feeling the anger rise, "is revealing Jackson's your son would cause too many problems for you and yours."

"You make it sound as if I'm looking for excuses to avoid claiming him." His mouth tightened. "Well, it's not like that at all. For a change, I'm trying to think of others and not myself."

"Well, you're not going about it very well!"

"What do you want from me then, Hannah? Do you want me to marry you, so I can legitimize Jackson and be able to call him my son in every way? Even then, sooner or later someone's bound to get hurt."

Hannah stared at him, speechless. Marry Devlin? Legitimize Jackson and become a mother to the other children in every way? The thought filled her with a wild joy. That solution would solve everything, including her heart's secret yearning.

Then reason, tinged with disappointment, returned. Devlin wasn't proposing. He was just venting his frustration at the situation and the untenable position it had placed him in. After all, he had just admitted someone was still bound to get hurt–maybe even him–in the process of his being forced into a marriage he didn't want.

"What, in the end, would us getting married solve?" She lowered her gaze to the pink-and-blue calico pattern on her dress. "It would only be a marriage of convenience for the children's sake. I think we both deserve better than that."

A marriage of convenience. Hannah's choice of words stung Devlin's pride. So, that's all the purpose that would be served marrying him!

"I suppose you're right." All the fight and anger drained from him, Devlin slumped back onto his elbows. "Maybe it'd be best to just give it more time." He didn't like admitting defeat, but this was one situation that didn't seem to have any easy answers. "Maybe, in time, something will present itself."

"Something like a miracle, perhaps?" Hannah sighed and shook her head. "Well, enough of that. How about that cup of cider you were offering? I've suddenly developed a terrific thirst."

Devlin hurried to comply, and they were soon sipping the thirst-quenching drink. They sat there for a while, savoring the moment, listening to the happy shouts of the children, and watching them play. Finally, though, Hannah decided the children had spent enough time in the hot sun and water.

She rose. "Five more minutes," she called to them. "Then head on in for some lunch."

The children took her at her word. She and Devlin had barely spread out the picnic meal before Beth and Devlin Jr., followed by Mary and Jackson, ran from the water to sprawl on the quilt and grab for food. After holding them off long enough to say grace, Hannah left Devlin to bring some order to the horde of ravenous children. Walking down to the water's edge, she retrieved Bonnie, who sat staring up at everyone in wide-eyed puzzlement.

When the feeding frenzy had subsided and the remnants of food were put away, Hannah insisted the children lie down for an hour's nap. Once they were quietly dozing, she turned to Devlin. "Care for a walk? I feel a need for some exercise after sitting for so long and eating such a big meal."

He nodded and climbed to his feet. "Sounds like a fine idea." He extended his hand to her.

For a long moment, Hannah eyed it warily. Devlin still refused to publicly acknowledge Jackson, had casually suggested wedding her, then blithely discounted the idea. Yet now he stood there, gazing down at her with the most devastatingly tender look. Whatever was she to make of him and his true feelings for her?

She took his hand and allowed him to pull her to her feet. He didn't let go once she was standing. Instead, his hand still clasping hers, Devlin led her toward another stand of cottonwoods about fifty feet away.

The trees in this particular spot were twisted and bent, some into grotesque shapes. Glancing up through the leafy branches, Hannah pictured the winter winds swooping down the hills with great force, battering the trees mercilessly. It would account for the malformed trunks and branches.

Hannah disengaged her hand from Devlin's. Strolling over to a gnarled, low-lying branch extending from one of the cottonwoods, she hopped up to sit on it. The trees here reminded her a lot of Devlin. Life had also battered him. Like these trees, his soul was twisted and bent in many ways. It would take God's work to untangle him.

Devlin came up to lean on the trunk of the tree she sat in. A sad, thoughtful look darkened his eyes.

Concern filled her. "What is it, Devlin? What's wrong?"

A smile twitched at one corner of his mouth, but he said nothing.

"Are you still thinking about Jackson?" she ventured.

He exhaled a weary breath. "If it were only me, I'd gladly claim Jackson before the whole world." His mouth twisted grimly. "But then, if it had only been me to begin with, I wouldn't be in half the trouble I'm in right now."

"The Lord will help us, if only we trust in Him."

"That's fine for you to believe," he muttered, "but I prefer to rely on my own efforts."

Hannah gripped the trunk on either side of her, and began to swing her legs to and fro. "What happened with you and God, Devlin? Why do you despise Him so?"

"It's a long, sordid story."

She glanced in the direction of the children. Tired by their swim and full from their lunch, they had all apparently settled down and were sound asleep. She turned back to Devlin. "Looks like I've got the time, if you care to tell me."

"And why do you want to know?"

"Isn't that obvious by now?"

He grimaced. "Yeah, I reckon it is, though I don't know why you've taken such an interest in me. Or why you care."

"You're a good man, Devlin MacKay. Don't let anyone tell you otherwise."

"And you're a good-hearted little fool," he retorted, grinning at her to soften his words. "And don't you let anyone tell *you* otherwise."

She smiled. "Well, are you going to tell this little fool, or not?"

His grin faded. He joined her on the tree branch, leaning against it, his long legs bracing himself on the ground. "My pa and his older brother, Robbie, who was Conor's pa," Devlin finally began his tale, "were the two youngest children of Sean MacKay, a Highlander who emigrated from Scotland during the horrible years of the Highland Clearances." He turned to her. "That was the time near the beginning of this century when the Scots peasants were thrown off their ancestral lands to make way for more profitable sheep," he explained. When Hannah nodded, he continued. "Sean died six years after my pa's birth, and his wife soon remarried to a man who was very cruel to the two boys, especially when he drank.

"Robbie ran away to Colorado when he was fifteen. By the time he joined Robbie here at Culdee Creek, my pa was already a hard, embittered man. He didn't trust anyone, and pretty much justified any means that served to his personal advantage. That outlook, combined with his anger at his brother for running away to come out West, led him to believe Robbie owed him a big debt."

Devlin paused to kick at a stone near the tree's trunk. "You can imagine how long that brotherly reunion lasted. My pa wasn't particularly successful at endearing himself to most of the folk in Grand View either. Pretty soon, the only work he could find was in the town saloon. It was there he met my ma."

Hannah's heart lurched. "Your mother worked in a saloon?"

Devlin's mouth clamped shut, and he nodded. "Yeah, she wasn't much more than a dance hall girl, and probably a prostitute on the side, if my pa can be believed. But she was a pretty little thing, from the one print I have of her, and my pa wasn't too particular by then. Conor said he heard from his pa that my ma was looking to get out of her line of work, and not too particular either."

Abby had never mentioned that detail about Devlin's mother. "So that's why you hated me so," she said. "And why you were so set against Evan and me getting married."

Devlin's laugh was harsh. "Maybe partly. But the main reason was because I was scared of being called to face what I had done. You—and my ma and pa—were just excuses I used to hide behind. Funny thing is, even though I hated my parents and what they did, I started to become the same kind of person." He sighed.

Hannah sat quietly, not knowing how to respond to Devlin's admission.

"You know what else was funny?" His mouth twisted in derision. "As much as I came to hate my pa for his brutality and self-destructiveness, in many ways, I hated my ma even more."

"For having left you?"

He shrugged. "Maybe. If she'd lived . . ." Momentarily, his voice faded. "But then there are other times when I think I hated her for being the woman she was, a woman of loose morals who maybe didn't even love my pa or want me, but just needed security and a better life for herself."

His words, so reminiscent of her own secret thoughts when she had first come to Culdee Creek, pierced Hannah's heart. "She could've just wanted it all. A better life, a man to love, *and* a baby to cherish."

Devlin lifted himself off the tree branch, strode to a big, split cottonwood opposite where Hannah sat, and wheeled about. "Yeah, maybe so. I'll never know. My pa refused to talk about her, except to set me straight about her past so I wouldn't harbor any romantic notions about a saintly mother."

Hannah frowned. "That was mean of him. What harm would it have done to speak kindly of his wife?"

"By then my pa's mind was so pickled by all his drinking, I don't think he even knew what he was saying half the time." Devlin gave a snort of disgust. "If it weren't for the food I could scrounge or steal, we wouldn't even have been eating. By the time I was twelve, he had even been fired from his job at the saloon."

Devlin had lost both parents, Hannah realized, one in death and one in despair. No wonder he found it hard to get close to people–to trust or take in the love offered him. How could he be certain it wouldn't fail him when he needed it the most?

"You're a brave man, Devlin MacKay," she said, filled with a growing admiration. "You've survived such terrible disappointments, yet still you fight on. You gave love a chance, and look what a wonderful woman you found in Ella. And you're giving me a chance."

He lowered his head for an instant, then lifted it to look at her. "I'd like to think my ma was a lot like you."

Joy swelled in her. "Thank you for that compliment." Hannah paused, chewing on her lower lip in indecision. "Your story told me a lot about you, Devlin. But I still don't understand what turned you against God. Or when. You used to attend church with Ella."

"I went because she wanted me to, and because it set a good example for the children. I never did it because of any love for God on my part. Most times, I find God cold and heartless."

"I suppose it could seem that way at times when life circumstances are bleak. I know I've had a hard time trying to understand why God lets certain things happen. I'm not sure I'll ever really understand, but I still want to trust Him." She leaned toward Devlin, her face now alight with growing fervor. "We find such great rewards in risking all to find God."

"You make it sound so easy," he growled, his face clouding over. "But it's not like that at all. There are many obstacles . . . many reasons for not even attempting such a foolhardy, hopeless–"

"Name one," Hannah challenged. "I dare you."

Devlin's eyes narrowed. "This isn't some game. This is serious, personal, and you might not like what you hear. Might not," he added darkly, "like me so very well by the time I'm finished."

"No, it isn't some game, and it *is* serious," she agreed, choosing her words with care. "But I would very much like to know and understand what keeps you from the Lord, Devlin."

He stared at her for a long moment, and Hannah began to fear he wouldn't say more. Finally, though, Devlin sighed, a long, deep, weary sound that filled her with compassion.

"I've wandered so far from the path of salvation and joy," Devlin finally began, "that I don't think I can ever find my way back. Indeed, I sometimes don't even know if I really want to. But mostly, I keep myself from God because I know He won't find me worthy. And why should I set myself up again for failure? I've managed, in some way or another, to disappoint everyone who ever needed me. I don't want to disappoint God, too."

"You can't disappoint God, Devlin, save to turn from Him and His love."

He laughed bitterly. "God doesn't love me!" He lowered himself to sit on the ground. Leaning back against the tree, Devlin closed his eyes and encircled his knees with his arms. "I've never done anything to deserve His love. Never!"

Hannah slid off the tree branch and walked to him. Kneeling before him, she placed her hands on his knees. "Do you know what Noah told me one day, when I came to him for lessons? He said that you don't have to do anything to deserve God's love. He loves and accepts you just as you are. You don't even have to change or mend your ways to get His love, though He obviously wants for you to lead a holy life. You already have His love, though, right now, just as you are, even before you decide to change—and whether you ever change or not."

Devlin opened his eyes. In their dark depths she saw his torment and confusion.

"You're not making any sense. You know that, don't you, Hannah?"

She laughed then. "Just like God loving us without any guarantee we'll ever love Him in return doesn't make sense? Yet He does it anyway. He can't help it. He *is* love!"

"And when did you get so wise in the ways of God?"

Even as a sad smile twisted his lips, his words held a note of hope and wonder. It gladdened her.

"I learned about God living at Culdee Creek. I came to know Him through all His people here. I saw His love in the kindness and compassion shown me, by reading of Him in the Bible, and by hearing about Him in the lessons Abby and Noah taught me." She smiled. "As my faith grew and my relationship with God blossomed, so did my certainty of His unconditional love and acceptance."

She saw the struggle in Devlin's eyes as he tried to sort through all she had said. He wanted to believe. She could see that. But as both Abby and Noah had warned her, a faith journey wasn't always straightforward or easy.

"Unconditional love . . . That's a pretty tough piece to chew on." Devlin exhaled a deep breath. "Well, I'm happy for you, Hannah. Truly, I am. But I'm still not so certain that's the road I wish my life to take."

"But you'll think about what I've said, won't you?"

He laid a hand over hers, a big hand rough with calluses but a hand strong and comforting nonetheless. "Yes, I'll think about it. When you get that special glow in your eyes, it's hard to ignore anything you say. And I must admit I find it harder and harder to discount you, or the effect you're having on my life."

"You're very kind to say that," she murmured, feeling warmth flood her cheeks.

His fingers encircled hers, squeezing her hand. "Hardly. I pretty much call things the way I see them." Devlin eyed her with frank admiration. "Do you really have any idea how very special you are, Hannah Cutler?"

Hannah's eyes widened. Her mouth went dry. She tried to say something—anything—but the look in his eyes melted all her resolve. All she knew was she wanted Devlin to kiss her.

His head lowered, moved toward her, but then he suddenly stopped. A curtain fell across his eyes and he withdrew his hand.

"Sounds like the children are stirring," he said, his voice gone low and husky. "Best we head on back before they come looking for us."

Hannah's emotions reeled, careening from the heady heights of anticipation to the depths of disappointment. She swallowed hard and forced herself to nod. "Yes, the children," she croaked. "I'd almost forgotten . . ."

She made a motion to rise, when his hand once more settled on hers, staying her.

"One thing more, Hannah," Devlin said, his gaze turned suddenly serious. "Have a care with that tender heart of yours. Nothing in life goes along easily for long. And that includes your idealistic search for God."

"No, nothing does," she softly agreed, "but when it comes to the Lord, the effort is worth it." She took his hand. "Can't you at least begin to believe that, Devlin?"

He stared at her for a long moment, then nodded slowly. "Maybe I can, Hannah. Just maybe."

18

Whoso keepeth his mouth and his tongue keepeth his soul from troubles.

Proverbs 21:23

On the evening of August 31st, Hannah, with Abby's help, threw Devlin a surprise birthday party. Due to space constraints as well as the difficulty of keeping his party a secret in his own home, the celebration was planned for the main house. Devlin was appropriately surprised when the entire MacKay clan, plus most of the ranch hands and their families, showed up to greet him as he walked in with Conor. When he learned who the chief instigator was, he threw his arms about Hannah and gave her a big hug.

Almost as soon as he had done it, though, Devlin drew back, embarrassed. Hannah gazed up at him in shock and blushed furiously. Then Abby stepped in and laughingly gave Devlin a big hug herself.

The party proved a huge success, lasting well past dark. After a time, though, the hands began heading for their bunkhouse, or riding home with their families. Hannah tucked Jackson and the other children into little pallets on the floor in Beth's bedroom, then rejoined Abby, Conor, and Devlin on the front porch.

She took a seat in one of the wicker chairs next to Devlin. "Where's Evan?" she asked, noticing his absence. "I haven't seen him for the past hour or so."

Abby and Conor, sitting together on the porch swing, exchanged an enigmatic glance. "Reckon he wasn't feeling too well," his father finally replied.

Hannah turned to look out over the ranch. From the front porch, one could see down past the two barns and livestock pens, out over the rolling, barbed-wire fenced pastures, all the way to the first of the four Culdee Creek ponds. In the moonlight, the broad swath of water gleamed with a luminous sheen.

Was she worrying unnecessarily, she wondered, that Evan still harbored hopes they'd someday marry? He didn't say much to her anymore, or try to seek her out, but there were still times—tonight in fact—when she had caught him watching her with the most intense look of longing. She had also seen the pain in his eyes earlier, when Devlin had hugged her.

It was hard to view his anguish and know she was the cause. There were times when Hannah wondered if it would ever resolve, as long as she remained at Culdee Creek. There were times when she even considered leaving for Evan's sake.

Her little dresses were selling so consistently now that she could well support herself and Jackson. But she hated the thought of taking her son from this stable, loving environment. She hated the thought of taking him away from his father. And she could hardly bear the thought of leaving the other children. Or Devlin, for that matter, either.

Voices on the porch slowly drew Hannah back as talk turned to more neutral things, the approaching autumn, the remaining ranch projects still to be completed, and baby Sean's amazing locomotive abilities now that he had mastered crawling. After a while, Abby pretended to stifle a huge yawn. Hannah grinned.

"Time for bed?"

Her friend nodded. "I need all the rest I can get to keep up with my son these days."

Hannah laughed. "Oh, you'll adjust in time. We mothers don't really have much choice, do we?"

Conor exchanged a long-suffering glance with Devlin. "Guess we'd better see to it, then, that the womenfolk get their beauty sleep." He took hold of Abby's hand and rose, pulling her with him.

"It's not that we want to run you off or anything . . ." Abby hurried to explain. "Sit out here as long as you want."

Devlin chuckled. "It *is* a nice night. But we won't be long. I need to help Hannah gather up my children and carry them back to the house."

"Well, enjoy yourselves. Good night."

Hannah watched Conor and Abby, arm in arm, head into the house. She smiled, then turned to Devlin. "I don't think I've ever seen two people more in love. I'm so happy for them."

"Yeah," Devlin agreed, "Conor couldn't have found a better woman. She was sure a long time in coming, though."

"Which goes to show that you shouldn't ever lose hope, doesn't it?"

He arched a brow. "Please, Hannah. No lectures on my birthday. Don't I get even one day off a year?"

"Oh, you get plenty more than just one day off, Devlin, and you know it!" At the smile twisting one corner of his mouth, Hannah giggled. "Besides, however you choose to take it, what I said is meant to be encouraging. You'll find another woman who'll make you feel happy and complete someday."

At her words, Devlin stared at her hard, then stood and walked to the porch railing. "Sometimes," he said, his back to her, "you can't always have what you want."

At the poignant note in his voice, overlaid as it was with a deep resignation, Hannah's heart went out to him. She climbed to her feet and moved to stand beside him.

"No, you can't always have what *you* want." Taking his hand in hers, she clutched it close to her side. "You can, though, if God wants you to have it. Just be sure then, that you don't turn your back on His gift and walk away."

He made a soft sound of disgust. "And why would God want me to have anything?" Devlin sighed. "Don't bother answering that. I already know what you'd say."

"But you've yet to believe it yourself."

"Something like that," he muttered.

"What would it take? For you to believe God loves you?"

His face an inscrutable mask, Devlin stared straight ahead. "I don't know. Probably some miracle."

"There are miracles aplenty every day, present in some of the smallest things, and in the most surprising places. We just have to want to find them, then be open enough to recognize and accept them."

"Ah, Hannah." The despairing sound seemed to be wrenched from the depths of Devlin's being. "I don't know how to do that. I never have."

"But God does, if only you let Him, Devlin." She lifted his hand, brought it to her lips, and kissed it. "Open your heart to Him. Set aside your fears, and trust."

243

"It isn't that easy! Don't you understand that yet?"

She turned her face to gaze up at him. "No, it isn't easy. Still, we have to make a beginning sometime, somehow, or we'll never find what we truly seek."

Devlin sighed. "You care so much for my salvation. If a man wasn't careful, he could very easily imagine . . ."

With his free hand, he lightly stroked the side of her face. His touch, so gentle, so tender, sent shivers down Hannah's spine. Yet it was his unfinished sentence, rich with unspoken possibilities, that stirred her hopes, sending them spinning wildly.

"What would a man begin to imagine?" she whispered, taking his hand to clutch it to her chest. "That I might care as much for him as I did for his soul? That I might harbor secret dreams, foolish as they might be, that the man might also feel something for me?"

"Hannah." Devlin's voice went husky and strained. "You'd do better to dream about any other man than me."

"Why, because you don't want me?"

An undisguised look of yearning flashed across his face, then was gone. He pulled back, disengaging his hand from her clasp. "As I said before, you can't always have what you want."

His words, suddenly so cold and devoid of emotion, were like a slap in the face. It was too much to bear. Not now, not after all this time, Hannah decided angrily, was she going to let him off so easily. "And I say," she countered with a fierce emphasis, "you're letting your fear unman you."

Devlin grabbed her by the shoulders and jerked her to him. "Don't lecture me. If you only knew the torment wanting you causes me, you'd turn and run as fast and far away as you could."

At the contact of their bodies, Hannah went rigid, then forced herself to relax. With an impish smile, she lifted

244

her arms and encircled his neck. "I'm not so sure who's more afraid of who."

He scowled. "Hannah, I'm warning you for the last time."

"Land sakes alive!" She expelled a frustrated breath. "Are you going to kiss me or not?"

Eyes wide, he stared down at her in disbelief. Then a slow, lazy grin touched his lips. "Well, don't ever say I didn't warn you."

Devlin gathered her to him. His head lowered; his mouth covered hers, and he kissed her, long, hard, and passionately.

Fire kindled within Hannah. Her hands slid from behind Devlin's neck to clench in the corded strength of his shoulders. A low moan escaped her.

The sound must have plucked at Devlin's conscience. With a heartrending groan, he pulled back and pushed Hannah from him, holding her at arm's length.

"What . . . what's wrong?" she asked, still confused and aroused by the short, fierce intensity of his kiss. "I . . . I didn't want you to stop."

"Well, *I* did."

"Why?" Hannah fought to still her racing heart, calm her befuddled mind. *"Why?"*

"Someone's got to be strong, do what's best for the both of us."

She opened her mouth to question him as to his meaning, when someone strode past the house from the back, heading resolutely toward the barn.

In the darkness, it was at first hard to make out who it was. As she watched the long-legged stride and sway of broad shoulders, though, Hannah finally realized it was Evan. Stetson on his head, a set of full, leather saddlebags slung over his shoulder, and a bedroll and jacket tucked beneath his arm, he appeared to be packed for a trip.

She frowned. Wherever was Evan going this late at night?

Devlin must have been thinking the same thing. "No one told me anything about Evan heading out somewhere." He released her and turned toward the porch steps. "Reckon I'd better go have a look-see."

"No." After what had just transpired between them, Hannah suspected he far preferred running after his cousin to staying here and working things out. "Evan didn't seem in the best of moods this evening. Let me go instead. Considering your and Evan's ongoing problems, you're not the best person to go after him tonight." She laid a hand on his arm. "Please, let me do it, Devlin. It won't take long. Then we can go up and fetch the children."

For a long moment he stared down at her hand, small and white in the moonlight, then sighed his acquiescence. "Fine. Suit yourself." He walked back and threw himself into a wicker chair. "Just remember I'm waiting on you."

"I won't forget." Releasing his arm, Hannah spun around and hurried down the porch steps. "I'll be back soon. I promise."

As she headed across the yard and down to the barn she had seen Evan enter, Hannah put her upsetting encounter with Devlin aside and composed her thoughts. She and Culdee Creek's foreman still had unfinished business to settle, but what mattered now was Evan. Whatever would she say, once she reached him? Small talk about the birthday party seemed trite. Questioning him about his sullen manner all evening was pointless, and could well lead to an argument. The best thing, Hannah finally resolved, was just to spit it out and ask him where he was going.

By the time she found him, Evan had finished saddling his favorite mount, a big buckskin gelding named

Culdee Gold. At the sound of her hard-soled footsteps on the dirt floor, Evan wheeled around, a startled, guilty look on his face. When he saw it was Hannah, his expression changed to one of irritation.

"What do you want?" he growled, turning back to give the saddle cinch one last, firm tug before looping the leathers through the cinch ring. "Tired of waiting on Devlin hand and foot, are you?"

"I hardly think throwing Devlin a birthday party constitutes waiting on him hand and foot. Besides, if I recall correctly, you had your own very nice party in February."

"Yeah, reckon I did, even if it wasn't some surprise one, thrown by you. But then, by that time you'd pretty much tossed me over, and set your sights on Devlin, hadn't you?"

He finished looping the cinch and lowered the stirrup, temporarily hooked up over the saddle horn, back to hang at his horse's side. After tying his bedroll to the back of the saddle and throwing his saddlebags across his mount's withers, Evan glanced briefly over his shoulder. "Move out of the way, will you? I'm going to back Culdee Gold from his stall."

"No, Evan. Wait." She touched his arm. When he stiffened, Hannah immediately withdrew her hand. "Where are you going? No one said anything tonight about you leaving. And the way those saddlebags are packed, it looks like you're aiming to be gone for a long while."

His back to her, Evan stood there for several seconds, then turned. "And why would you care, Hannah?" His expression had gone stony, his gaze hard. "You don't need me anymore. You've all but got Devlin wrapped around your little finger. Why, I expected to hear wedding bells by now."

Shocked by the anger in his voice, Hannah took a hasty step back. "Evan . . . it's not like that," she managed to choke out. "Devlin and I haven't—"

247

"Don't lie to me! I saw you two kissing on the porch. After all we've been to each other, don't ruin even that by lying to me!"

"Evan . . . don't!" Hannah recoiled in fear. "I wasn't lying. Devlin's never said one word to me about getting married."

As the words left her lips, a sudden memory of Devlin at the pond only a week ago, demanding to know if she wanted to marry him and legitimize Jackson, filled her. With that memory, hot color flooded her face.

Fury flashed in Evan's eyes. "Just as I suspected! You used me until you thought something better had come along—though for the life of me I can't understand what you see in Devlin. Reckon it serves both Devlin and me right, though. What else can a man expect from a woman like you?"

With a snarl of disgust, Evan began to back his horse from its stall. As he led the animal toward the open barn door, Hannah finally recovered her composure. Running to him, she grabbed his arm and held on with all her might.

"Where are you going?" she cried, digging in her heels to no avail. Evan just kept on walking, all but dragging her behind him. *"Where are you going?"*

At that moment Devlin stepped out in front of Evan and his horse. Culdee Gold gave a snort and reared. Before Evan could even react, Devlin's hand shot out. Grabbing hold of the reins, he wrestled the horse back down.

"The lady asked you a question," he then said, his voice low. "Where do you think you're going?"

The younger man glared at him. "I don't have to account to you—or her—for my actions or whereabouts!"

The big foreman met him glare for glare. "Does your father know what you're planning on doing?"

"He will when he reads my letter."

"And how much did you clean him out for this time?"

Evan's face mottled with rage. "You low-lying scum! I didn't take a cent from my pa. All I've got is the wages I've saved and my belongings."

"But you didn't have the decency to tell him to his face why you're running out on him. How do you think that's going to make him feel?"

"I'll be back." Evan's jaw worked, and he looked away. "I just need to put some distance between me and Culdee Creek for a while, that's all."

"And why's that, Evan?"

"You've got nerve asking me that after what you've done!" He pulled hard on the reins, trying unsuccessfully to free them from Devlin's clasp. "But I don't owe you, of all people, an explanation. Now let go, and let me be, before I do something I might regret."

"I'll let you be," Devlin countered with quiet emphasis, "if you give me your word you'll put up your horse and go talk to your pa. You're right. You don't owe me anything, but you owe your pa a whole lot."

Evan stared at Devlin and, for a moment, Hannah thought he'd back down. Then, in a lightning quick move, the young man swung out with his free hand. Before Devlin could react, Evan's fist caught him square in the mouth.

Devlin staggered backward, slamming into the doorframe. Blood spilled from his split lip. Fleetingly, surprise widened his eyes. Then anger rushed in to take its place.

With a snarl, Devlin leaped at Evan, knocking him to the floor. The big buckskin, freed of the hold on its reins, gave a whistling snort and bolted from the barn.

Hannah rushed to where the two men now grappled in ferocious struggle on the ground. "Stop it!" she screamed. "Devlin! Evan! Stop it, I say!"

Pounding at each other's faces and bodies, they seemed not to hear. Hannah watched them for a moment longer, saw all the pent-up animosity and resentment they had harbored against each other unloosed at last, and knew it would take more than her pleadings to break through their rage. She turned and ran for the main house.

By the time she reached the front porch and bolted up the steps, her breath came in gasps. She raced into the house. "Abby! Conor!" Hannah screamed. "Come quick! Devlin and Evan are fighting!"

Overhead she heard footsteps. A door opened and more footsteps sounded along the hallway, then clattered down the stairs. Conor rounded the corner first, stuffing his shirttails back into his denims.

"What happened?" the big rancher demanded. "Devlin and Evan are fighting?"

"Y-yes," she panted, suddenly on the verge of tears. "In the b-barn. Evan was trying to leave Culdee Creek, and Devlin tried to stop him. Then they got into a f-fight."

She couldn't help it. The tears began to pour down her cheeks. "I-it's all my fault," Hannah sobbed. "They hate each other because of m-me."

At that moment Abby joined them. She took Hannah into her arms. "Go on," she told her husband. "Break up that fight between those two, hotheaded fools."

Conor shot Hannah one final, frowning look, then turned and hurried from the house. Hannah clung to Abby for a brief, blessed instant of comfort, then pulled away. "I need to go to them. Need to explain."

"Hannah, maybe it'd be better to stay here." Abby reached out toward her. "Your being there might just add further fuel to the fire."

"No." She shook her head and stepped back. "If I'm part of the problem, then I need to be there to help solve it." She turned and ran out the door.

250

There was no sign of Conor, Hannah realized as she rushed back the way she had first come. As she drew near, she heard the sound of male voices lifted in anger. Fearfully, Hannah pulled up, hesitated, then squared her shoulders and entered the barn.

Conor, both arms outstretched, held back two bleeding, disheveled men. "That's enough!" he commanded. "Do you two hear me? *That's enough!*"

At his words Devlin appeared to respond, backing away. Evan, however, did everything but crawl over his father trying to get to Devlin.

"It's not over by a long shot," he cried, glowering at his older cousin. "That backstabbing, low-down snake stole Hannah from me. And he's never once kept his nose out of my business!"

"I didn't steal anyone from you," Devlin snarled in turn. He pulled a handkerchief from his back pocket and dabbed gingerly at his split lip. "You just need to grow up, and take your knocks like any other man."

Conor shot his cousin an irritated look, then turned back to his son. "This obsession of yours with Hannah has got to stop. She told you months ago it was over between you two." He looked to Hannah. "That's right, isn't it?"

She nodded. "Yes, that's right." Taking that as her cue, she walked up to stand beside Conor. "Please, Evan. Stop this fighting over me. Devlin's your cousin. He's family. It breaks my heart to see you two so angry with each other."

"You love him, don't you?"

The unexpected, outrageous question took Hannah aback. She stared at Evan, momentarily speechless.

"Well, don't you?" The young man's eyes narrowed, and he studied her with sullen intent. "Come on, Hannah. It can't be that hard to figure out. It sure wasn't when it came to me."

251

"Leave her be, Evan!" Grasping Hannah by the arm, Devlin pulled her to stand beside him. "When it comes down to it, she's not and never has been the real cause of our little feud. We've been at each other's throats for years, and you know it."

"Yeah, maybe so," Evan drawled, never taking his eyes off Hannah. "But what's wrong with hearing the truth from her? If she even knows *what* the truth is these days."

Conor grabbed his son's arm. "That's enough, Evan. Hannah doesn't owe you or any of us an explanation." He tugged gently. "Come along now."

With an abrupt jerk, Evan freed himself of his father's hold. "I'm not going anywhere until I hear what Hannah has to say!" His furious, smoky blue gaze bore into her. "Well, do you love Devlin, or not?"

An answering anger swelled in her. "That's none of your business!"

Evan gave a careless shrug. "Maybe so, but after all that cooing and kissing tonight, I'll bet Devlin's itching to hear your answer." With a final seething gaze at his cousin, the younger man strode past the pair back toward the house.

Conor quickly cast an anxious look at Hannah and Devlin, then hurried after his son.

Hannah slanted a nervous, uncertain glance at Devlin. He stared back at her, an uneasy look in his eyes. After what they had left unfinished on the porch just a short time ago, Hannah wondered if he wasn't indeed wondering about her true feelings. She knew *she* wanted to know how he had felt about kissing her. What was the point of pretending it hadn't affected her?

"It's true, you know," she said softly, meeting Devlin's gaze. "I do love you."

In the stunned silence, Hannah watched as a wild riot of emotions flashed in Devlin's eyes—joy, a deep satisfaction, then growing horror. He shook his head, staggered back. "Oh, Hannah . . ." He swallowed hard. "It won't work. I-it can't."

With that, Devlin turned on his heel and rushed from the barn. She stared after him, shocked and humiliated. What had she done? *Dear Lord, what had she done?*

Tears filled her eyes. Her stomach lurched, and the barn interior began to whirl crazily. For a moment, she thought she might either faint or retch. Then everything righted itself–everything but the reality of Devlin's rejection.

With a low cry, Hannah turned and ran from the barn.

19

When I looked for good, then evil came unto me; and when I waited for light, there came darkness.

Job 30:26

She had to find Devlin. Had to find him and explain. He cared for her. Hannah knew that from the myriad ways he had shown it in the past months, and from the kiss they had shared on the porch this evening. Now she needed to hear what he truly felt for her.

Even if, for him, it never went past caring.

A quick glance to the front porch of the main house revealed that Devlin hadn't returned there. Hannah looked up the hill, hoping to catch a glimpse of him striding to his own house. She saw nothing.

There were sounds, though, emanating from the second barn as she hurried past it. Hannah slowed, drew to a halt, and listened. A horse snorted. Leather creaked, metal jingled. Then came the sound of a saddle protesting, as if someone were mounting.

In a rush of movement and rapid hoofbeats, a rider and big bay bolted from the open barn door. Hannah jumped back.

"Devlin!" she cried, recognizing his powerfully muscled form. "Don't go! We need to talk!"

"No," he yelled as he rode past. "Not tonight!"

Clutching her skirts, she ran after him. "Where . . . where are you going?"

"To town," he flung back.

With a flurry of dust and pounding hooves, Devlin headed down the road. The moonlight illuminated his dark figure as he rode through Culdee Creek's front gate and topped the hill. Hannah watched until he disappeared, then turned and walked slowly back to the main house.

Swathed in shadows, Abby sat on the porch in the wicker rocker. "What happened in the barn?" she asked at last, when Hannah said nothing.

"He apparently didn't like hearing that I loved him."

Abby was silent for a time. "No, I don't suppose Devlin *would* like knowing that," she finally said. "Loving you scares him witless, and he doesn't know what to do about it."

At her friend's words, renewed hope sprang to life. Then, with a weary sigh, Hannah quickly banished it. "Well, he isn't helping things any, telling me it can't work between us"—she walked over and sank into the other chair—"then riding off to Grand View to get away from me."

"Devlin's always had trouble accepting happiness into his life. Ella told me once that even after they married, for a long while Devlin was as wild-eyed crazy as a cow at branding time. He had a hard time settling down to a normal, happy family life."

255

"Well, he's never going to have another normal, happy life with a woman if he doesn't start having a little faith in himself," Hannah muttered, frustration welling in her.

"You've helped him a lot since you came to Culdee Creek. Helped him open his mind and heart to far greater possibilities–in himself and in others."

"It makes me mad, though, that he ran tonight, instead of staying to work things out between us. Mad and frustrated and of a mind to–" Her thoughts racing, Hannah rose from her chair and strode to the porch railing. Once there, she whirled around to face her friend.

"Whatever are you thinking?" Abby asked, staring up at her in suspicion.

"I need to talk to Devlin. Tonight."

"Well, I don't think he'll be getting home any time soon. I'd bet he's planning on a long sojourn in Sam Green's saloon."

Hannah turned. Her hand gripping one of the porch's support pillars, she nodded with firm resolve. "Then I'll just have to pay the saloon a little visit."

Abby stood and joined Hannah at the railing. "Can't this discussion with Devlin wait until morning? Nearly everyone's abed, and Conor's still talking with Evan. There's no one to take you to Grand View tonight."

"No, I suppose there isn't." Hannah's shoulders sagged. "Guess that settles that."

"At least for tonight." Her friend patted her hand. "Besides, it's best you give Devlin time to cool down."

"Yes, that's probably a good idea." She paused. "Well, now that Devlin's gone, I guess I'll need some help getting the children home."

Abby turned to her. "Why not leave them in Beth's room for the night? She won't mind and, since they're all asleep by now, there's no sense disturbing them 'til morning."

Gratitude at her friend's thoughtfulness filled Hannah. "It probably would be best. Thank you so much, Abby."

"Go on. Head back to the bunkhouse and make yourself a cup of chamomile tea, then go to bed and get a good night's sleep." She squeezed Hannah's hand, then released it. "Tomorrow's soon enough to deal with all this."

"Yes." Hannah nodded firmly. "Yes, it is. I'll see you in the morning then."

"In the morning."

Sleep for Hannah, however, didn't come as quickly or easily as she had hoped. As the next hour passed, thoughts of the evening kept creeping into her head, stirring wild emotions and endless unanswered questions. Fear stole in as well. Fear of the morning and what it would bring. Fear that the wonderful future she had hoped was building with Devlin was over. And a fear that, at long last, because she didn't think she could bear to be near Devlin if he didn't love her, she'd have to leave Culdee Creek.

Finally, Hannah gave up on sleep. She rose to pace her bedroom with fast, jerky steps. Her tension, however, only grew. Thoughts of going after Devlin rose once again.

"I can saddle a horse and ride," she muttered, clutching her wrapper tightly to her. "Grand View's less than a half hour away. Besides, the moon's bright enough to light the road." She nodded with growing resolve. "I'll be fine. No one will even know I'm gone, and surely Devlin will ride back with me."

The decision made, Hannah hurriedly dressed in a divided riding skirt, shirtwaist blouse, and boots, then quietly left the bunkhouse and headed toward the second barn. Abby's horse, Culdee Fire, was stabled there. The animal was gentle and steady, and Hannah knew her friend would forgive her borrowing it.

After tacking up the mare, Hannah led her from the barn and mounted. For an instant she stared up at the main house, renewed uncertainty flooding her. Then she squared her shoulders, nudged Culdee Fire in the side, and rode out after Devlin.

The night was warm, the moonlit countryside bathed in a soft, velvety glow. If the journey had been for happier reasons, Hannah would've enjoyed the ride. But she was scared to death of Devlin's reaction to being confronted in the saloon. And she didn't know what she would say to him. One way or another, though, they needed to get things settled between them tonight.

As Hannah neared Grand View bright lights and voices from Sadie Fleming's, and the dimmer illumination and piano music pouring out through the Prancing Pronghorn's half doors, shattered the dark, silent night. Passing the bordello, Hannah stiffened reflexively. That life was over now, she firmly reminded herself, letting her gaze settle on the saloon. Over forever.

Several horses already filled the few spots at the hitching post before the saloon's entrance. Hannah rode Culdee Fire around to the west side of the building, and secured her to the fence separating the saloon yard from the expanse of land between it and Sadie's big, ornately wood-trimmed house and landscaped grounds. That done, she strode back around, climbed onto the boardwalk fronting the saloon, and drew up before its two half doors.

The acrid smell of cigarette and cigar smoke mixed with the scent of unwashed male bodies. A piano tinkled plaintively in one corner of the large, open room. The giggles and soft laughs of several gaudily clad women mingled with the discordant shouts and calls of the men within. It wasn't a place Hannah had envisioned entering ever again.

But Devlin was in there. Culdee Star was one of the horses tied before the saloon. And it was for Devlin that she had ridden all this way.

Hannah dragged in a fortifying breath, then braced herself to push past the swinging doors and walk into the saloon. As she raised her hand to the door, an arm snaked out of the shadows and clamped around her wrist.

"Finally decided to come back where you belong, have you?" a familiar voice drawled.

Hannah wheeled around and her gaze slammed into that of Brody Gerard. With a low gasp, she stepped back.

"Let me go, Brody," Hannah said through gritted teeth. "I've got no business with you."

His hand remained where it was, gripping her firmly. "Maybe not, but I've got some unfinished business with you." As he spoke, Brody's glance slowly, suggestively slid down her body.

Uneasy, Hannah tried to free herself from Brody's grasp. When he snickered at her futile struggle, icy talons of fear clenched around her chest.

She opened her mouth to call for help, but in a split second Brody's hand twisted her arm behind her. Another hand slammed down over her mouth.

Terrified, Hannah elbowed him hard in the side and bit down on the muscled palm covering her mouth. Brody grunted in pain, and momentarily loosened his grasp.

Hannah wrenched free. She took two steps forward, and opened her mouth to scream. Then, with a brutal grip, Brody grabbed her and jerked her back around. His other hand fisted, slamming into her jaw.

Pain exploded in her head. A colorful kaleidoscope of whirling lights flashed before her eyes. Then, like a curtain, darkness fell, obliterating everything.

∂

The sun was blindingly bright. A flock of crows flying overhead made a deafening cacophony. His horse's jarring gait sent Devlin's stomach to roiling and his head to pounding. And, to add insult to injury, his split lip and bruised face throbbed. If he didn't get to Culdee Creek soon, Devlin decided, he'd never make it at all.

Finally, blessedly, through the morning mists rising off the land, he blearily made out the ranch entrance's gateposts. "Just a little while longer," he mumbled to his mount. "Hang in there, old boy."

Culdee Star's ears flicked back. Devlin knew the big bay was listening. He seriously doubted, though, that his horse bore him any sympathy.

After all the other occupants of the Prancing Pronghorn had departed late last night, Sam Green had taken pity on Devlin and made a pallet for him behind the bar. This morning the Presbyterian Church's bells, peeling out a greeting to the churchgoers attending the early Sunday service, had nearly sent Devlin flying straight into the air. As it was, he had managed to break several bottles of Sam's finest whiskey, which had ended up costing a pretty penny.

No, he admitted, the day hadn't begun well at all. And it didn't promise to get any better. Not only did he have a ferocious hangover and splitting headache, but he still had Hannah to face once he arrived back at Culdee Creek.

And face her he would. That much he had determined last night between shots of whiskey and bouts of bitter self-recrimination. At the very least, he owed her the truth. He owed himself the truth, too.

Last night Hannah had admitted she loved him, an admission Devlin know had required an enormous amount of courage. She deserved the same from him—the courage to confront his own needs and fears, and be man enough to fight for what he wanted.

Fight for her.

He loved Hannah, had for a long while now. So did his children. Devlin wagered he pretty much needed her as much as they did, too. A man would have to be a fool to turn his back on a woman as fine as Hannah. Even a man as bullheaded and thick-skulled as he.

But what would it take, then, to finally be worthy of her? Devlin reined in Culdee Star and, with his free hand, massaged his aching forehead. What *was* it about him that drew Hannah so strongly that she now seemed convinced she loved him? And could he truly live up to her lofty expectations?

He knew he wanted to. He'd do everything in his power never to disappoint her. But if he tried and still failed . . .

With a fierce swell of rage, Devlin swept aside the old, insidious doubts. What had happened in the past was over and done. No amount of guilt or wishing it had been different would change what had occurred. It was time to move on, to regain control of his life and not look back. He had always been a man who did well when he took charge and relied on himself. He would do so again, but this time with Hannah at his side.

Joy surged through him. "I think you'd approve, Ella," Devlin whispered, lifting his thoughts briefly heavenward. "In fact, I wouldn't be surprised if you hadn't plotted out all this yourself. It'd be just like you," he added with a tender smile. "I thank you for loving me that much. I thank you from the bottom of my heart."

As Devlin headed down the road toward the ranch buildings, Conor, followed by Abby, walked out onto the main house's front porch and down the steps. Even before he had reined in his horse and begun to dismount, Abby ran to him.

"Where's Hannah?" She glanced up at him with anxious eyes. "She left last night without telling me, and when you and she didn't come home, I thought . . . well, I thought you two were together."

Devlin all but fell off his horse. Wincing in pain, he turned to face her. "Could you lower your voice a mite?" He pulled off his Stetson and massaged his temples. "I'm not deaf, you know."

"You may not be deaf, but you sure look to have a walloping good hangover," Conor offered, joining his wife.

Abby shot both men a quelling look. "At this moment, I could care less whether Devlin has a hangover or not. I want to know where Hannah is!"

As the gravity of the situation slowly permeated Devlin's befuddled mind, he forced his thoughts to focus. "I don't know. I haven't seen her since last night."

"Well, she's not here," Abby snapped. "She went after you and never came home!"

Devlin shot Conor a questioning glance.

His cousin nodded in solemn agreement. "She's not here, Devlin. We've searched the whole ranch."

Concern in her eyes, Abby stepped closer. "What happened last night at the Prancing Pronghorn, Devlin? What did you say to Hannah?"

Devlin's gut clenched. "I didn't say *anything* to her. She never came into the saloon."

Conor turned to his wife. "Do you think it's possible she decided not to go to the saloon, and spent the night with the Starrs, or maybe with Russell Gates and his wife?"

Abby's eyes brightened with renewed hope. "I suppose that's possible. Will you ride to Grand View and see?"

"No, it's my fault Hannah went to town in the first place," Devlin cut in with as much firmness as his pounding head would allow. "It should be up to me to find her and set things straight."

"From the looks of you right now," Conor muttered, casting a disgusted glance at his cousin, "you couldn't manage that by yourself if your life depended on it. So, while I saddle up, why don't you head into the house and have a couple cups of coffee? You'll need it for the ride back."

Devlin stifled a groan. What more could go wrong? Still, when Conor used that tone of voice, it was pointless to argue. Besides, he didn't know what he would do if he didn't have a chance to set things right with Hannah, to tell her he loved her. Now that he had taken the final step that would free him from his past, Devlin didn't want it to be a journey begun–and ended–in vain.

On the return trip to town, Conor informed Devlin that, despite all arguments to the contrary, Evan had insisted on riding out first thing in the morning. He had to get away for a while, his son had explained. Get things put back in the proper perspective. Where and how he presumed to accomplish that, Conor added grimly, Evan didn't say.

Beneath the sparse words and flat tone of voice, Devlin could hear his cousin's pain. "I'm sorry, Conor," he said, shaking his head in disbelief. "I know Evan and I had our problems, but I never thought it would come to this. And I swear to you. It was the furthest thing from my mind to try to take Hannah away from him."

"Well, there's no accounting for women and their choice of men, is there?" Conor shot him an agonized look. "That's a lesson Evan's going to have to learn sooner or later. It's also a lesson you need to learn real soon, too, before you destroy any chance you have with Hannah. You hurt her last night by running out on her."

"I didn't know what else to do. She deserves better than me, Conor. But I didn't know how to make her see that."

"Do you love her?"

Devlin closed his eyes against the bright sun, willing the throbbing pain in his head to ease. "That's a fool stupid question," he growled. "Who wouldn't love Hannah? She's an angel, a rare, sweet, beautiful angel."

"Then why are you trying so hard to destroy what you have with her?"

"Why else?" Devlin's laugh was unsteady. "I'm afraid. Afraid I'll disappoint her. Afraid to let myself hope I can ever be happy again."

"Well, that's a foolish way to go through life. Are you bound and determined to end up like your pa?"

Devlin's head jerked around, and he glared at Conor. "I never want to end up like my pa. Never!"

"So that's why you got drunk at Sam's and ran off on Hannah? 'Cause you don't want to be like your pa." Conor shook his head in renewed disgust. "Sure makes a heap of sense to me."

To shield his bloodshot, burning eyes from the sun's glare, Devlin tugged down his Stetson's front brim even lower. "Yeah, I reckon it does," he muttered. "Just about as much sense as it makes to me."

With that, he spurred his mount on to a gallop.

Hannah wasn't at either the Starrs' or Gates' house. After scouring the town, Devlin finally found Culdee Fire still tied near the saloon. Their anxiety rising, the two men headed for the sheriff's office.

When he heard the news, Jake Whitmore wasn't any more pleased than Devlin and Conor. "Considering her horse is here and she's nowhere to be found," he said, scratching his jaw, "I reckon some foul play's afoot. Any ideas who might wish her harm—aside from a passel of the women in this town, of course?"

At the memory of the day he had dragged Brody Gerard's carcass into this very office, a cold horror flooded Devlin. If Gerard had finally managed to carry her back to Sadie Fleming's . . .

He slammed on his Stetson and headed for the door. "Just one idea," he growled over his shoulder, "and if she's there, the man who took her is going to wish he was never born!"

20

Out of the depths have I cried unto thee, O Lord.
                                                    Psalm 130:1

Hannah woke to feel herself being rocked to and fro. She squinted at the bright light shining in her eyes. Disoriented and nauseated, she struggled to make sense of her surroundings. Slowly, the sky came into focus above her, bright blue and full of fluffy white, wind-swept clouds.

The creak of wood ... the jingle of traces ... the scent of horseflesh assailed her. A wagon ... she was in a wagon going somewhere.

She struggled to sit up, and found her hands and feet tied. She tried to cry out, and found her mouth gagged with a filthy, foul-smelling rag. Finally, the memory of the previous night returned.

With a sickening rush, Hannah recalled Brody's attack on her. The awful sense of helpless panic against his greater size and strength gripped her once more.

And now he had her. Had her, and was taking her to heaven knows where.

Anger filled her. Hannah cried out and fought violently to free herself, but to no avail. Finally she fell back, panting against the wagon's hard floor, tears of frustration in her eyes.

"Ah, I see you've finally woken up."

Twisting around, Hannah caught sight of Brody on the front seat, glancing back at her. As her furious gaze met his, he grinned and gave a low laugh.

"Don't care much, do you, for being trussed up like a lamb to the slaughter? But that goes with living with those high and mighty MacKays. Reckon they went and put some fool ideas into your head, ideas that you had miraculously become some fine lady, rather than the trash you really are." Brody turned back to stare at the road ahead. "No matter. I helped teach you your place before. I can sure do it again."

A stiff breeze blew past, nearly relieving him of the big, tan plantation-style hat he liked to wear. With a curse, Brody grabbed for it in the nick of time. He slammed the hat down hard on his head, then jerked its rawhide ties a little tighter beneath his chin.

"Yeah, that's exactly what I aim to do, too," he said, picking up the thread of their one-sided conversation. "After all the grief you've caused me, what with Sadie and then MacKay, I'd say you owe me plenty. And I just happen to know a madam up in Breckenridge who's been after me to go into business with her. When I bring her a sweet little filly like you, I'm betting she'll be more than willing to cut me in for half interest in her brothel."

Hannah had heard more than she cared to know. There was no sense continuing to stare at his back or, for that matter, listen any further. She jerked around until she was once more gazing out at the trail behind

267

them. Like tumbleweeds racing to the four winds across the prairies, her thoughts scattered.

She had always known Brody wasn't a man to show anyone any mercy. From the first day Sadie had hired him on at her place, he had been trouble. When he wasn't trying to cheat Sadie's girls out of their earnings, he was the first one, in the pretense of playing the bodyguard, to walk in on them at any time, and claim favors even he should've paid for. Few ever complained to Sadie, though. Brody was mean as a snake. He'd always find some way to get back at them.

Remembering the horrible bruises he had repeatedly left on her—bruises that took weeks to heal—Hannah shivered in revulsion. She had seen the results of Brody's beatings on some of the other girls, too. And the last time she had finally been dragged back, after she had run away . . .

Thank goodness Brody had never hit her in the belly, or he might have unwittingly killed the child growing there. And thank goodness Doc Childress was such a talented physician. Not only had he set her nose so well only a tiny bump now marred its perfect line, but he had also seen to the three broken fingers on her left hand and two toes of her right foot. But there had been little he could do for her swollen scalp, tender from Hannah being dragged endlessly about the room by her hair, or for the welts across her back.

In time, everything had healed. Few could ever imagine the horrible extent of her injuries that night. Yet the worst wounds of all had been inflicted on her soul. The sheer terror, the pain, the complete and utter degradation were hard, even now, to recall.

Even worse to consider was the fact she was, once again, totally under Brody's power. Anger welled anew. This time, though, Hannah directed it at Devlin. It was all his fault she was in this predicament. If he hadn't ridden off to Grand View, Brody Gerard would've never had the opportunity to abduct her.

Hannah inhaled a shuddering breath. What a stupid fool she had been. She had fallen in love with a man who had run away like some frenzied steer in the midst of a stampede, just because a woman loved him.

No more, though, Hannah vowed with a fierce resolve. If she managed to get free of Brody Gerard, she wasn't about to go back and take Devlin's abuse ever again. She might have harbored foolish dreams for a time, but not now. Repeatedly, Devlin had shown his true colors. He didn't have the guts it took to risk his heart. Or, leastwise, Hannah amended sadly, not for her.

She would return to Culdee Creek, get Jackson and the now sizable nest egg saved from her sewing business, then move to Colorado Springs. Several times already, Mrs. Waters had offered her a room upstairs from her millinery shop, and more orders than Hannah could ever hope to fill. No one knew her in the Springs. She would have her respectability and security at last. And she would be free of her hopeless, dead-end relationship with Devlin MacKay.

Yes, they were all wonderful dreams, Hannah thought, if she could only escape. That was a mighty tall order, though. A mighty tall order indeed, she added, the panic rising, yet again, to clamp about her heart with a vise-like grip. Yet, this time, the stakes were even higher, the consequences far more terrifying to contemplate.

This time, she had finally tasted of a life she had long and deeply yearned for. A life made rich with her sweet little Jackson, her friendship with Abby, Conor, and Noah Starr. A life that had restored her hope and sense of self-esteem. A life that had led her to God and the discovery of herself as a woman of value and grace.

All were precious beyond words. And this time, the loss of them would surely be impossible to endure.

♄

At Wilkerson Pass high in the Rockies, Devlin drew up on his horse beside Sheriff Jake Whitmore, and scowled at the heavy, gray clouds building in the distance. Like angry giants, they hung over the next range of peaks awaiting them across the wide expanse of level valley, threatening and potentially lethal to all who dared approach.

"I don't like the looks of those clouds," Jake muttered, as the three other deputized men finally reined in alongside them. "The temperature has dropped fast in the past four hours. Even if it *is* just the beginning of September, I think we're in for an early snowstorm."

"Maybe so." Devlin leaned back in his saddle and lifted his feet from the stirrups to stretch his legs. "We still have a few more hours of daylight left, though. I think it's worth the risk to ride on."

Jake glanced around at the other men. "I think, maybe, it might be better to camp up here in the trees, and wait out the storm. Down there on the park's open plain, we'll be completely exposed for the next thirty or forty miles."

Simon Nealy sidled his horse up to them. "We've been on the trail now for three days, MacKay. Bob's sicker than a dog, and Ned's not feeling any too chipper either. I'm with the sheriff. Best we make camp for the night, and head out again tomorrow."

Devlin shot the burly blacksmith a sour look. He had feared this was coming, especially when Bob Farley and Ned Teachout turned sick. "Fine. We can all meet up in Breckenridge then." He slid his feet back in the stirrups and reined his horse around. "Me, though, I'm heading out."

Gritting his teeth, Devlin fought back his own frustration and burgeoning despair. Gerard had her. That they pretty much knew after learning the man had disappeared the same night as Hannah. In the bargain, after Sadie Fleming discovered that Brody had stolen her extra cash and all her jewelry, as well as her brand new buckboard, she was most forthcoming with the news that her bodyguard had formerly worked for a madam in Breckenridge.

What the rest of them—save maybe Jake—didn't know was that Gerard had a long-standing grudge against Hannah. But then, the rest of them hadn't had a private, heart-to-heart with Sadie either. The older woman had expressed grave concern for Hannah's safety.

No, it was impossible to consider leaving Hannah to Brody Gerard's mercy any longer than was absolutely necessary. She was the mother of his son. He loved her and wanted her for his wife if she'd still have him. If it took three days or three months, Devlin was determined to find her. In the meanwhile, he didn't plan to let some snowstorm that might not amount to much slow him down.

"Devlin," Jake said gently, "I think you should stay the night with us."

He closed his eyes and stubbornly shook his head. "No. I'm going on. I've got a feeling I'm getting close to them. Don't ask me how I know, but I feel it, deep down inside me."

The sheriff eyed him dubiously, then shrugged. "Well, suit yourself." He neck-reined his horse into a half circle, facing back the way they had just come. Then Jake hesitated and glanced over his shoulder. "If you do get lucky and find Gerard before we meet back up, watch yourself. He's a desperate man. He won't go down easily."

Devlin nodded in grim agreement. "No, I don't suppose he will. But I've had plenty of experience with desperate men. I know how they think. Gerard won't put anything past me."

Jake touched a finger to the brim of his hat in farewell. Devlin returned the salute. Then he signaled his horse out into a slow lope. The clouds lowering over the mountains were blackening with each passing second. He needed to make as much time as he could, while he could.

Besides, Devlin reminded himself as he left the other men behind and headed down from the pass, there was no telling how Hannah was faring. Jake was right. Brody Gerard was a desperate man. If Hannah didn't see things his way, Gerard could get mean.

Desperate men were like that. He should know. He had lived nearly his whole life in quiet desperation.

"No! I don't care *what* you say or do. I won't work as a prostitute ever again!"

"And *I* told *you!*" His handsome face twisted in fury, Brody Gerard threw down his half-empty whiskey bottle and advanced on her. "Don't you ever tell me what you will or won't do!"

Terrified, Hannah fought frantically to free herself from the rope bonds holding her, hands tied above her head, to one wheel of the buckboard. She was exhausted, weak from hunger, her body bruised and battered from days of bouncing around in the back of the buckboard. Until tonight, though, just one day from the booming mining town of Breckenridge if the threatening storm didn't further slow their journey, she hadn't dared defy her captor.

But tonight was the last night before he took her into town and brought her to the bordello. Tonight, after four days of hoping and praying for rescue, or for some opportunity to escape, Hannah had finally faced the fact there was little chance of either. What she had secretly feared for the past two years had, despite all her efforts to the contrary, come to pass. She would soon be forced back into a life of prostitution.

Yet, as Brody leaned over, grabbed a handful of her hair, and jerked Hannah to her knees, an unexpected strength of spirit flooded her. She met his enraged gaze with a steadfast one of her own.

"Yes, I *will* tell you," Hannah said with quiet determination. "It's my life, my body, not yours. And no one will ever, *ever* use me again."

His grip tightened. He twisted her hair with brutal intent. "And *you* forget," he sneered, "that I know how to make you do exactly what I want, when I want it." He jerked her hard. "I always win. And I don't care what it takes either. Had you forgotten that, Hannah?"

Pain shot through her head. Hannah bit back a cry. She refused, however, to give him the answer he sought. She refused to let him intimidate and manipulate her once more. Never again, she vowed. Never again would she betray her heart, her principles, or her God.

"It doesn't matter what you think you know." She gritted her teeth against the pain. "You can't make me do anything anymore!"

Brody slapped her full across the face. "Can't I? Are you so keen on dying, then? You'll never see that precious little boy of yours again, if you do." He chuckled malevolently. "And here I thought a mother's love was strong enough to endure most anything."

Jackson . . . Even the consideration of losing him, of never being able to see or hold him again, was beyond bearing. But now Brody's words stabbed clear through to her heart.

Her love *was* strong enough to endure anything for her son. But something else—something even greater than her love for Jackson—was at stake here. To give in, to acquiesce to Brody's demands would threaten her immortal soul.

At her baptism she had renounced Satan and all his works. She had promised to follow and obey God, to put her whole trust in His grace and love. Though Hannah now fought constantly against the fear He had abandoned her in allowing her to fall into Brody Gerard's hands, she clung to Him nonetheless. He had given her so much; she could at least render Him her trust—even in this—in repayment.

"You'd never let me see Jackson again anyway," Hannah forced herself to reply. "But if I remain true to the Lord, I know I'll at least see my son again in heaven. That much, no matter what you do to me, you can't ever take away."

He slapped her again, so hard this time it split Hannah's lip. The warm, metallic taste of blood filled her mouth. She blinked back the tears as, around them, a frigid wind careened suddenly through the camp.

"What's happened to you?" Angry frustration now tautening his voice, Brody tugged hard on her hair. "What kind of fool ideas have the MacKays and that spineless preacher gone and put into your head?"

She gazed steadfastly up at him, refusing to reply. Brody didn't really want to hear the truth; he only cared to discover any weakness he could use against her.

He tugged all the harder. "Answer me, Hannah. You know what will happen if you don't." Gerard leaned close, his whiskey-soaked breath drenching her. "How is this time any different then before? Isn't life, however it's lived, better than dying?"

Wasn't it? Hannah asked herself. As long as there was life, there was always hope. There was still a chance of escape, of eventually returning to Culdee Creek and her son. But if she persisted in this stubborn battle of wills, Brody would finally lose patience, kill her. And, in destroying her, he would also destroy all her hopes and dreams.

Yet what was the value of anything in life without God?

The tears spilled down her cheeks. "Would you have me sacrifice even that, then, Lord?" Hannah whispered softly. "My hopes, my dreams, the child I love with all my heart?"

I would have it all, Beloved, a voice seemed to answer from the very depths of her being. *Only when you empty yourself of all earthly attachments can you finally and most fully open yourself to My grace.*

Empty yourself . . .

The words were strangely familiar, reminding Hannah of something Abby had once said, after reading a verse from Matthew. Something about . . . something about to lose one's life for God's sake was to find it.

Had that then, always been her stumbling block—her fierce desire to regain control of her life, to make something of it, and show everyone she was as good as they? Had her pride, her newfound sense of self-worth and independence, qualities she cherished as things hard won and precious, placed then a barrier between her and the Lord? But to give them up when they were now so much a part of her—what would be left of her? Who would she then be?

It wasn't fair. Angrily, Hannah lifted her protest heavenward. It just wasn't fair! She, who'd had so much taken from her, must now relinquish even what had been so dearly—and rightfully—regained. Yet, in the end, what was the value of it anyway, if it could so easily be taken and destroyed by a man like Brody Gerard?

Lay up for yourselves treasures in heaven, where neither moth nor rust doth corrupt, and where thieves do not break through nor steal . . .

As a gentle snow began to fall, Hannah closed her eyes against the renewed surge of tears. Her treasures, she realized, were no longer of this world. Her treasures couldn't ever be taken from her—not by thieves, and not by a man such as Brody Gerard. He no longer possessed any power over her. No man did. At last she was truly, blessedly, free.

And that, Hannah thought, a deep, heart-sustaining peace flooding her, was the difference between the last time . . . and now.

About five in the evening the storm broke, catching Devlin in the middle of the flat, open park. True to Jake Whitmore's prediction, the snow began to fall, first in light flakes that danced on the wind, then in thicker, denser showers sleeting down from the leaden skies. Soon, a covering of white blanketed the land. As darkness descended, and clouds totally blocked any light from the moon and stars, Devlin was forced to admit he was in trouble.

If he lost his bearings and got turned around, he had no way of knowing which direction he was headed. Out here in this barren, grassy plain there was no shelter, no wood to start a fire to warm himself. Though they had brought heavy jackets and thick woolen blankets, well aware of the vagaries of Colorado weather, Devlin knew even those items wouldn't be enough if the storm lasted long. And even this early in the autumn, Rocky

Mountain snowstorms had, on occasion, been known to last several days.

As time passed, the wind began to shriek. The snow now pelted him and his horse like stinging needles. It swirled and blew, distorting the landscape until Devlin could barely make out five feet in front of him. He pulled up his bandanna to cover his nose and mouth, then hunched down as best he could within the shelter of his Stetson and jacket, and rode on.

The hours ticked interminably by in the whiteout of blowing snow. Head down against the wind, Devlin's big bay gelding plodded on, his movement increasingly slowed by the ever-deepening drifts. Ice began to coat them. The reins in Devlin's gloved hands grew stiff. More and more frequently, he caught himself dozing.

"Wake up, you fool," he muttered through numb, awkward lips. "You thought you knew better than Jake and the others. You thought you could brave whatever the Rockies threw your way. Now you got what you deserved, so take it like a man!"

For a time, his disparaging words seemed to work. Devlin forced himself to think of things other than his agonized muscles, numb hands and feet, and bones throbbing with the cold. He forced himself to think of home—and of Hannah.

Had she given up hope of rescue? If so, what must she think of him? He had failed her when she needed him more than she had ever needed anyone before. Likely, by now, her affection for him was beginning to die, just as he could die this night.

Not that he wanted to die, Devlin was quick to add, especially now when he was so close to gaining the happiness that had eluded him for so long. But if he did, perhaps it was just recompense he should die out here, alone in this dark, dangerous storm.

His current predicament mimicked his existence in so many ways. He staggered blindly through life without much hope of a lasting happiness. Indeed, even when good fortune seemed to all but hit him square in the face, Devlin knew he had repeatedly turned his back on it and headed off to his own self-destruction. Or, even worse, God had seemed to intervene and take that happiness from him.

God hadn't taken Hannah from him, though. If he lost her, he lost her solely through his own cowardice and sheer stupidity. Indeed, if he'd had the sense ever to enlist God's aid, he might now be safe at home with Hannah and his children at his side.

But he never could find it in his heart to ask the Lord for anything. He had always been a man who relied on himself. To turn to God would make him vulnerable, once again, to rejection. His own father had rejected him, and Devlin had been flesh of his flesh. What would some distant, all-powerful God want with the likes of him?

And what, for that matter, would *he* want with the likes of God? Humility and abasement had never been Devlin's strong suit. Such traits were only for fools, the weak and unsure.

He smiled in grim irony. In the end, the only person who had been weak and unsure—a fool—had been him. He had been too afraid to see the truth that had been there all along . . .

After a time, Devlin discovered he couldn't feel his body. The reins dropped from his fingers; his feet slipped from the stirrups. The drowsiness grew heavier and increasingly harder to fight.

Then, with a snort of surprise, Culdee Star stumbled, went down. Devlin sailed headfirst into the snow. It was cold, but strangely soft and comforting, too. He lay there, the will to go on seeping from his body.

Not far from him, his gelding fought to regain his footing. Finally the big animal staggered upright. Devlin watched him, curiously uncaring.

It was over then, he thought in resignation.

At the admission fear flared, growing with each passing second until it flamed at last into a conflagration. He was going to die, and he would die a failure. He had failed Ella. Soon, he would also fail Hannah, his children, and even God.

Strangely, the consideration of failing God, of never having seized the opportunity to come to know Him, disturbed Devlin most of all. What if He *had* always been the loving Father his friends had spoken of? What if *he* had squandered his whole life running from the only love that truly mattered?

Anguish welled in him.

Be of good courage . . . and I will strengthen your heart . . .

Devlin lifted his head, glanced blearily around. He had heard a voice—hadn't he? The wind wailed, mournful and sad. With a sigh, he laid his head back on the snow. He must truly be near death. He was hearing voices in the storm.

Arise, Beloved. The joy of the Lord is your strength.

He shut his eyes, closed his ears against the voice reverberating through his skull. Had he died then, Devlin wondered, and already gone to stand before the throne of God? If so, he was afraid to find out. He had done nothing to deserve God's mercy or love. The Lord's judgment of him would be swift and pitiless.

You don't have to do anything to deserve God's love. You already have it, right now, just as you are . . .

Unbidden, Hannah's sweet words that day at the pond filled Devlin. "You're not making any sense," he brokenly stumbled through the words he had said to her. "You know that, don't you, Hannah?"

In reply, her gentle, loving laughter surrounded him once more. *Just like God loving us without any guarantee that we'll ever love Him in return doesn't make sense? Yet He does it anyway. He can't help it. He is Love!*

Ah, more than anything he had ever wanted to believe, he wanted to believe that now! Tears filled Devlin's eyes, trickled down his cheeks and froze. He needed that love with all his heart. Not just because he was on the verge of death, but because he also needed it to make some sense of his life.

It was the last—and the greatest—gift he could give himself.

From somewhere deep within, that realization stirred Devlin to one final, superhuman effort. Strength swelled, flooding his nerveless limbs. He shoved to his hands and knees and began to crawl, inch by excruciating inch.

Miraculously, the whirling snow suddenly seemed to slow, circle more languorously. In the vault of darkness overhead, Devlin almost thought he could pick out a star or two.

Then the wind died, and a faint whiff of wood smoke scented the air. Nearby, Culdee Star snorted and pawed at the snow.

Devlin's crawl quickened, sending blood surging through his veins to his nerveless arms and legs. He climbed to his knees, then his feet.

Far away he saw a faint light. "Thank you, Lord," he whispered. Grasping hold of his horse's saddle he staggered onward, toward the beacon flickering in the rapidly fading darkness.

21

Where sin abounded, grace did much more abound.
Romans 5:20

By dawn, the storm began to abate. Hannah lay there in the snug pine branch bower Brody had put together in the shelter of the dense ponderosa pines, wondering how much snow had fallen the night before. If it was deep, it would seriously impede any escape she might make–if the opportunity ever presented itself.

Brody lay beside her, snoring softly, his body blocking the way out. Though her feet were free, with her hands still tied she doubted she could crawl over him without waking him. Still, it was worth a try. Anything was better than the fate that lay before her.

As Hannah rolled over and pushed to her knees, their buckboard horse whinnied loudly. The shrill sound was quickly answered by another whinny, this time from further away. With a curse, Brody jerked upright.

"What the–?" His hand gripping his holstered revolver, he flung the blanket covering the bower's entrance aside and peered out.

Hannah's heart pounded a wild rhythm beneath her breast. Another horse . . . Was is possible someone else was riding up on the camp? Someone who might rescue her?

Then Brody gave a snort of disgust. He sat back and looked at her. "Nothing more than a riderless horse. Most likely some fool out in the storm lost him. Probably froze to death for his troubles."

"Shouldn't you go out and see if the man's nearby?" she asked, fighting hard to master her renewed despair. "The poor man could still be alive and need help."

"If he is alive, the only help he'll get from me," Brody drawled, "is a bullet to the head. I don't need anybody sticking their nose into my business." He paused to eye her consideringly. "Still, you've made a good point. If that horse's rider's alive, I can't risk him showing up later, can I?"

He crawled from the bower. "Stay put if you know what's good for you. I'll be back in a minute."

Hannah watched Brody stand and stride off through the knee-deep snow. She scooted to the bower's needle-framed doorway. About twenty yards away, just where a few scraggly pines met the open plain, a saddled horse stood.

The animal was a bay with a white star on its forehead. Hannah's heart skipped a beat. The horse looked a lot like Devlin's mount. But then, there were many bay horses out there with white marks on their foreheads.

Well, help or no, she resolved, using her bound hands to climb to her feet, this might be the only chance she ever had to make a run for it. If she could just put enough distance between herself and Brody before he noticed she was gone . . .

Hannah glanced around. Her best chance stood in finding some way to hide in the trees. She turned and sprinted for the densest, darkest part of the forest.

It felt good to move, to run again, to feel the wind on her face. The deep snow, however, combined with muscles stiff with disuse to impede her progress. Hannah shot a quick look over her shoulder, just in time to see Brody turn from the horse. As their gazes momentarily met, rage darkened his features. With a hoarse shout, he dropped the big bay's reins and raced after her.

Terror sent the blood shooting through her veins, fueling Hannah's sudden burst of speed. She ran, dodging through the closely spaced trees, her breath coming now in sharp gulps. Her long skirt, however, was her undoing.

As she leaped over a rotted log, her hem caught on a protruding limb. Hannah tripped and fell. Before she could struggle to her feet, Brody was on her.

"I told you to stay put!" He grabbed Hannah by the back of her jacket collar and jerked her upright. "Did you really think you could get away from me?" Brody shook her hard. "Did you?"

"It d-didn't matter," she replied between panting breaths. "I'll never st-stop trying to get away. N-never!"

His face a mask of fury, he lifted his hand to hit her. "Why, you insolent little–"

"Lay one finger on Hannah, Gerard," another male voice intruded just then, "and you're a dead man."

At the sound of Devlin's voice, relief flooded Hannah. Thank the Lord, she thought.

With a feral snarl, Brody dragged her around to face in the direction they had just come, her body providing a shield before him. There stood Devlin, his Colt revolver aimed at them.

Her hungry gaze took in the sight of him. He looked half-frozen. Ice encrusted his hat and the dark stubble that shadowed his jaw. It stiffened his canvas jacket, denims, and boots. Though he gripped his revolver tightly, his gloved hand trembled. Exhaustion hung visibly over him, dragging him down.

Brody must have seen the same thing, for a low chuckle rumbled in his chest. The hand not holding her by her jacket moved surreptitiously. Hannah found the end of a gun barrel pressed to her head. Her breath caught in her throat.

"Toss your gun to me, MacKay, or *she's* a dead woman."

A guarded look in his eyes, Devlin went very still.

"Don't do this, Brody." Hannah twisted in her captor's grip. "It's over. Just let me go."

"No it's *not* over until I say it is," he rasped, his lips close to her ear. "And don't think for a moment I won't kill you." He lifted his head and laughed. "You believe me, don't you, MacKay?"

For a long, tension-laden moment, Devlin said nothing. His gaze, full of frustrated yearning, met Hannah's. Then, slowly, a look of defeat clouded his eyes. "Just let her go, Gerard," he finally said. "Do what you want with me, but just let Hannah go."

"Toss me your gun. Then we'll talk."

Devlin exhaled a weary breath, then threw his revolver toward Brody. It landed at Hannah's feet.

Brody wouldn't let her go. Hannah knew that instinctively. Just as she knew he would kill Devlin. But she couldn't let that happen. She'd do whatever it took to stop him, even sacrifice her own life.

Brody chuckled again, and moved the gun barrel away from her head. "A hero to the bitter end, aren't you, MacKay?" he asked as he directed his revolver at Devlin. "Well, this time it's not going to do either you or Hannah any good."

Once more, her gaze met Devlin's. Through the sudden sheen of tears glazing her eyes, she saw him smile.

A surprising look of peace softened his rugged features. Then Brody's gun clicked as he cocked it to fire.

With a fierce cry of protest, Hannah flung her bound hands back into the air, hitting the gun. At the same time, she rammed her body into Brody's.

He grunted in pain, stumbled backward, then fell, pulling her with him. The gun slipped from Brody's grip and sank in the snow. In the next instant, he shoved Hannah roughly from him and pushed to his knees.

By then Devlin was upon him, slamming into Brody with such force both men fell back into the snow. There they fought. Fists struck hard. Bodies twisted and turned. Grunts of pain mingled with those of exertion.

Hannah climbed to her feet and backed away from the two battling men. It soon became evident that Devlin couldn't long prevail against his opponent. He was just too worn out. He'd need help or Brody would yet win the day.

Frantically, she began searching for the revolvers. Both had fallen somewhere in the deep drifts, and trying to find even one of them in the now trampled snow was like looking for a needle in a haystack. Still, Hannah scooped and swiped with bound hands at any likely spot, her unprotected fingers soon turning cold and painful.

Then, with a jarring blow, Brody hit Devlin square in the jaw, sending the big foreman flying backward. His gaze snagged on something lying nearby and, as he bent and extricated the object from the snow, Hannah saw it was one of the revolvers.

Panic-stricken, she groped wildly about where she thought she had seen the other revolver fall. Her hands numb now, she almost missed recognizing the hard metal of the gun when her fingers glanced off it. Then, blessedly, she had it in her hands.

Even as she lifted the weapon and turned toward the two men, Brody was aiming his gun and cocking it with deliberate purpose. Devlin, climbing to his knees, froze when he heard the deadly sound. His gaze resolute, he stared up at his enemy.

"Say your prayers, MacKay," Brody said with cold disdain. "For all the good it'll do you."

Hannah aimed, closed her eyes, and fired.

The gun blast sent her reeling. In the next instant, Brody Gerard gave an agonized cry, wheeled around, and pointed his gun at her. She was going to die, Hannah thought in a split second of recognition. Then Devlin threw himself into Brody. The revolver fired, piercing the mountain air with a quick, sharp, deadly sound.

Late that morning, Jake Whitmore and the rest of the posse rode up to the camp. After taking one look at Brody, tied to the buckboard's front wagon wheel with his right shoulder swathed in bandages, they turned to see Hannah and Devlin seated around a blazing campfire and sipping steaming cups of coffee. The sheriff shook his head, then dismounted.

"Looks like you've kept yourself well-occupied since we parted yesterday," he observed with a wry smile. Jake ambled over to the campfire to warm himself. "Any coffee left?" he asked, indicating the blackened tin pot hanging over the fire.

Devlin took another swallow from his cup, then nodded. "Sure, enough for all of you, I'd reckon." He smiled. "Glad to see you finally made it."

"Yeah, we thought we'd just make it in time to help you tie up any loose ends." Jake glanced at Brody. "See you had to shoot him."

286

"Actually, Hannah shot him. I just beat him up a bit."

The sheriff graced her with an admiring look. "Well, congratulations. Didn't know you were an expert marksman, Miss Cutler."

"I'm not. That was the first–and hopefully only–time I've fired a gun."

"Are you okay, Hannah?" Concern in his eyes, Jake looked her up and down.

She had thought she'd had enough time to calm down and regain her composure. But in the ensuing time since they had finally subdued Brody, tied him up, then treated his shoulder wound, Hannah realized she had just barely begun to realize she was finally free. Soon, she would be heading home–to Culdee Creek and her son.

Tears filled her eyes. "Not really, but I will be once I'm back home. I'm just . . . just so g-grateful–" Her voice cracked and then the tears came.

Devlin poured his coffee into the fire, stood, and gently took Hannah's cup from her. Setting it down, he grasped her hand. "We need to talk. Really talk." He pulled her to her feet. "Come on. Jake and the others can see to Gerard now. Let's take a walk."

Startled, Hannah wiped away her tears and nodded. "Okay, Devlin," she answered cautiously. "If that's what you want."

He led her from the camp, out of the forest, and back onto the open plain of the park. Before them spread an endless sea of white. The sun, climbing now into the clean, clear blue sky, caught in the myriad tiny snow crystals, causing them to glint like so many precious diamonds. After the terror and ugliness of the past several days, it seemed to Hannah the scene before them was surely something like heaven must look.

They walked for a time along the base of a rocky bluff, until they were far from sight and earshot of the others. Finally, though, Devlin pulled her to a halt.

287

"I nearly didn't live to see this day," he began suddenly. "I almost died out there in the storm."

She gave a small jerk, filled anew with the realization of how close Devlin had come to losing his life. "I-I didn't even know you were out here, or that close."

A long silence ensued.

Why was she suddenly so afraid of him, or what to say? Hannah wondered. Conversation, even in their most hostile times, had never been lacking. And it wasn't as if Devlin didn't have some feelings for her. He had risked his life to bring her back. But then, Devlin was a man who unflinchingly met his responsibilities. And he had most certainly felt responsible for what had happened to her.

She needed more, much, much more, though, than that. Yet she feared . . . she feared Devlin's unflinching sense of responsibility might color, distort even, their relationship from now on, changing it into something neither of them would ultimately want. Something God wouldn't want either.

After a time he continued. "If I had died, it would have been worth it in trying to rescue you." Devlin's mouth lifted in a wry, sad little smile. "I know it may come too late to mean much, but I love you, Hannah. I love you, and want you to be my wife."

Ah, the pain, she thought, of hearing those longed for words now! Now, when she finally realized there was no hope for them, unless their love also encompassed the Lord.

Hannah closed her eyes. "Devlin," she whispered, "love isn't always enough." She sighed, the mournful sound wrenched from deep within her. "You still have so much pain and anger in your heart. I don't think I'm the woman who can help you. Indeed, I don't think any *person* can."

"But God can."

"Yes," Hannah agreed softly. "Yes, He can, if only you would let Him."

"I *have* let Him." Devlin laid a hand on her arm. "He came to me, spoke to me, in the midst of the snowstorm. And, for the first time in my life, I truly understood what Ella meant when she told me how important it was for me to accept full responsibility for my actions, and to forgive. That forgiveness, though, didn't just encompass my forgiving you. I had to forgive myself, too. And I couldn't do that until I first asked the Lord's forgiveness."

Hannah opened her eyes and turned to him. Wild hope warred with disbelief. It couldn't be. Yet the unmistakable confirmation of his words burned now in his eyes.

At last, she thought, the joy swelling in her. Thank You, Lord. Thank You.

"It's a miracle, I know. One just as glorious as me finding you out here in these mountains." Devlin's gaze was warm and full of certitude. "But, as you once said, there are miracles aplenty every day. The miracle of dreams long sought and finally fulfilled. The miracle of forgiveness, which you and Ella taught me with the example of your lives. But most of all,"–Devlin's eyes brimmed with tears–"there's the miracle of you, loving me, and of me, loving you. And that, I think, is the greatest miracle of all."

"No, my love," Hannah whispered achingly, reaching up to stroke his cheek. "The greatest miracle of all is God's grace and unconditional love. They have saved us both, and made us whole at long last. And that, I think is all the miracle anyone can ever hope to need."

Epilogue

With a sigh, Hannah leaned back in the wicker rocker on the main house's front porch, and tugged the knit afghan lying across her lap a bit tighter. It was a glorious Indian summer day for the first week of October, the sky an intense fall blue, the air temperate, the breeze mild. She still had yet, though, to recover from her sense of perpetual chill. Most likely, Hannah mused wryly, that problem would subside once she had a bit more meat on her bones.

The front door opened, then slammed shut. Beth, bright of eye and eager of countenance, hurried over. "Do you need anything?" she asked, peering down at her. "Abby said to come and check."

Hannah smiled and shook her head. "No, I'm just fine." She paused to examine the red polka-dotted dress the girl wore. "That's quite a pretty dress, Beth. Did Abby make that for you?"

The girl's chest swelled visibly with pride. "No, ma'am. I sewed it myself."

"You've got a fine eye for detail," Hannah said, noting the intricate smocking and lace trims. "Have you ever thought of becoming a seamstress?"

"Not in the way most folk might imagine." Beth grinned. "I favor the stitching up of people more than cloth. I think I'd like to be a doctor."

"A doctor, eh?" She cocked her head. "That's an ambitious plan."

"Pa always said we should never limit our dreams."

"No, we never should," Hannah concurred with a quick, resolute nod, "no matter how hard it may seem at first to achieve. Your pa's a very wise man."

"Yeah, he is." A sudden memory clouded the girl's eyes. "Sure wish, though, he could've known what to say to keep Evan here. I miss him."

Evan . . . Abby had reluctantly broken the news of Evan's departure to Hannah soon after she and Devlin had returned. Even now, Hannah's heart twisted every time she thought of him. Poor Evan. Would he never find the peace and happiness he so ardently sought?

"I miss him, too," she whispered, "and say a little prayer for him every night."

"Pa says he's down in Texas, working some cattle drive. Maybe Evan will come home after he's done with that."

"Yes, maybe he will." Somehow, though, despite all their prayers, Hannah feared Evan wouldn't be home any time soon. He wouldn't be home, this time, until he had found what he was seeking.

Once more the front door swung open and Devlin walked out. His glance met Hannah's and a tender smile lifted his lips. "Beth," he said, "Abby's wondering when you're coming back. Seems there's something about a cake needing icing . . ."

The girl's hand flew to her mouth. "Oh, yes. I'd forgotten." She turned back to Hannah. "If you want anything, just send Devlin in for it, okay?"

"Okay."

She watched Beth depart, then turned to Devlin, who had pulled up a chair to sit beside her. "Is Bonnie finally asleep?"

He laughed wryly. "Yes, finally. I had a devil of a time getting her to take her nap, though. She insisted on getting up to play with Jackson, who had already fallen asleep. I don't know how many times I caught her just as she was toddling over to wake him."

"Guess we could move Jackson in with Devlin Jr.," Hannah mused. "That way we could separate Bonnie and Jackson for naps." She twisted in the rocker. "Do you think Devlin Jr. would mind sharing his room?"

Devlin grinned. "On the contrary. I think he'd be thrilled to have his brother bunking in with him. Of late, he's been complaining long and hard of feeling outnumbered by his sisters."

"And for good reason," Hannah agreed with a laugh.

The first thing Devlin had done when they'd arrived back at the ranch was to announce that he and Hannah would be married at Thanksgiving, and to officially claim Jackson as his son. His fears about how Devlin Jr., Mary, and Bonnie would take the news had been unfounded. In typical childlike fashion, once the two oldest children had confirmed that Hannah would now also be their mother and had finally finished cheering, they had gone back to playing their game of cat's cradle.

Yes, Hannah thought in contentment, it seemed as if all her dreams had finally come true. She had a good home blessed with many friends, a father for her son, and soon a husband for herself whom she loved and who loved her. She had rebuilt her life from the shattered pieces of her past, and rebuilt it into something beautiful and fulfilling. But above everything else, she had found the Lord and would strive to do His will for the rest of her days.

Once, she had wondered how anyone knew for certain when it was God's will manifesting itself in one's life, and when it was just one's own selfish, misguided desires twisting things to seem so. Hannah realized now that for those who loved and truly tried to follow Him, God made His will manifest in all things that really mattered. Things like love, forgiveness, dying to self, and storing up one's treasures in heaven rather than on earth.

At long last, Hannah knew and understood this. During those dark days when Brody Gerard had taken her away, she had thought God was asking her to give up everything, to relinquish all that was truly precious to her. But now she knew her deepest desire had always been for Him. He had, in truth, asked for so little. He had asked only that she give up everything that kept her from Him, and from her truest heart's desire.

God was so very, very good.

Devlin laid his hand on hers. "You seem full of thoughts today. Is anything bothering you?"

Hannah shook her head and smiled. "No, nothing's bothering me. Everything is finally perfect, just perfect."

He squeezed her hand and nodded, his eyes brimming over with love. "Yes, yes it is."

Watch for Book 3 in the Brides of Culdee Creek series

Lady of Light

by Kathleen Morgan

The Village of Culdee
Highlands of Strathnaver, Scotland
May 1899

Even before he opened his mouth, Claire knew the tall, dark-haired stranger with the unusually wide-brimmed, black hat wasn't a native Scotsman. Something about him had caught her eye as she swept the parish church steps. Something she noted even while he was only halfway up the winding road leading through Culdee to the seven-hundred-year-old stone church at the top of the hill.

Perhaps it was his fine dark suit. Dust-coated as it was from his long walk from the coach stop just outside the village, it accentuated his broad shoulders and skimmed his long, lithe legs. Then again, perhaps it was the way he moved, his stride smooth, effortless, powerful. Or perhaps, just perhaps, Claire thought as the stranger finally reached the base of the church steps and paused to squint up at her, it was his sheer masculine beauty–

from his tanned face and strong jaw to his straight nose and striking, smoky blue eyes.

One thing was certain. She had never seen a more handsome, physically impressive man.

"Do ye think, lass," a rusty old voice rose unexpectedly from behind her, "ye might do well to greet our guest? 'Twouldna speak well o' our fine village to gape and stare overlong at every stranger who comes our way."

"Och, Father MacLaren! I didna hear ye come up," Claire cried, losing her grip on the broom as she wheeled about to face him. In that same instant she realized her error. With a gasp, she spun back around and grabbed for it, just missing the wooden, wheat straw implement. End over end, the broom tumbled down the long course of steps to land at the stranger's feet.

With a grin he stooped, picked it up, and offered it back to her. "Have a care, ma'am, or you might be the next thing landing at my feet."

She could feel the heat flood her face. This was daft, the way she was acting, Claire scolded herself. 'Twasn't as if she had never met a fine-looking man before. And 'twasn't as if she had never had a masculine glint of admiration directed at her either.

Claire managed a taut smile. "Ye're from America, aren't ye? I can tell by yer accent."

His gaze never wavered from her face. "Yes, I'm from America. Colorado to be exact. Funny thing is, though, where I come from it's you who'd be branded with having the accent."

Claire laughed. Despite the stranger's attempt at bravado, she could see a deeper glimmer of uncertainty in his eyes. Her strange unease dissipated, and she felt confident and in control again.

"Well, ye're in the Highlands now, my braw lad, and ye're the foreigner, not I." She glanced over her shoulder at the old priest. "If ye havena further chores for me, Father, I'll be on my way now. Ian should be heading home soon. I've a fine pot of colcannon simmering and a loaf of bread yet to bake for supper."

"And havena ye a wee moment more to spare for our new friend, lass?" The gray-haired cleric cocked his head and arched a shaggy brow. "Dinna ye wish to hear what his needs might be?"

If the truth be told, Claire wished she were as fast and far away from the tall American as she could get. As pleasant and well-mannered as he seemed, there was just something about him—something disturbing that she couldn't quite put her finger on. But she couldn't very well admit that to his face now, could she?

"I didna wish to pry," she forced herself to reply. "It appears he came to see—"

"Reckon you might as well stay, ma'am," the stranger cut her off. "In fact, you may be as much help as the padre here. I'm looking for some kinfolk, and I haven't any idea where to begin."

Reluctantly, Claire turned back to face him. He was a stranger in their land, after all, and no true Highlander would deny anyone hospitality. "Well, if ye could tell us the names of yer kin, mayhap that would be the best way to begin. 'Twould be nigh impossible, even for a man as knowledgeable as Father MacLaren, to help ye without names."

The American pulled off his hat and ran a hand roughly through black, wavy hair in dire need of a trim. "That's just the problem, ma'am. The last kin of mine who lived in Culdee left here in 1825. His name was Sean MacKay, and he was my great-grandfather."

"That was seventy-three years ago, lad." The priest's glance skittered off Claire's. He scratched his jaw. "'Twill be a challenge to find yer true kin, though if ye be a

MacKay, in a sense these hills are filled wi' yer kin, for these are MacKay lands."

"I've got time," the American muttered cryptically, with what Claire imagined to be an edge of bitterness. "It's why I came all this way north from Glasgow."

"Did ye now?" Father MacLaren grasped his cane and climbed awkwardly down the steps to stand beside Claire. "And who be ye, then?"

"I'm Evan MacKay, son of Conor MacKay, the owner of Culdee Creek Ranch near Colorado Springs, Colorado." He held out his hand.

"Well, I've heard o' Colorado, but no' o' this Colorado Springs." The priest accepted the American's proffered hand and gave it a hearty shake before releasing it. "I'm Father MacLaren of St. Columba's Kirk. And this bonnie lassie," he added, turning to Claire, "is Claire Sutherland, my wee housekeeper."

The man named Evan rendered her a quick nod. It wasn't quick enough, though, Claire realized with a twinge of irritation, to hide a freshened gleam of appreciation.

"Pleased to meet you, ma'am." He shoved his hat back on his head, lifted his face to the sun that was even now dipping toward the distant mountains, then frowned. "Well, as you say, the search for my kin might be a challenge. And it certainly isn't one I care to take on today."

"Nay, I'd imagine no'," the priest agreed amiably. "The morrow will be soon enough. If ye wish, ye can then begin wi' our church records. Mayhap a wee look into the baptismal and wedding register will provide ye wi' additional clues to solve yer mystery."

"I'd be much obliged, Padre."

Father MacLaren stroked his chin and eyed him speculatively. "Do ye have lodging then, already arranged for the night?"

"No." Evan MacKay gave a swift shake of his head. "But if you could direct me to an inn or boarding house . . ."

"There's no inn, leastwise no' in Culdee," The old priest's brow furrowed in though. "Indeed, the closest inn's in Tongue, a good sixty miles north o' here. He turned to Claire. "Doesna yer landlord have another small croft to let?"

"Aye," she replied slowly, not liking where the conversation seemed suddenly to be heading. "But the dwelling is shabby indeed, and no fit dwelling for such a fine man as Mr. MacKay."

"It's Evan. Please, call me Evan." He gave a low, husky laugh. "And believe me, Miss Sutherland. I'm not all that fine. I can handle just about anything that provides me with a roof over my head."

"This isna America, ye know," Claire protested, not at all pleased with the idea of the tall man residing so near to her. "The wind blows bitter off the sea and when it rains, the chill can sink deep into yer bones."

Once more, Evan laughed. "And you, pretty lady, haven't lived through a Colorado winter either. I'd say as bad as your Highland weather might be, it's no worse in comparison."

"Ye see, lass?" Father MacLaren offered just a little too eagerly. "'Tis the perfect solution. If Mr. MacKay . . . Evan . . . lives nearby, he might even be willin' to earn a bit o' his board by helpin' ye and Ian in the garden plot, and carin' for Angus's sheep and chickens. 'Twould take a load from yer shoulders, wouldna it?"

"Aye, I suppose so," Claire admitted. "Just as long as Angus doesna raise our rent in the doing."

"Och, dinna fash yerself. I'll have a talk wi' the mon. He's a MacKay, after all. 'Twouldna hurt him to extend a wee bit o' hospitality to kin, now wouldna it?"

"Nay," she muttered. Angus MacKay was as tight-fisted as any Scotsman could get. Odds were, though, he just might lower the rent for one of his blood, even if he had never seen fit to do so for her and Ian. But then they were Sutherlands, she reminded herself with a twinge of resentment, and not even from these parts.

"Then get on wi' ye, lass. Escort Evan 'ere to Angus's." The old priest gave her a gentle nudge. "As ye said, ye'd best be on yer way. There's that pot simmerin', and the bread ye've yet to bake."

She stared at him in disbelief. Did he really expect her to lead this stranger—this American—through Culdee and all the way home? Why, she'd be the talk of the village for weeks to come!

Yet what else could she do? It wouldn't be polite to refuse. Indeed, what plausible excuse could she give? She exhaled a frustrated breath, then turned to the American. "Well, shall we be goin' now, Mr. MacKay?"

He grinned up at her. "Evan. Please, call me Evan."

"I prefer Mr. MacKay, if ye dinna mind." Claire rendered the priest a curt nod. "I'll see ye on the morrow then, Father."

"Och, nay." The priest held up a silencing hand. "Take the next day or two off. Assist Evan in discerning who his true blood kin are. 'Tis the hospitable thing to do."

Once more the heat warmed her cheeks, but this time it was fueled by rising irritation. If she didna know any better, Claire thought, she'd swear Father MacLaren was playing the matchmaker. Well, his well-meant efforts would fail yet again. She didna want a man in her life. Not now, and not ever.

"As ye wish, Father," she gritted out her reply. Someday soon she'd have to have a wee talk with the priest about his marital interference. But not just now. Her first priority must be for her totally unexpected and unwanted guest. The sooner she helped him ascertain who his true kin in Culdee were, the sooner she could be rid of him.

If all went well, she'd have to endure him, at the very most, another day or two. As much as she didn't care to have men hanging about and fawning over her, the ordeal would soon be over. And it wasn't as if she had to spend time alone with him or worry about his causing problems. There were neighbors aplenty about, and Ian would be near at night.

Aye, Claire reassured herself, just another day or two of the American's presence at the very most. How hard could that possibly be?

**Also look for the first book
of the Brides of Culdee Creek series,**
Daughter of Joy

Abby and Conor each thought

love would never again

stir their hearts.

But the One who knows

them best may have

other plans . . .

Infused with spark and warmth,
Daughter of Joy tells a compelling, perceptive tale
of one woman's faith journey. In the wake of losing both her
husband and young son, Abigail Stanton is searching for a
way to make sense of her losses. She takes a job as housekeeper for Conor MacKay, a confusing, often volatile man
who also carries deep pain–and secrets–in his inscrutable
heart.

As the volatile rancher's new housekeeper, Abby is supposed
to keep his affairs–and his equally capricious little girl–in
order. Why, then, does she feel confusion, desire, and anything but order every time they are together? Conor tries to
hide his own seething emotions beneath a cold facade, but
there is something about his prim new housekeeper that sets
him on edge. As Abby and Conor draw closer to the flame of
their attraction, they risk opening their hearts again for a
chance at the greatest love of all.

Kathleen Morgan is a successful romance writer whose work includes fifteen published novels. She is a member of the Romance Writers of America and has been a popular conference speaker. Morgan lives with her husband and son near Colorado Springs.

If you would like to be included on a mailing list to notify you of future books in The Brides of Culdee Creek series, please write to Kathleen at P.O. Box 62365, Colorado Springs, CO 80962, or e-mail her at kathleenmorgan@juno.com. If you wish to receive a newsletter, please enclose a self-addressed, stamped envelope.